THE COURIER

THE COURIER

Derek Kartun

St. Martin's Press
New York

Library of Congress Cataloging in Publication Data

Kartun, Derek.
  The courier.

  1. World War, 1939-1945—Fiction.   I. Title.
PR6061.A78C68   1985   823'.914   85-25089
ISBN 0-312-17044-0

First published in Great Britain by Century Publishing Co. Ltd.

First U.S. Edition

10 9 8 7 6 5 4 3 2 1

For Debbie and Sally

Author's Note

The 3½ litre Bentley drophead coupé which is the chief pro-
tagonist – the heroine, if you will – of the events described here
has been devotedly rebuilt and refurbished since the days of her
heroic run from Paris to Lisbon in the rogue summer of 1940.
Early in 1984 she was sold to a new owner through the London
market in classic cars. She was looking magnificent, running
like a dream, her elegant French bodywork glistening discreetly
in the sun. She smelt of mature leather and beeswax. She was
fifty years of age. But whereas her natural habitat is among
the Lamborghinis in the Place Vendôme or running down to
Henley or Goodwood on their appointed days, she has actually
gone where the new money is, to California. May she end her
days there in dignity and peace.

Derek Kartun
Highgate, London, 1985

Chapter 1

'You're wanted,' old Charlot said, poking his head round the door. 'The *patron* wants you in his office.' He sniffed and scratched his backside in a way that he had. 'Better make it sharp. He's got a big shot from Paris with him. Looks official.'

I stopped what I had been doing, which – to be frank about it – was hunting for bedbugs. I'd long ago concluded that they bred faster than I could catch them anyway. I got up from bed, straightened myself and accompanied old Charlot down the corridor.

The place was like a mausoleum. Most of the prisoners had been evacuated south to other penal institutions and the building was half empty now. 'Maybe this is your turn,' old Charlot said as we passed through our third set of locked gates. 'About time, isn't it?'

'Overdue.'

'What is it, four years?'

'Three years and thirty-one days, *if* you please.'

'Another year to go.'

'Damn nearly.'

'Excessive punishment.'

'It's what I've always said.'

'You are a man with a deep sense of justice and concern for the human condition,' I told him. We were fast approaching the office of the *Directeur*.

'I am a man of principle'.

'Precisely.'

'Later, I'll have the new socks for you.'

'Thank you.'

Monsieur le Directeur of the *Maison d'Arrêt* at Reims was a former army major with a beard. The beard was his most significant feature, luxuriating as it did around a petulant mouth and beneath eyes which blinked pinkly at you as if they were full of seawater. He appeared to love the beard as he loved nothing else. He would handle it affectionately even as he condemned some hapless half-wit to three months' solitary for flinging the contents of his pisspot over the place. When I arrived in his office he was stroking it very much as if it were a favourite cat to which he was about to offer a saucer of warm milk.

The beard was offering no surprises. But there was something odd about his tone of voice. Normally, he'd address us collectively as '*mes enfants*' or individually as 'you swine'. In my case it would be 'English scum'. Recently he would seek me out at our morning parades in order to make it clear that he held me personally responsible for the failings of General Gort and the entire British war machine. '*Les Anglo-Saxons*,' he would say, his mouth twitching angrily deep among the hair on his face, '*sont des lâches* – cowards!' He knew the odd word of English.

But now he rose from his chair, blinked in my direction and extended a hand. 'Monsieur Quinton, *cher ami*, you have a visitor.'

I ignored the hand and by force of habit came to something resembling attention in front of his desk. The beard quivered a little, seemed a bit offended.

'Please sit down, Monsieur Quinton. You have a visitor who has brought you good news.'

I sat on the hard wooden chair and glanced at Max, of all people, seated at the far end of the desk. Something in his expression warned me that I wasn't supposed to know him from Adam. I looked blank.

'This gentleman,' the beard was saying, 'is from Paris. He has come here under difficult circumstances entirely on your account. You appear to have friends in high places.'

'Not high enough or I'd have been out of here years ago.'

'He has come with this, from the Ministry of the Interior,' waving an official-looking bit of paper. I could see stamps and a couple of signatures. So far so good.

'You are to be released under the jurisdiction of the Courts according to Article . . .' – he adjusted a pair of gold pince-nez and peered with his rheumy eyes at the paper – 'yes, Article 141, paragraph 17, according to the terms of which the prisoner may at the discretion of the minister . . .'

But, naturally enough, I was no longer listening. I glanced again at Max and the merest trace of a nod of that vulpine head told me that all this was the real thing.

'May I see?'

The *Directeur* passed me the bit of paper. I read it carefully. I am exceedingly cautious by nature, save when I take ridiculous chances. The paper seemed in order.

'Monsieur here is authorised to take me out?'

The beard nodded.

'And I am no longer under your jurisdiction?'

'No longer, *cher ami*.'

I turned to Max. 'Come on. Get me out of this filthy dump.'

They appeared to have been warned of my departure, for my things were waiting for me. Oddly, my watch from Cartier (it was a genuine Cartier – in those days they hadn't learned how to fake them) – my watch, I say, had not gone missing, which I considered odd. Odder still, it showed the correct time and was ticking away in its ineffably discreet manner. Someone must have been using it for the past three years. Soon old Charlot turned up with the stuff from my cell in a bag. In his other hand he clutched a pair of socks.

'I suppose you won't want these now. It's back to silk and cashmere, eh?'

'Any use to you?'

'Thank you.'

'Keep them as a souvenir, and here, drink my health some time.' I handed him a note from the wallet they'd returned to me.

'You are an English gentleman. I wish you good luck.'

'Thank you.'

We shook hands.

'They say the English armies have taken to the boats somewhere around Dunkirk. The *Tommies* aren't what they were in my day. The *Boches* will be here soon.'

'What will you do?'

He drew himself up and I thought for a moment he was going to salute. 'My duty, *face à l'ennemi*,' he said, and turning smartly on his heel he stumped off about his business.

'Hurry, please,' Max said. He was still keeping his distance. But later, as the great iron door of the *Maison d'Arrêt* closed behind us, he dropped the pretence.

'For Christ's sake get a move on. I thought you'd never finish with your sentimental farewells in there.'

'Sorry Max, but that was a whole chapter of my life.'

'I don't read books.'

He led the way to a Citroen which was parked on the far side of the street. There was a driver at the wheel.

'A local car,' Max said. 'We'll talk later. Now hurry, we have to get to the airfield by six. It doesn't leave us much time.'

We drove north out of Reims and soon the driver left the main Rethel road and headed the car down a narrow side road. The road signs had all been removed and I had no idea where we were or where we were headed. Not that that bothered me: I was too absorbed in the astonishing things that were going on around us. Nothing at all was heading our way, but flooding southwards and almost filling the entire width of the Rethel road was a dense stream of humanity. Men, women and children were straggling on foot. Some were on bicycles. Many had loaded farm carts with what appeared to be all their worldly goods and were perched on top of the great piles. There were baskets with live chickens and geese. There were old men pushing prams full of their possessions. There were lost dogs. There were farmers driving cows. Interspersed with all this were cars and trucks of every description, their cursing drivers trying to make progress in the human melee. By the roadside we passed dozens of vehicles which had overheated in the broiling June sunshine and were standing there, radiators steaming, their disconsolate occupants looking on hopelessly. Most of the cars had mattresses tied to their roofs. It was only later that I came to realize why.

What was truly alarming was not the flood of Dutch, Belgian and French refugees on the French roads but the very large admixture of French troops among them. The French line, we were being told, was still holding up on the Somme. But if this was so, how come that this gaggle of haggard and dispirited French soldiery, some carrying their rifles, some not, some motorized after a fashion, some on what must have been stolen bicycles, some on foot – how come that they were retreating in no kind of formation at all? And how come quite a few were patently drunk?

'Doesn't look good,' I said to Max as we finally managed to turn off the main road to our left.

'It doesn't look good because it *isn't* good. What do you expect, a flaming victory parade?'

'They say the Germans are at Laon and somewhere south of Sedan,' the driver said. 'They're dropping their men by parachute in civilian clothes. My brother lives at Rethel. He told me on the phone this morning that they'd dropped nuns.'

'What do you mean, nuns?'

'That's right. Stormtroopers in nuns' habits. And they have a fifth column which signals to them at night and spreads rumours. That's what causes this panic on the roads, the rumours.'

'Rumours like your nuns?'

The point was lost on him.

We passed through a deserted village which he said was Betheny and soon came to a hamlet.

'Modelin,' the driver said. 'The airfield's on our left.'

There were a few military aircraft on the field and very little sign of activity. I could see craters in neat rows where the place had been bombed and a couple of wrecked planes which had suffered direct hits. A gang was filling in a crater without feeling the need to hurry.

The car stopped at the gates and a very young soldier looked at the driver's papers and waved us through.

'Hurry,' Max said. 'The plane's waiting.'

The plane proved to be a worn-looking Amiot 143 which could have done with a coat of paint. The pilot, a freckled youngster with a cheerful face, installed us aboard and they got the propellors turning and the whole sorry contraption moving out to a runway.

'This is the slowest aircraft in the entire French air force,' the pilot shouted as he drove the thing out to the far side of the airfield. 'In fact, it's the slowest thing in *any* airforce, and that includes the *Luftwaffe*, I'm afraid. I'm sorry, it's all we had available for you.'

'Where are we headed?' I asked. No one was telling me anything.

'Villacoublay. We could land at Le Bourget but the conditions on the roads are impossible. You'd never get into Paris tonight.'

'Thanks,' I shouted as the engines were revved up and the Amiot strained and shuddered, ready to get into the air where it clearly felt more at home.

It was Friday 7 June 1940, and I had the feeling it might well be my last summer of all.

At 10.30 a.m. on 5 June the French War Committee had met in Prime Minister Reynaud's office. The Commander-in-Chief, General Weygand, reported that the enemy had opened the second phase of his offensive. As the Dunkirk evacuation was being wound up, General von Bock's Army Group B was preparing to attack across the Somme and although Weygand didn't know it at the time, a series of disasters for the French was to occur on the sixth, with the Panzers breaking out of bridgeheads at Abbeville and St Valèry. Between Condé and Hangest two railway bridges had not been blown and were held by Hoth's XV Panzer Korps. The German rifle regiments had been flooding across during the night, and behind them the rails would be torn up to allow the Panzer armour to follow. On the same day, further east, von Kleist's armour was about to smash across the Aisne east of Compiègne. The mood of the War Committee was black and would have been blacker still had it known what was to happen later that day and on the morrow. For the first time there was talk of a cease-fire and the possible conditions for an armistice. There was bitterness about the British. In response to an abusive letter demanding greater fighter support, Churchill replied in a memorandum to the French premier that 'Your request for fighter aircraft is completely unreasonable . . . The letter made the worst possible impression here.'

As the British were finally forced to leave the mainland and the French armies started to crumple and collapse, the population of Paris was drawing its own conclusions. The first air raids had been on the first and second. On the third a raid on the west wing of the Citroen works had caused a thousand casualties. The tone of the French press and radio was uncertain and hollow. And so the exodus from Paris of close to two million people would shortly get under way.

Chapter 2

Max had his own car parked at the military airfield at Villacoublay and we travelled fairly easy north-eastwards towards Paris. Nothing much was going our way but plenty was passing us going southwards in the direction of Chartres and Orléans. It was much like it had been at Reims.

'Now, what is all this?' I asked him.

'I got you out, that's all.'

'If you could do it now, why couldn't you have done it sooner?'

'I'm not the President of the Appeal Court, you know. And we haven't got the minister in our pocket. These things aren't always easy.'

'So what suddenly changed all that?'

'There was a change of Under-Secretary at the Interior. What with one thing and another we were able to swing it. We had to be careful.'

'You still in the *Police Judiciare?*'

'With the rank of Inspector.' I glanced at him and caught the trace of a smirk on his sallow face. The light was failing and it might just have been his effort to see the road ahead without benefit of headlights.

'Congratulations,' I said, and he grunted. We drove in silence for a while, passing through the respectable outskirts in that part of the Ile de France. After Petit-Clamart it was Chatillon.

'Getting you out,' Max was saying, 'cost a lot of effort. A lot of influence. A lot of money.'

'Are you asking me to pay anyone back?'

'Not in cash.'

I was beginning to understand. Three years and thirty-one days inside had dulled my wits but Max was the man to sharpen them up again. 'In what, then?'

Max took his time answering. We were approaching the city through the little-used Porte de Vanves and the going was pretty fair.

'All in good time. The old man wants to see you tomorrow morning.'

'You know,' I said, 'I don't really think I need all this – old man Schlesser, you, debts to be repaid. All right, the thing came unstuck and some of us – not all of us, but some of us – had to face the music. Three years and thirty-one days inside with that lousy beard and the bedbugs just about repays society for what I'm supposed to have done to it. Just now I think I'd like to be left alone to get out of this Godforsaken country of yours, much as I used to love it, and back to England, where they do not, as far as I know, have a warrant out for my arrest.'

'Like hell,' Max said.

'Like hell, the warrant?'

'Like hell, getting out.'

We were inside Paris, it was close to 10 p.m. and the great city was unnaturally quiet and deserted. Cafes which would normally be open were closed and shuttered. The blackout had turned the place into a ghost town.

'Where are you taking me?'

'We've booked you into a place in the Rue Vavin. The Hotel des Arbustes.'

'I know it. A dump.'

'The *patron* owes us a favour. We have him by the balls.'

'So he'll keep an eye on me?'

Max shrugged. 'Put it like that if you want to.'

We had arrived at the hotel, which was gaunt, minimal and

very depressing. It was scarcely out of the category of *hotel de passe*, where they charged you by the hour, use of towels extra. After my quarters in Reims, of course, it was going to be paradise.

'I'll call for you tomorrow morning at ten,' Max said. 'We'll go over to the Senate to see the old man and he'll tell you what all this is about.' He slammed the car door, pulled out and was away. He hadn't said goodbye, let alone to sleep well or anything sentimental like that.

I checked in and got my key from a sinister character in a pullover and a beret who indeed looked much as if someone had him by the balls. I can't remember the name I used. Twenty minutes later I was in a hot bath and half an hour after that I was fast asleep.

It should perhaps be said at this point that I am neither by nature nor by normal occupation a crook. The episode of the prison in Reims should not be allowed to loom too large in my life story. Such a thing had never happened before and would not, if I could possibly help it, happen again. I was, if I may so express myself, a victim of exceptionally venal times, with a range of opportunities and temptations which, in my judgement, are unlikely ever to confront me again. The ramshackle Third Republic, in which democracy had become a grinning caricature of itself, was staggering, a corrupt and exhausted political whore, to its unseemly end in Vichy. Who was I, when faced with the temptation of easy money, to resist it more successfully than senators, prefects, senior policemen and sundry mayors? The only difference between us was that I, and very few others, got caught. High-ranking policemen and officials had done very well out of the business and most of them were still honoured public servants. And so was the old man – now in the Senate after twenty years in the Chamber of Deputies and still making his famous speech about democratic values. And so, of course, was Max with his *Inspecteur's* pips and his solid connections in the *milieu*.

12

When I first got into the thing I had no idea it was fraudulent. Naive? Not really: the mayor and what looked like the corporation of the town of Bayonne were in it too. So was a distinguished prefect, a senior policeman or two and at least one member of the Chamber of Deputies. It concerned a matter of French Municipal Bonds – respectable enough, you'd have thought. At first I did not know they were forged. Then there were the Hungarian bonds. Now they were not forged, though it appeared there was something else wrong with them. I am not a financial wizard, and as for being a psychologist, well I was not the only one to be taken in by the persuasive Serge Alexandre, dubbed by the press 'The King of Paris' and known on his birth certificate as Alexandre Stavisky.*

I sold a lot of bonds for him

Someone has remarked that it is marvellous what you can do with an investment trust if you know how to work it. I don't know about investment trusts but it was certainly marvellous what Stavisky could do with a bond. It made him vastly rich

---

* For those with an interest in the attractive country town of Bayonne, or in municipal bonds, or maybe both, Stavisky's little scheme went like this: bonds were issued in Bayonne as elsewhere in France to finance municipal pawnbroking services designed to help worthy citizens who might be temporarily embarrassed. Sums were advanced against the usual security: interest was charged at 6½ per cent. To finance the operation the bonds were issued to the public, earning interest at 4½ per cent, a copper-bottomed investment, to which insurance companies and private investors were happy to subscribe. But instead of investing these funds in loans to the needy, Stavisky was milking the Bayonne bonds on a lavish scale. Also, he'd found a useful little man in Italy who made pretty fair imitation emeralds. These he deposited in bagsfuls in Bayonne, getting advances far ahead of their value. Thus, he milked both ends. All he needed was a corrupt mayor, which he had, and a corrupt director of the Bayonne enterprise, which he also had. And friends in the *Police Judiciaire* and in the prefect's office. He had both, and both were glad to let him know when things got unhealthy. As for the matter of the Hungarians, that was designed to plug the holes in Bayonne as and when they needed it. It worked very well for a while.

13

and it made several others pretty rich too. When the crash came and Stavisky, who was left-handed, committed suicide by shooting himself in the right temple from what appears to have been six feet away, with policemen all over the place at the time, a number of people breathed a sigh of relief that he wouldn't after all appear in court with his little address book. But by then they were rioting on the streets of Paris and a court case there would have to be. The mayor of Bayonne and the member of the Chamber of Deputies, one Garat, received sentences. So did I and a few others. The big fish did not. And they included the old man – Senator Jean Paul Schlesser. Also my friend Max, who was working on the case and, for a consideration, had done his best for me – which was little enough. Also the *Inspecteur* at the *Sûreté* who had given Stavisky two days' warning that a warrant for his arrest had been sworn. It was the only opportunity that poor old Stavisky muffled in his remarkable career. As for me, they stopped me at the Swiss frontier.

Political parties are much like the classier type of brothel in this respect: there has to be someone presentable on the front desk. Whatever the depravity going on in the back bedroom, the front of the house has to look good. For this you need someone who epitomises rectitude, public spirit and utter trustworthiness. (I am speaking now, let there be no misunderstanding, about political parties.) You will wheel this person out to head a list at election time, to face impertinent investigative journalists or to join a coalition in some anodyne past – say as Minister of Transport. Or Social Welfare, if the Government proves capable of cobbling together a brief to go with such a title. Senator Jean Paul Schlesser, *Officier de la Légion d'Honneur*, was such a one. He had been in half a dozen coalitions, starting with Briand's government of 1929, and he had ranked among the top three or four men of his party for some twenty years. He was a public orator of great persuasive powers and looked every inch the family man at the service of his country. So much the worse, I always thought, for his country.

14

Peering out between the heavy folds of adipose tissue which made his face both chubby but strangely alarming, his eyes were appraising me carefully. Schlesser, I had noticed, seemed always to give his eyes first refusal. They would look you over – often for an uncomfortably long while – before he allowed himself to say anything. It was as if the look of you was more important to him than anything you might say in your own defence. He had been a provincial lawyer of the hard school, like most of his political associates, and one would not care to be on the other side in any case in which he chose to involve himself.

Having sized me up, he spoke: 'You look none the worse for it, I must say.'

'In fact, I am considerably the worse. I'm underweight, lousy and broke.'

All of this was true. It would be tedious to describe what had happened to the money I made with Stavisky beyond saying that a financial wizard had advised me to place the bulk of it outside France against just such an eventuality as had in fact overtaken me. 'Switzerland?' I asked innocently. 'They say the banks there are very discreet.' The wizard had sneered. 'In Switzerland,' he pointed out, 'the up-side is discretion; the down-side is lousy rates of interest.' Where then? I asked. 'Ah,' said the wizard, 'rates are very good just now in Belgium, and the discretion thing can be looked after. Especially in one of their provincial banks.' And he looked wise and actually winked. What had been left of my modest and certainly ill-gotten fortune was therefore in the *Banque Agricole des Flandres* which, in its turn, was now in the hands of the Germans. For practical purposes I was broke.

'Perhaps I can help,' Schlesser said.

'I am glad to see you again, Monsieur Schlesser, but I would be gladder still if I knew what all this is about and why I've been flown down to Paris by bomber and then booked into a squalid dive with a minder in a beret.'

Schlesser raised his eyebrows. 'Where did you put our

friend?' he asked Max.

'We have something in the Rue Vavin.'

'Get Monsieur Quinton out of there the moment you leave here.'

Max looked discomfited. 'I thought . . .'

'Don't think, it always lands you in trouble. Put him in the Crillon.'

'If you say so.'

'I do say so. And advance what he needs for the bill and expenses.'

'How much?'

'Whatever he needs.'

Max shrugged in a minimal and only slightly impertinent fashion. He clearly wanted to save what face he could, but he wouldn't be taking risks.

'Tell me, *mon cher*,' Schlesser said, 'that famous car of yours, you still have it?'

'I hope so, but . . .'

'Excellent, very good indeed. I would count it a great personal favour if you could retrieve it right away from wherever it has been these past years and get it into condition for a long journey.'

Schlesser had a personality which ran over you like a steam-roller and flattened you into the aggregate. It was a personality that easily held its own, and often more than its own, in the savage rough and tumble of French political life. I felt myself being flattened. I was moved to make what protest I could.

'Monsieur Schlesser . . .' I began, and got no further.

'Of course, I will pay whatever it costs. Spare no expense – tyres, overhaul, spare parts . . . I know nothing of cars but do what has to be done.' He was looking me over and appeared to find me wanting. 'You will pardon me . . . you have other suits?'

'I left my stuff with a friend. I shall be going to fetch it later this morning.'

'Good. For what I have in mind one must look, what shall I say, prosperous? As you always looked in the old days. I re-

16

member that impeccable style of yours: Quinton at Fouquet's with one of his magnificent women. How could one forget that, eh?'

'You flatter me,' I said weakly.

Schlesser waved a strangely delicate, almost feminine hand. It didn't fit the shrewd, plump face and heavy body. 'Not flattery – merely the truth. You, at Fouquet's, with your women, and in that car of yours – again with your women. What was the name of that blonde creature . . . Francoise?'

'Francine.'

'No doubt you'll be after her again, eh? I wish you luck.' A brief laugh came from somewhere deep inside him and stopped as suddenly as it had started. All it lacked was mirth.

'Monsieur Schlesser,' I managed at last, 'will you please tell me what all this is *about*. There has to be a payoff somewhere, and I think I ought to tell you . . .'

'I know precisely what you are about to say, *mon cher*. You are about to say that you are not interested in business propositions just now. You simply want to rest after your ordeal, is that not so?' He did not pause for an answer. 'Of course it is so. A very human reaction from a man who has been sorely tried. So let us leave business discussions until later, eh? Get yourself into shape, entirely without obligation – you understand, no obligation whatsoever – and then we'll see. I shall have a little project to offer you that will not be without its charm. A seductive proposal, let us say, from which you could emerge with some profit to yourself and with great advantage to our poor country.'

He actually paused for breath. 'I'd have to know what this thing of yours is. All I really want,' I said, 'is to get out of here and back to England.'

'Precisely, my dear fellow, and so you shall, with my blessing. And I can assure you that what we have in mind does not exclude an early return to your country, not for one moment. To the contrary, indeed, to the contrary.'

'Good,' I said.

17

Schlesser looked carefully at me again. 'In, h'm, prison, there is very little exercise, no?'

'Very little.'

'France is due for an overhaul of her penal services. We are backward in these matters, I'm afraid. So, very little exercise. From which I have to conclude that you are not in the best shape?'

'Correct.'

'At the Sporting Club in the Avenue Gabriel there is an excellent gym. I used to go there myself, but that was some years ago. I think you should arrange to attend for a daily workout, starting tomorrow. Again at our expense. That is something you will find useful if you want to get back to England.'

'I don't plan to swim.'

Again the brief, mirthless laugh. 'Fix it,' he said to Max. 'Mr Quinton will want at least a couple of hours a day.' Max nodded, glad to be brought back into the conversation.

'I propose,' I said, 'to report to the British consul tomorrow.'

The eyes narrowed a fraction. 'Unwise.'

'Why unwise?'

'The British here know all about you. And that will not encourage them to render your return home any easier. After all, if you will forgive me, you are competing for time and transport with several thousand British residents who, perhaps, commend themselves more readily to their embassy than you with your unfortunate recent experiences.'

There might be some sense in it. 'Your passport,' Schlesser was saying. 'You have it?' I nodded. 'It has not expired?' I shook my head. 'Good.' He got to his feet. Max and I did the same. The long, delicate fingers were extended for me to take. 'I estimate,' he said, 'that we have five days at the most in which to do all the things we have agreed upon.'

We had agreed upon nothing whatever, but I let it pass. He continued as we edged towards the door of his office: 'Do all I ask and you will find a situation very much to your liking. And I

18

promise that if what I have to propose is unacceptable to you, why then we shall just shake hands like the good friends we have always been and I shall be a disappointed man.' He spread his arms in a kind of whooping movement to express either my delight or his dismay, I knew not which. 'Restore your famous elegance. Together, we will have to see some bankers.'

With that we were outside and on our way down to the street.

I got Max to drive me to the apartment of a friend on the Quai St Michel where I had left my gear for safe keeping. My friend, it transpired, had left for the south two days ago. But my cases were in the basement. We got them out and loaded them. As we drove back to the Rue Vavin, Max sulky and aggressive at the wheel, I told myself that any scheme of Schlesser's was likely to be dubious at best, highly objectionable at worst. But was there any harm in hearing more? There was no harm, I decided. Also, I had to get the car back on the road. After three years on the blocks it might cost a franc or two. With the Germans rifling the till at the Belgian bank, it was now my only tangible asset and I was not to be parted from it.

Max was saying nothing. I tried to cheer him up. 'Perhaps you'll dine with me at the Crillon this evening, Max?'

'My wife expects me.' His feelings had clearly been bruised.

'Well then, another night.'

'Maybe.' He wiped the sweat from his brow, cursed a cyclist through the open window of the car and drove savagely down the Boulevard Raspail. 'This afternoon,' he said, 'I will take you to the car. Where is it?'

'You will not take me to the car, my dear Max, and I will not tell you where it is.'

'I have my orders.'

'I don't give a damn for your orders.'

'We can find out,' he said darkly.

'Try,' I said.

He shrugged and turned sharply into the Rue Vavin and jammed his foot down on the brake as we drew level with the Hotel des Arbustes.

'Never mind, Max,' I said. 'I'll get my gear and then you can take me to the Crillon. You'd better tell your friend in the beret that I'm free to go.'

Later at the imposing entrance to the Hotel Crillon on the Place de la Concorde, I bid Max good-day. 'Don't have me followed, Max,' I said. 'It would be a waste of manpower.'

I could hear the screech of his tyres as I followed the doorman into the hotel lobby, grasping firmly in my hand the wad of bills that Max had handed over with a sigh.

At dawn on 7 June the so-called Weygand line was breached by the German Panzers along its entire length. The seventh also happened to be the birthday of General Erwin Rommel's wife. 'Your birthday was a real day of victory,' he told her in a note hurriedly scribbled at his mobile command post north-east of Rouen. 'We gave a good account of ourselves. More and more signs that the enemy is collapsing. We're all fine. I slept like a dormouse.' He had reason to feel fine: his 7th Panzers were slicing through the remnants of General Besson's divisions east of Rouen like a hot knife through butter. The Germans would soon be standing on the Seine.

The War Committee, meeting at 10.30 a.m., heard a report of un-relieved gloom from General Weygand. The telegraph wires between Paris and London were humming through most of the day. Premier Reynaud complained to Churchill that General Fortune with his remnant of British troops was refusing to take orders from the French C-in-C. Churchill replied that British fighters had flown 144 sorties along the French front on the previous day. Reynaud told the British in confidence that there were now only two members of his cabinet — Georges Mandel and himself — who still believed in fighting on until victory was won.

At 10.30 that night General Weygand's chief assistant telephoned the prime minister's office to say there had been 'an accident of a technical nature' on the Tenth Army's front and two Panzer divisions were now installed in Forges-les-Eaux, a watering place on the road to Dieppe well-known to Parisians. The news brought the developing catastrophe home to those in the know in Paris in a graphic and personal fashion: Forges-les-Eaux was a place one visited very readily from the capital for a weekend with one's petite amie.

The newspapers announced that a little-known colonel — a tank expert — who had only recently been promoted to general, had been appointed Undersecretary for War. His name, new to the Frenchman in the street, was Charles de Gaulle. At the Sacré Coeur there had been a mass prayer of intercession for France in the hope that God might do better than the French High Command.

Chapter 3

Through those three years and thirty-one days I had memorized three numbers. One was the number of my account at the *Banque Agricole des Flandres*. And there were two telephone numbers: Jacques and Francine. I have said somewhere that I am very cautious by nature. Now my caution told me not to use the phone in my splendid room at the hotel. So I walked down to a nearby *bistro* and dialled the number in a call box. It rang for quite a while before the receiver was lifted and an irritable female voice said, '*Oui?*'

I asked for Jacques.

'Who wants him?'

'Tell him it's an old friend.'

I heard her shouting: 'You're wanted. Sounds like the Englishman.' Then the receiver was banged down on a hard surface and I waited.

'*Allo, oui.*'

I recognized Jacques' thick Toulouse accent at once.

'It's Bill Quinton,' I said.

'*Monsieur William, quel plaisir!*'

'How are you, Jacques?'

'Very well, very well. And you?'

'I'm fine, Jacques. Back in Paris.'

'You come at a bad time.'

'I know. Listen, I'd like to come over, but discreetly, you understand?'

'Of course. Come this evening.'

'What time?'

'I suggest after dark. Say ten.'

'I'll be there. And listen, you haven't heard from me, right?'

'Right, Monsieur William. *Au plaisir.*'

I walked back to the hotel, and as I was making for the lift the sirens started wailing. There was a general movement towards a door marked *Personnel*. Staff and a sprinkling of guests made no pretence of an orderly progress. Eventually we all stood around looking at each other with a kind of guilty complicity in the whitewashed corridors of the old building's basement. There was a smell of garlic and hot oil. No one said anything. An old lady who might well have been a duchess was quietly sobbing into a fine lace handkerchief while a put-upon companion kept murmuring, 'There, there, Madame, you are quite safe down here, quite safe.'

After ten minutes or so there was a rapid succession of fairly distant thumps and somewhere glasses rattled. I waited for the *crrump* of anti-aircraft fire but it never came. Thirty minutes later the wail of the all-clear reached us and we emerged looking shamefaced, as if we had all behaved like cowards. I went out on to the Place de la Concorde with its sandbags placed at random on roads and pavements, presumably against the landing of light aircraft. Over to the left, in the direction of the Gare de Lyon, a thin column of black smoke was rising into the perfect blue sky. I could hear the bell of an ambulance or a fire engine somewhere far off. People were emerging from whatever shelter they had been able to find and were going about their business. It all looked pretty normal, as if a bare week of air raids had already hardened the population.

There were leaflets scattered on the pavement opposite and in the roadway. I walked over and picked one up. On one side it said:

To the people of Paris

The armies of your allies, the British, have returned safely to their homeland, save for the many divisions which the invincible German armies have destroyed. Your own troops are fighting valiantly, but they have been betrayed by their leaders and their allies. Is it not time to end this senseless war?

On the back was a cartoon. There were three frames. The first showed a British and a French soldier, standing before a sea marked 'blood'. 'Let's jump,' says the Briton. Frame two showed the Frenchman jumping. In frame three the Briton stood smiling at the edge while the Frenchman drowned.

I crumpled the bit of paper and deciding I could use some exercise, made my way back to the Rue Royale. Half way up towards the Madeleine church, on the right-hand side of the street, is the world's most expensive florist. Because it brought back memories of the days when I could afford to use the place, sometimes at a rhythm of three dozen red roses per week, I stopped to admire the riot of flowers in the window. Who, I wondered, was still thinking of bouquets as the Nazi tanks rumbled through Normandy? A farewell to an incomparable woman? A corsage for a last, last dinner across the road at Maxim's? I looked at the flowers, and then I glanced back towards the Concorde. The young man in a brownish suit who had been walking along rather aimlessly behind me had also stopped and appeared to be deeply interested in the display in the world's most expensive china shop. Max was not one to overlook the routine side of police work.

I strolled up to the boulevards and so did my young man in brown. We both got back to the Crillon by five, in time for another air raid. This time they appeared to be aiming at the industrial suburbs to the north of the city. It lasted nearly an hour and again I heard no anti-aircraft fire. Then I went to the Sporting Club for my first workout and a swim. The young man sat on a bench beneath the plane trees out in the Avenue Gabriel, bored and no doubt wanting to go to the lavatory.

Back in my room I stretched out on the bed and thought about my life. Through the wide-open windows the strangely muted sounds of the city drifted in. The traffic across the Place de la Concorde was sparse and there were hardly any pedestrians. The sun blazed away over towards the Arc de Triomphe

24

and the room was airless and uncomfortably hot. We were having one of the most perfect summers of our time – ideal for an air force which had gained total air supremacy as the *Luftwaffe* had, and appalling for the masses toiling along the roads of France. And there I lay in the Louis XVI splendour of my room – former man-about-town and jailbird, frequently pictured in the London *Tatler* and the *Tout-Paris*, my name often linked with this or that heiress and on one misinformed occasion a princess of one of the better European royal houses. It all sounded a bit tawdry and pointless now, though there was as usual a sub-text to all the surface glitter, the sleepers on the Blue Train and the wild parties at the Embassy Club.

I considered the sub-text, lying there in beleaguered Paris, and found it wanting – as thin and pointless as the rest. How did I end up in France in the mid-thirties with no visible means of support? The answer was a knack: I had the gambler's knack, which I suppose is a cross between an untutored flair for mathematics and a certain psychological insight, plus the ability to sit patiently for hours at a baize-covered table and never, never make an unpremeditated move. Down from Oxford, in and out of an advertising agency where I showed a tiny flair for writing persuasive advertising copy, then in and out of a broker's office where I failed over a space of twenty months to sell either stocks or shares, and so to France in pursuit of a girl I was much taken with. And in France I lost the girl but discovered that I could beat the hostile odds in the card games in the casinos often enough to live thereby. I never touched roulette or *boule*. But at *trente-et-quarante, vingt-et-un* and at side games of bridge and poker at Enghien, Deauville and Le Touquet I could win and win consistently. And that was how I lived until friend Stavisky had wandered one day into my field of vision at a pricey restaurant at St Cloud, had scraped acquaintance and introduced me to his magnificent wife, and drawn me into his wretched scheme.

It all seemed infinitely stupid and socially negative now, and so, no doubt, it was. And the question posed itself: was I being drawn yet again into a doomed and dishonourable scandal?

Of course, I could turn my back on the Senator and Max and the others and simply take my chance with the rest of the Britons stranded in France. But it would certainly cost me something to get my car roadworthy and one thing I would not do was leave her behind. If the Nazis planned to pick France dry – and it didn't even occur to me now that they might not win the war – one thing they would not get their hands on, I told myself, was my car. So what did I stand to lose by getting her ready and then hearing what Schlesser had to say? Very little, it seemed to me. When it came to my turn to say something I could always say no. That evening, on the bed, I did not face up to what might happen if I said no and Schlesser said all right, but you owe me money, so pay up.

I had a couple of hours to kill before setting out for Jacques' place. Maxim's was just round the corner. What could be more nostalgic, pleasanter, than strolling round there for dinner?

I made myself look presentable and just before eight I was being carefully scrutinized by Monsieur Alphonse, the maître d'hôtel, who remembered me well enough from the old days but was carefully concealing the fact. I expected him to put me in the back room, where the riff-raff was always tucked away so that their presence should not discomfit the celebrities who squabbled for highly visible tables in the front room near the door. But to my surprise he led me to a highly prized table beneath the mirror on the right-hand wall – a table at which they normally seated nothing less than cabinet ministers or dollar millionaires. I soon discovered why. By the time I had finished my meal at 9.30 only one other table was taken. What I did not know then was that a couple of weeks later Goering and his cronies would be sitting under the mirror on the right-hand wall with the same Monsieur Alphonse recommending the *noisette d'agneau Edouard VII*.

When I came out of Maxim's I noticed they'd changed shifts and the young man in the brownish suit had given way to a plump, middle-aged colleague with *Police Judiciaire* written all over him. The *Police Judiciaire*, I should explain, was one of the three separate police forces heading up to the Prefect of Police in

Paris. It was supposed to chase villains and, where a wire could not be successfully pulled, bring them to justice. It had plenty of dossiers, I knew that much. It also had, for its sins, Inspector Max Boni, formerly of the *Police Municipale* in Ajaccio, Corsica. And this was doubtless his man, pretending to read a newspaper beneath the nearest lamp post. My task now was to get over to Jacques' place near the Quai de Berci, losing this policeman on the way.

I have no great experience of being tailed and losing my pursuer but I had little doubt that I could manage the present task. The man was clearly overweight and not at all happy in the stifling heat. He probably wanted to get home to his wife and children. He didn't look all that bright. And as far as I could see Max hadn't given him a sidekick.

I decided I would lose him in the Metro by nipping in and out of trains at the last moment until I'd shaken him off. The technique requires no great agility, just care and persistence. It took twenty minutes before I fooled him at the Châtelet interchange and found myself on my own. A half-hour later I emerged into the dusk at the Berci station. Ten minutes' walk along the mean streets lying between that part of the river and the railway marshalling yards brought me to the Rue de la Garonne. This was a street of workshops and small lorry parks. On the far side lay the blank walls of the bonded warehouses in which dutiable goods arriving by rail were stored for customs inspection. In the blackout the area was not attractive.

Jacques ran a car repair workshop. Beyond a forecourt a wall bore the legend: *J. Favet. Réparations Auto.* There was a down-at-heel office reached through a glass door. There was also access to sheds and a workshop at the back.

I crossed the forecourt, tried the office door, which was locked, and rang the bell. It sounded distantly. In a moment Jacques appeared, grinning and waving through the glass panel of the door as he unlocked it. Then I was inside and he had clasped me in his great hairy arms, laughing and thumping my back as if I were his long-lost brother from Toulouse. He wore a tight red sweatshirt over his massive torso and I noticed he had even less hair on his head than when I'd last seen him. The big unshaven face glistened with sweat. A good man with whom to go on that tiger hunt.

'*Alors, mon vieux! Alors, hein?*' He kept repeating it as he locked the door behind me and led me to an inner office. He sat me down on a bench, grasped a bottle of cognac which he had clearly opened for the occasion, and poured a couple of fingers each into two tumblers. We clinked and drank.

'*Alors*, so we're back among the living, then. How was it? No, I don't suppose you want to tell me. So what next, eh? What about the *Boches*, eh? *Nous sommes foutus!* We're done for! Isn't that right, eh? Done for! *Ah, les salauds!* The swine!'

The words tumbled out, thick and guttural, in the rhythms of the south-west. He refilled our glasses.

'I must say, I'm glad to see you, Jacques.'

'*Et moi, alors.*'

'How's the wife?'

He pulled a face. 'She knew it was you on the phone.'

'So I gathered.'

'She doesn't like you, you know.'

'I gathered that too.'

'Matter of fact, she's pretty hostile to the English these days. Says Germany's bound to win the war so we might as well learn to go to bed with 'em. The cow!'

'I hope she doesn't mean it literally.'

Jacques laughed. 'Couldn't care less, to tell you the truth. If it weren't for the kids . . .' He didn't finish the sentence.

'I've got an urgent job for you.'

'The car?'

'Obviously.' I suddenly panicked. 'You have still got it?'

Jacques grinned. Then he got to his feet. 'Come on.'

She was resting on her blocks, gleaming and magnificent, in an ancient shed. We had closed the door behind us and Jacques had turned on the light. Even by the pale light of a single 100-watt bulb, she was superb.

I ran a finger lightly along the contour of a wing. 'You've looked after her,' I said.

'A beautiful woman must be looked after or she'll lose her looks. I polish her myself. She's in fine condition, eh?'

'Magnificent.'

She was a 3½-litre Derby Bentley close-coupled drophead coupé. I had imported the chassis from England and had her delivered to Franay, the coachbuilders, to have one of their incomparably elegant bodies built on to her. My idea had been to drive her in the Paris–Nice run the following year, but that was just about the time when events overtook me and we never made Paris–Nice though I had had a few months of joy out of her. And here she was, her lithe black body gleaming, the rich red leather as inviting as ever.

Neither of us said anything as I walked round her and was seized with an absurd desire: just to sit in her again.

'Go on!' Jacques knew what was going through my head.

I climbed in, rested my hands on the wooden rim of the steering wheel, pushed into the yielding seat back, fiddled for a moment with the gear lever – getting the feel of her again. 'Marvellous,' I said. 'Bloody marvellous.'

'Like finding a new woman, eh?'

'No, no, a woman one has known but not yet closely enough. A touch of familiarity but true delight yet to come.'

'A poet, eh?'

We laughed like a couple of schoolboys.

'We have to get her ready for the road,' I said.

'No problem. A day or two.'

'Expect any snags?'

'You're going to tell me the clutch may have seized up and we'll need new clutch plates.'

'Could happen.'

'In *my* workshop? *Voyons!*'

'Okay, Jacques, if you say so.'

'I do say so. We'll get her wheels on tomorrow morning. Tickle her up a little, put in some juice and you can drive her away by evening. It's a promise.'

'I owe you a lot of money.'

'A fair sum.'

29

'How much?'

'I've no idea. We'll talk tomorrow. For old times' sake it won't be a bomb. And I've enjoyed having her here. Perfect manners – the ideal house guest.' He patted her affectionately. I took a last look. She was still wonderful. And she smelt good.

By the time I got back to my room at the Crillon it was midnight. I wasn't sleepy. The car had aroused in me a kind of sensual, even erotic excitement. But however beautiful a car – even a Bentley with *carrosserie* by Franay – you cannot make love to it. They say when you come out of prison two things obsess you: food and sex. I had had a very good meal at Maxim's . . .

I suddenly felt a deeply sincere desire to go to bed again with Francine. She had been the one who had helped me to cut a sizeable swathe through the Stavisky money. We'd done it in Paris and in Le Touquet, Deauville and Cannes during the respective seasons of those altogether delightful resorts. We'd done it in the hotels – the Royal Picardie, the Normandie, the Carlton – and in the casinos. And we had got there in my Bentley, had enjoyed her together, laughed and sung the songs of the day in her and, on several occasions – albeit with difficulty – had made love in her. Having retrieved my Bentley, I now wanted Francine.

If I am describing her at all now it is not because she was at home when I phoned: she wasn't. But she, and a number of her friends, were what had made Paris so irresistible to me, and what had made it so necessary to acquire those sums without which Francine would not have been available at all. She was a mannequin at Lanvin, where they didn't object to breasts and a woman didn't have to look irritable. Francine had quite splendid breasts and her disposition was entirely cheerful. She would laugh over a lobster supper at Larue and purr with pleasure as she lost my money at the high table at Deauville. And since she never went to bed, even with me, before one or so in the morning, I dialled her number now and waited nervously like a callow youth for the phone to be answered.

It seemed to ring for a long time. She could be out; she was

30

unlikely to be asleep. Then the receiver was lifted and I heard a sleepy voice.

'*Allo.*'

'Francine?'

'No, it's not Francine.'

'Is she there?'

'No, she doesn't live here now.'

The voice was shaking off its sleepiness.

'Did I wake you?'

'You did. May I go back to sleep now?'

'Wait a minute. Can you give me Francine's number?'

'She's in America.'

'When will she be back?'

'I don't know. She married an American. When they divorce, I suppose. A couple of years?'

There was the hint of a giggle. A pause. No clear signal that the conversation was over.

'Who are you?'

'Who are *you?*'

'I asked first.'

A brief hesitation. 'I'm Francine's cousin.'

'I never knew she had a cousin.'

'I'm sorry, but we weren't close. Now tell me who you are?'

'I was a good friend of Francine's, some three years ago. I've been away since.'

'You sound English.'

'I am.'

'No harm in that.' Another pause. 'My name's Marie Antoinette.' Something new was working its way into the voice.

'Are you a mannequin, too?'

'A mannequin?' She sounded puzzled.

'Yes, like Francine. All her friends were at Patou, Lanvin, Alix . . .'

'Oh no, not a mannequin. I'm her cousin. From the country.'

'You sound very beautiful indeed.'

'I am.'

'My name,' I said, 'is Bill – Bill Quinton. That's short for

31

William. Let's go to the *Poisson d'Or*. I believe it's still the best *boite*.'

'What, now?'

'When else?'

There was another pause, as if she were tempted.

'No.'

'Not ever?'

'Perhaps ever, but not now. I am very sleepy, you woke me and have still not apologized. I have to sleep now. Call me in the morning but not before ten. Goodnight, Mr Bill.' And she rang off.

I went to bed and had the greatest difficulty in getting to sleep.

As Rommel and his Panzers raced for the Seine they were often taken for British troops as they passed through towns and villages, and were frequently cheered by the local population. As they approached the river near Elbeuf they drove unchallenged past French military installations where lights were on and guards came smartly to the salute. In Elbeuf itself they were delayed by traffic jams. Meanwhile, the second phase of the German advance was opened with Von Rundstedt's Army Group B attacking from Bourg-et-Commin to the Meuse.

'The army is fighting its last defensive battle,' Weygand told Reynaud. Members of the War Committee moaned about the situation and Prime Minister Reynaud and the aged Marshal Pétain argued and snapped at each other. Pétain proposed an approach to Roosevelt to negotiate an armistice but the Committee lacked the energy to accept or reject the proposal and it lay on the table. Later in the day de Gaulle, the new Undersecretary for War, had an interview with Weygand and reported to Reynaud that what he needed was a new commander-in-chief. Weygand had talked about defending the line of the Seine while de Gaulle brushed aside the whole question of local defensive battles and tried to get the C-in-C to talk about the whole country, the colonies, the world. 'There was nothing in our conversation worth noting,' Weygand wrote later.

On the eighth and ninth Italy was mobilizing and Mussolini promised to speak to his countrymen on Monday, 10 June.

Refugees from the north and east continued to stream southwards through Paris and the exodus from Paris itself was now rather more than a trickle, though it had not yet reached the flood tide which would burst from the tenth onwards.

Chapter 4

Next morning my breakfast was served by an elderly maître d'hôtel. 'Your floor waiter has been called up,' he told me. 'Monsieur will forgive the inadequate service.'

'A bit on the late side to start calling people up?'

He sighed heavily as he fussed over the things on my tray. 'I'm afraid this country is done for. We can only wait for the Germans and learn to live with them.'

'Difficult.'

'I was in the grillroom at your Savoy Hotel for six years,' he said. 'The British have more resilience. We French are magnificent in attack. In defence, we lose heart. If Monsieur will permit me to say so, the British do not know when they are defeated.'

'A failure of imagination,' I said as I poured my coffee.

He bowed a bit and edged out of the door.

It was just after ten by the time I had eaten so I called Marie Antoinette. There was no reply. An hour later there was still no reply. I was beginning to feel like a teenager with acne who had aimed beyond his class. Outside, the Place de la Concorde was almost deserted. Vast crowds, the concierge told me, were streaming through Paris on their way south. But the Concorde did not lie on their route. They were crossing the Seine further west at Grenelle or to the east over the Conflans and Charenton bridges. 'We're done for,' the concierge told me. 'They should put Marshal Pétain in charge. He would know how to get us out of this mess.' He sized me up, wondered whether he should rubbish the Third Republic, decided against. 'All politics,' he ventured, 'are corrupt, Monsieur. There is nothing wrong with our armies.'

'I'm sure there isn't.'

The hotel was almost deserted. The duchess and her companion were still there, huddled in a corner of the salon, and there was a group of Dutchmen.

'Sure they aren't Germans?' I asked the concierge.

'Not at all, Monsieur. They are from Rotterdam.' How did he know? 'Their passports are Dutch, I assure you.' Genuine passports? 'I believe so.' I noticed as I walked away that he was talking to the man in Reception. Had I started another rumour?

Shortly before eleven a call came through; it was Schlesser. 'Meet me at the Ritz for lunch at one,' he said. Then he rang off. It was less an invitation than a command. I called Marie Antoinette again before setting out and this time she answered.

'You said after ten but you haven't been answering,' I said.

'I went out at nine,' she said. 'Isn't Paris terrible? All those poor people on the roads.'

'Not round here, but they tell me it's very bad.'

'And there's hardly any food in the shops. This morning I couldn't get eggs. Can you imagine?'

'You'll have to eat with me this evening.' There was a silence. 'Did you hear what I said?'

'Yes, I was thinking about where I'd like to eat.'

'Why not leave that to me?'

'Aren't you interested in my wishes?'

'Yes.'

'I'd like to eat at the Grand Véfour at the Palais Royal. Do you know it?'

'Of course. Shall I pick you up at eight? After all, I know where you live.'

'No. I'll meet you at the restaurant at eight-thirty. I'll be the very beautiful one in the red dress.' She giggled slightly. 'Goodbye,' and she rang off.

In the great dining room of the Ritz only one table was occupied: there were two couples, talking quietly together. As we passed them on the way to our own table, Schlesser nodded and both men greeted him. 'The head of Reynaud's personal staff and his wife,' he said as we sat down. 'The other couple are the Baron and Baroness de Chenet. If I know anything, the Baron is after a couple of seats on a government train. He's too late: nothing's moving out of the main-line stations any more.'

As we ordered our food and then started to eat, Schlesser told me what he had in mind.

'You will know,' he said, 'that I am a member of the Council of the Bank of France – one of the seven councillors nominated from public life.'

I didn't know but I nodded. There is no point in diminishing a man's solid opinion of himself, even by a fraction.

'In that capacity I have naturally developed close – I might say intimate – relations with the high officials of the bank, in particular with Fresnoy, one of the two deputy governors. He is in charge of the bank's resources in precious metals. Gold and so on.'

I nodded. I had no comment ready to mind for any of this.

'You will realize,' Schlesser was saying, 'that our gold reserves, which amount to some two thousand four hundred tons, were shipped abroad last year when war was declared. An obvious precaution.'

I didn't realize it, but I could see it was an obvious enough thing to have done, given the way things were working out, and again I nodded. Schlesser had a habit of assuming that you knew things you were highly unlikely to know. It was, in its way, a kind of compliment.

'Also, the bank's archives left last month. Another obvious precaution.'

Again I nodded.

'Most people,' Schlesser said, 'would assume that with the departure of the bank's staff, which is already under way – they are going, I may tell you in confidence, to Saumur – that nothing more needs to be done here in Paris.' He wiped his mouth carefully. He had been eaten fillets of sole in a cream sauce. 'But they would be wrong.' He paused for some kind of dramatic effect. 'The bank has a problem.'

36

He wanted me to ask what it was, so I did.

'They have a problem, *cher ami*, which I must tell you with all the conviction at my command only you can solve.'

He brought a hand down on the glistening white napery to underline this startling assertion.

'Me?'

'Only you.' He leaned forward and dropped his voice, though there was not a living soul within ten yards of us. The waiters hovered distantly on the far side of the room and the party at the other table were deep in conversation.

'Only you. I have spoken to Fresnoy and he agrees. And now I will explain. It is little known outside the bank itself that we hold one of the world's great collections of rare coins, probably the greatest. Only the Krupp collection can compare. These have come into our hands over the years – ever since Napoleon founded the bank in 1804. Incredible things – you will see. Worth a great fortune.' His eyes seemed to shine behind the folds of fat. 'This marvellous collection is still in the bank's vaults in the Rue de la Vrillière. Also some ingots of platinum which for certain reasons were not shipped with the main consignments of gold. It is the gold coins and the platinum which you are to take out of Paris in your car.'

There was an interruption while waiters tended to our needs, which in Schlesser's case rather surprisingly was vanilla ice cream.

I took a long and careful draft of the excellent wine before commenting on what he had said. 'What,' I asked, 'is to prevent the bank from sending the stuff out by truck with its own employees? Who needs a Bentley for a job like that?'

'The answer is simple. The governor and his closest colleagues have decided that in the deeply disturbed conditions through which we are living, it would be unwise to trust any member of the staff with such a consignment. My advice was sought and I concurred in this view. There is the question of honesty. There is also the question of danger. Conditions on our roads will be highly dangerous in the coming weeks. Secrecy is our first requirement. Technical competence – the ability to

37

transport this treasure safely out of the country – is the second. When I was consulted I remembered you and your motoring feats. I recalled your splendid car. I put you forward as a safe man to take this treasure out of the country. I said you had been abroad for the past three years.'

'And where, for God's sake, would I be taking it?'

'Across our frontier with Spain and then on to Portugal. There you will contact the British Embassy, who must be persuaded to provide transport to London. You, an Englishman, will be able to achieve that.'

'Is that all?'

'That is all.' Schlesser didn't appreciate irony.

'Forget it,' I said.

Schlesser showed his considerable quality. 'Precisely what I would expect you to say. Perhaps what I would say myself at this stage of our little transaction.' He smiled and tapped my arm affectionately. 'Only a fool would say yes to such a project at once.' He smiled again. 'Or, of course, a villain.'

'Forget it, Monsieur Schlesser,' I said again.

'You would be rendering both our countries a great service. The money that such a collection can fetch would play an important part in rallying our forces overseas for eventual victory. I am talking about millions, you understand, millions.'

'Count me out,' I said.

'We will provide you with papers to cross the Spanish frontier. Your Spanish visa is already waiting for you. I arranged it.'

I shook my head.

'There are already twenty kilometre queues at Hendaye and the other frontier crossings. I am told no more visas are being issued. And there are no more ships putting out from French harbours. How will you get home on your own?'

'I'll take my chances like everyone else.'

'Also, I'm afraid you owe me rather a lot of money. I wouldn't dream of embarrassing you, *cher ami*, but a debt is a debt.'

'I'll repay you when I get my hands on my assets.'

'What assets?'

I told him. When he laughed this time it sounded nasty.

'Those can scarcely be called assets any longer,' he said. 'And there is another problem. Otto Abetz, the last German ambassador to France, is a very dear friend of mine. No doubt when the Germans reach Paris he will once again play an important role here.' He paused. He was eating his ice cream and had a blob of the stuff poised in his spoon. 'This is a line of thought that I do not care to pursue now, with you as my guest, but you will understand what I leave unsaid.' He popped the ice cream into his mouth and dug out some more from the silver goblet before him. 'I am bound to point out that I obtained your release from prison. I am also financing your, er, rehabilitation and the servicing of your car. I am even paying for your hotel. You cannot expect all that to go for nothing.' He ate the ice cream. 'I will leave you to reflect on all this and you will call me at my office tomorrow morning at ten. Meanwhile, I have fixed an appointment for us both to see Henri Fresnoy at the bank at eleven. You will think it over and you will tell me tomorrow that you accept my proposition.'

The party at the other table had left. We were alone, the sole beneficiaries of the great kitchens, the immaculate service and the palatial setting of the Ritz.

'You will at least talk to Fresnoy,' Schlesser was saying. 'I ask you that as an old friend, entirely without commitment. He is a charming and cultivated man.' He wiped the traces of ice cream from his mouth and called for coffee and the bill.

Taking my precautions, I went straight from the Ritz to Jacques' place. It was Sunday and the centre of Paris was even emptier than the day before. Few Metro trains were running and it took me an hour to reach Jacques' workshop. I went straight round to the back, and there was my car, flashing in the sunlight, every inch of her polished and buffed, her wheels on, her hood packed down, ready for adventure and romance. Jacques was giving a final rub to one of the great headlamps.

'I told you, eh? No problems.'

He climbed in, turned the ignition key and pressed the

39

starter, and the car purred into life. He climbed out. 'Go on, drive her.'

'I can't take her out now,' I said. But I got in, put her in gear and took her across the yard. Perfect! Then I backed her. No boy with his new train set could be more intoxicated.

'Jacques, you're a master! I expect to pick her up tomorrow. So how much?'

He told me, with a grin which said he hated taking money for her. It was little enough but vastly more than I had.

'All right,' I said. 'I'll have it by tomorrow.'

Later in the afternoon I spent a couple of hours at the Sporting Club, and being in rotten condition I found it extremely unpleasant. The gym instructor gave me a hard time and must have signalled the masseur to do likewise. Outside, one of Max's men waited perspiring and disconsolate in the shade of a plane tree against the fierce heat of the sun. There hadn't been a cloud in the sky for close on three weeks.

She turned up at nine in a blue dress and joined me at the bar.

'Don't say it,' she said as she tried to get on to the bar stool. She was a small girl with long, thin wrists and delicate hands. 'I know I said red but I caught sight of myself in a shop window after leaving home and decided against. Blue seemed to me appropriate, so I went back and changed. Hello, I'm Marie Antoinette.'

I kissed her hand because Englishmen aren't supposed to do it and I thought it might impress.

'Any friend of Francine's,' she said airily, 'is a friend of mine. I'll have a gin fizz, please.'

I attended to the cocktail and turned to look at her. She had been right: she was a very beautiful girl indeed.

'I am, aren't I?' She had a knack, I found later, of answering your thoughts.

'You are. Also a trifle disconcerting.'

'Surely not?'

'I think you set out to be.'

She laughed. It was carefully controlled for effect but genuine

40

in its slightly theatrical way.

The gin fizz and the menus arrived. She waved her menu away. 'Tell me, please.'

We wandered together through the hors d'oeuvre and entrées. 'I like the sound of the *salade Quimperloise*,' she said. 'I went to Quimper on holiday as a child. That was where I pushed my English nanny off a rock.'

'Was she hurt?'

'She nearly died. Terrible gashes. Blood everywhere. Hysterics, followed by punishment. It was awful. But I'll try the salad. What is it?'

I asked. It was pieces of lobster laced with cognac but it was off. 'No produce is reaching us from Normandy or Brittany,' the maître d'hôtel said. 'The war, you see.' He looked upset that the war had spoiled his salad.

'Damn,' Marie Antoinette said. 'I'd better have the caviare. You must also have caviare. And then the calves' kidneys with the three mustards. Why three mustards?'

The question went unanswered and I ordered wine.

'So you had an English nanny?'

She nodded. 'But I hardly speak any English. I hated her and so a resistance was set up and I refused to learn.' She drained her cocktail. 'You see, I have this very, very strong will. I get it from my father.'

'I can believe it. Would you like another drink?'

She shook her head. 'Let's go to our table.'

Side by side on the red plush *banquette* we had a full view of the splendid eighteenth-century room. Only two other tables were occupied and no one spoke above a whisper. It was as if civilization were to be quietly liquidated and hardly anyone was bothering to stay to see it happen. The waiters, all elderly, tried to look busy. A young *commis* scuttled about, doing nothing. A couple at a nearby table were deep in an examination of the delicately painted ceiling with its cherubs and garlands. We were on a ship which was going down without hope of rescue. Here, in the far corner of the Palais Royal, you could almost hear the waves lapping over the gunwales, the hiss

41

of steam as seawater reached the boilers . . .

'You don't talk much,' she said.

'Actually, I do. I was thinking. Sorry.'

'Tell me.'

'Let's get to know each other first. Tell me about yourself.'

'My name is Marie Antoinette de Bergemont. My father is the Comte Henri de Bergemont et St Hilaire. Those are two villages near Barbezieux. It's where we have our place.'

'Francine never told me she had relatives with a place.'

'Oh, Francine! She never mixed much with us. My father thinks that side of the family is common.'

'Nothing common about Francine,' I said defensively.

'My father has rigid standards. It was why I had an English nanny, the bitch, and wasn't allowed to talk to boys until I was eighteen. I was a virtual prisoner at the château. That's at Bergemont. Louis XIII. Garden by Le Nôtre. When I was sixteen I was caught in a barn with the farm manager. It was a difficult moment because he was forty-two and I was naked.' She giggled and sipped her wine. 'They beat me. I was black and blue. The priest made me confess everything and as he was clearly enjoying it I coloured it up a bit. Not that it needed much colour. God, that priest! I could tell you the most disgusting things about him.' She pulled a wry face in which disgust scarcely figured at all. 'Anyway, as I said, Le Nôtre did the garden. You know – parterres, fountains, a Greek temple or two. Very *ancien régime*.'

'Le Nôtre was a bit later, wasn't he?'

'The garden was laid out later.'

'And what are you doing in Paris?'

There was a pause. 'I work with, you know, a gallery.' A hand fluttered.

'Paintings?'

'That sort of thing. *Mostly* paintings. Very advanced stuff.' The hand again. 'And you?'

I told her what I thought she ought to know about me, changing the geography of the last three years a little. Switzerland came into it. And I thought Belgium could be appropriate.

Our food was served and she picked at hers with the deftness of a kitten, darting the tip of a pink tongue out to catch an egg or two of caviare from her fork.

Later, as she toyed with the kidneys in their complicated sauce, I said: 'So you live alone in Francine's apartment?'

She nodded. I glanced for maybe the tenth time at her profile – the delicacy of a terracotta by Greuze but with that hardness of edge which gives the women of Paris their fascination and their capacity to alarm. I noticed that her earrings were a very good colour match to her dress, but cheap. She wore no other jewellery.

'All my family is down at Bergemont,' she said. 'My parents – my mother is a darling but confined to a wheelchair – my two younger sisters and of course my father. I am the black sheep.'

'And what are your plans now that the Germans are so close?'

She shrugged. 'I don't make plans. I allow things to happen and then I decide.'

'But they're happening.'

'And I'm deciding.' She turned her head and looked at me. I noticed that the imperfections of her face, the tiny departures from the classical, were the real secret of her beauty. Her mouth was just a shade too wide, her lips a little fuller than you'd expect in a face whose main character was a fine and delicate bone structure, her unplucked eyebrows maybe thicker than proportion demanded, and there was an unexpected dimple in her chin. But it was the eyes above all, set rather deep and rather far apart, which held the attention. They had highlights, tiny flecks of what appeared to be yellow – almost gold – which caught the lights from the chandeliers in the restaurant. And when she smiled or produced that elusive giggle of hers, the eyes seemed to shine with their own secret mirth.

As we drank coffee I asked if I could take her home and she shook her head quickly. 'Not tonight. But you can find me a cab, of course.'

As we waited for it I said I would call her tomorrow. 'I don't know when I'll be in,' she said, 'but by all means try.' I had the impression that she had perfected a technique. It was neither

43

come hither nor go hence. It was aggravation. 'Thank you for a very nice dinner,' she said as she climbed into the taxi, and she offered me the upper part of her right cheekbone to peck at. I pecked. Round one to Marie Antoinette.

Chapter 5

The papers next morning appeared with large blanks where whole columns of copy had been lifted out by the censor and the editorial staff had presumably refused to put in alternative matter. They were signalling to their readers that they no longer had editorial control over their journals. What was left uncensored did not inspire confidence. German advanced units, said *Le Petit Parisien*, had entered Rouen but were being held north-east of the capital.

'People are leaving the city,' the concierge said. 'They say the stations are besieged. At the Gare Montparnasse I heard it's chaos and the police have lost control. It seems that half Paris wants to get down to the south-west.'

'I can understand it.'

'And Monsieur is not leaving?'

'I have things to do in Paris. I have no plans to leave.'

'The lady with her companion is leaving this morning. Perhaps we will have to close the hotel.'

'Give me notice,' I said.

'*Bien sûr, Monsieur.*'

'And the Dutchmen?'

'I believe they are staying.'

I caught sight of them later, chatting in the lobby and seemingly unconcerned at the plight of their own city. Were they selling something? Or buying? A forlorn mission either way.

The normally impassable social barrier between staff and guests was breaking down. I had seen the concierge deep in conversation with the duchess in the salon. A *chef cuisinier* in his white apron, neckerchief and cap appeared suddenly in the foyer and disappeared again. It was the briefest of interludes but it spelt either revolution or national collapse. Perhaps both.

And something had happened to the weather. It still promised to be in the eighties by midday but Paris was enveloped in a pall of dirty grey mist, smelling of petrol fumes and carbon. 'We have no idea what it can be,' the concierge was telling us. 'Perhaps the Germans dropped smoke bombs during the raid early this morning.'

It was one of the Dutchmen who said he had heard on the radio that the petrol dumps on the lower Seine had been hit and were still burning.

At nine I had called Jacques.

'She's ready,' he said.

'I'll be over at lunchtime to collect her.'

'I'll hate to see her go.'

'Come better days, I'll bring her back to see you.'

At ten I was in Schlesser's office. He came straight to the point.

'You have decided?'

'I'll listen to your banker, then I'll make up my mind.'

'Very sensible.'

'Tell me,' I said, 'is there any angle to all this?'

Schlesser, whose entire career had been Euclidean when it came to angles, pretended bemusement. 'I don't understand, *cher ami.*'

'An American expression meaning that there is some hidden significance, some advantage to unspecified persons.'

'I still do not understand.'

'I think you do, Monsieur Schlesser, but let me put it as delicately as I can. First, you go to considerable trouble and certainly some expense to get me out of jail and down to Paris in an air force plane at a time when your armies are begging for more air support. Then you take me to the Ritz to persuade me to undertake a mission which seems singularly inappropriate, given my *dossier* at the *Préfecture de Police*. And all this is done with the very active participation of that sinister villain Max

46

Boni, who is having me tailed like a common crook. Then you plan to take me to see a high official of the *Banque de France*, who is to be persuaded to entrust an enormous fortune to me. And I have no doubt that between now and the moment you introduce me you will actually tell me he thinks my name is John Smith.'

'Robinson, actually. David Robinson.'

It stopped me, but only for a moment. 'Sorry, Robinson. And as I was saying, you do all this and then you don't understand when I ask about angles. So let me put it another way. Is there anything about this project which is in any way different from what your friend Monsieur Fresnoy at the bank imagines it to be?'

Schlesser allowed a smile to crease his face without in any way affecting his eyes. He took a moment to reply.

'Very good, my dear Quinton. Very good in the English empirical style of reasoning which we French so much admire – I would even say envy.' He chuckled. 'Analytical, devoid of subjective emotion, but based, I fear, on a false premise: that Jean Paul Schlesser is motivated only by self-interest.' He drew his great bulk upright in his chair and I began to feel like an audience. '*La patrie*,' he said, '*est en danger!*'

I could scarcely believe my ears. That hoary cliché about the fatherland, and from this rogue who must even now be estimating how his friendship with Ambassador Abetz could keep him afloat in a humiliated and occupied France!

'So?' I asked.

'It is our duty to save our precious reserves so that the fight may go on elsewhere. I saw the prime minister yesterday and it is his express wish. Fresnoy will confirm it.'

'So why that crook Max, and why am I to be David Robinson?'

Schlesser shrugged his great shoulders. 'I use Max Boni because I can trust him. He is obligated to me in certain ways and so I am sure of his loyalty and his discretion. And of course, being in the police, he can get certain things done. As for you and your name, the thing is obvious. We need you because we need your car. Also, you are English. And if the people at the bank knew of your recent little troubles, clearly it would . . .' He spread his hands eloquently and it became another of his unfinished sentences. He was a master of that difficult genre. 'So,' he said, pulling himself up from his chair, 'it is time for us to go to the bank. You will see, it is a very fine building, well worth a visit.'

Old man Schlesser puffed his way into the impressive entrance hall of the *Banque de France* a few steps ahead of me, acknowledging in the curt French manner the bow of the uniformed flunkey. We made our way slowly up the magnificent staircase.

'We will go to Fresnoy's office,' he said. 'He will tell you what it is all about and when he has finished, *cher ami*, you will say yes because you are a patriotic Englishman and this is your duty.'

I had only come to listen, I said to myself.

Schlesser was giving me a conducted tour. 'This was the mansion built in 1620 by our finest architect, Mansart, for the Councillor of State Phelypeaux de la Vrillière. Napoleon gave it to the Bank in 1808. See, the tapestries are very fine.' We had reached the first floor. 'There you will see a portrait of the emperor and another of the unfortunate Duchesse de Lamballe, who had lived here. And now,' as we walked down a corridor, 'we come to the famous golden gallery.'

Actually the place hurt your eyes. Almost every inch of the panelling and mouldings was covered in gold leaf. Everything gleamed. Everything cried excess, ostentation and arrogance. It was from here that they tried with only intermittent success to defend the value of the franc.

We passed through this preposterous ballroom – which is what the golden gallery had once been – and on to a door marked *Monsieur le Sous-Directeur de la Banque*. Schlesser knocked firmly and had the door open before the response from beyond had been uttered.

Another splendid room: oak panelling, a high ceiling with mouldings and a painted panel, an oil painting of what I took to be some former bank official, and the absurd and inescapable official photo of the current President of the Republic, Albert Lebrun. Henri Fresnoy rose from behind his desk and the introductions were made. I was one David Robinson. He was the very model of a high French functionary, as smooth as his own magnificent marble chimneypiece and quite probably as hard. A man to defend the franc and admonish the government for its extravagance.

'The Senator has recommended you to us, Monsieur Robinson,' he said. 'Permit me to explain our problem.'

He brought the tips of his fingers together in a neat pyramid above the polished surface of his desk and I noticed that they stayed like that, motionless, as he talked. This was the kind of Frenchman whose existence the English deny.

'Our gold reserves have been suitably disposed of. But we still have here in our vaults some very valuable specie which was retained for reasons I am not at liberty to divulge. These our Board of Governors has decided must now be removed to safety. The confidential view of the Ministry of War is that the enemy will be in Paris within four or five days, possibly sooner. Before then, this treasure must be on its way out of France.'

'What weight are we talking about?'

'Possibly a ton.'

'I don't think my car will carry a ton.'

'What modifications would it need?'

'My guess is that we'd have to look at the wheels and the springs. I can get expert advice.'

'Good. So let us assume the technical problems can be solved. We would want you to secrete this consignment in your car, drive it down to Portugal and arrange its transfer to England.'

'Senator Schlesser told me as much.'

'We will designate a member of our staff to travel with you. A young man from my private office in whom I have confidence.'

I nodded. I glanced at Schlesser. The watchful eyes appeared to be fixed on the indifferent portrait hanging on the wall behind Fresnoy's head. It was difficult to tell if he was listening.

'Of course,' Fresnoy was saying, 'we will finance your journey. I would simply ask you to keep an account of your

49

expenditure. You will understand . . . we are a government department.'

I had a quick vision of the bank's accountants, years hence, running their slide rules over my expense account and knocking off 'refreshments' and 'miscellaneous'.

'Also, we will meet the costs of modifying your car, fuelling it, and allowing for depreciation and so forth.'

The ship of state was settling by the stern and this absurd functionary was costing the lifejackets. Looking at the man, at the immovable hands and the pedantic tidiness of his desk, and listening to his accountant's view of how to save the last pathetic remnants of the nation's treasure, I positively warmed to him. In a world over-endowed with Staviskys, Max Bonis and Schlessers, here at any rate was an old-fashioned servant of the state: blinkered, narrow and honest.

'I would like to help,' I said, looking not at the hard little man on the other side of the desk but at Schlesser. If I had hoped to detect a clue to this or that, I was disappointed. Schlesser did not move his gaze from the portrait on the wall.

'The bank is deeply obligated to you, Monsieur Robinson. Can you arrange for the necessary work on your car?'

'I can.'

'And how long do you think it will take?'

'I will know later today. I have a good mechanic.'

'I will introduce you in a moment to my young colleague, Marcel Bellon, who will look after all financial matters and act as liaison between us.'

'Perhaps you'll tell me what exactly I am to carry.'

The fingertips separated and a sheet of paper which had lain face-down on the blotter was carefully lifted and passed across the desk to me.

'You will observe,' Fresnoy said in his precise voice, 'that the consignment consists of two categories: the first is made up of sixty ingots of platinum of twelve kilos each; the second is our collection of rare coins, of which there are some sixty thousand, of a total weight of two hundred and seventy kilos. Whereas the coins are of lesser weight, they are of the greater value, given the extreme rarity of many of the items.' He had embarked on a subject which appeared to light some spark in the grey recesses of his soul. 'We have some very remarkable items. No less than seven of the ten Louis d'or known to have been issued by the royal mint in 1640 and unpriced in the catalogues since there is no market in them. If we have to sell, they will fetch many thousands of dollars each. Similarly, a unique – I repeat, unique – twenty-rouble piece of Catherine the Great, 1755. Or a group of fifty excellentes minted in Spain in the reign of Ferdinand and Isabella, probably 1511, also exceedingly rare. In short, probably the finest collection in the world. We have a full catalogue on file and I will ask you to accept that what we place in your car will correspond precisely with that catalogue. Your own list there, of course, deals only in weights.'

I could not conceive of this man getting a decimal wrong.

'We are entrusting great treasure to you, Monsieur Robinson. France, in her extremity, must rely on her friends.'

'If the stuff reaches London at all,' I said, 'it will check against your lists.'

Marcel Bellon proved to be an eager young man who clearly would never achieve the level of desiccation required to step into his boss's shoes. I told him I wanted to see the cargo. Leaving Schlesser, still motionless, in Fresnoy's office, he led me back through the golden gallery to a narrow lift which had been tucked into a recess and whose doors had been panelled to match the original panelling. When we emerged, we were in the vaults.

'Everything is in one room, ready to be moved,' he said. 'You have a van?'

'I have a car.'

'Good heavens . . .'

'Let's see anyway.'

A man in a grey smock was called and at the end of a passage we found the room. Grey smock had the key to a mortice lock and friend Bellon had another key which unlocked a mechanism I didn't understand. Between the two, the heavy steel door swung open.

51

If I had expected to be thrilled by the sight of treasure trove I was to be disappointed. Rows of rather dull-looking platinum ingots, each about ten inches long and maybe a couple of inches high, rested on battens against a wall. On wooden shelving there were rows of metal bins, each containing rolls of coins tightly packed in brown paper like so many sticks of rock. Each was about a foot long.

'There you are,' Bellon was saying, 'but I don't know how you're going to get all that into a car.'

'Nor do I, but we'll try.'

We went back upstairs. 'You can reach me here at any time, day or night,' Bellon said. 'I am permanent duty officer now. Nearly all our staff except security have left.'

'As soon as your car is ready,' Fresnoy said, 'you can load it here in the courtyard.'

'We can't drive out of Paris with boxes of gold and platinum on the back seats,' Bellon said.

'I never thought we would,' I said. 'The stuff will have to be hidden in the car – a ton of precious metals invisible to the naked eye or the casual marauder.'

'Can it be done?'

'Possibly. The car's chassis is essentially two girders running from front to back. We'll have to see if the ingots can be strapped along their length. The coins will be a bit harder. We'll see what space we find behind the interior trim or maybe under the seats.'

'And your car will take all that weight?'

'Not as it stands, but we'll work on it.'

'Your mechanic, can he be trusted?'

'Yes.'

'But you won't tell him what the car is to be used for.'

'I won't but I could.'

Bellon handed me an envelope of money for which I signed, then we took our farewells.

I parted from Schlesser outside the bank. 'Let me have progress reports,' he said.

I took the Metro to Berci, again taking my precautions. But

outside Jacques' yard there was a Citroen with police number plates and a uniformed man at the wheel. And in the dismal office Max was sitting, his hat on his knee. He was smoking a *maïs* and seemed perfectly at ease. Jacques sat in the other chair, looking miserable.

'What's this?' I asked.

'Good day,' Max said. 'I was waiting for you.'

'The car,' Jacques said miserably, 'it's gone, Monsieur William.'

'Stolen?'

'My men have taken it,' Max said. He didn't bother to remove the cigarette from his mouth.

'Why?'

'We think modifications will be needed. We'll do them in the police garage at the *Préfecture.*'

'Under what statute do you remove private property like that?'

'I've no idea,' Max said lightly. 'We have our orders.'

'Where from.'

'Not your business,' Max said as he lighted another cigarette from the butt of the first.

'The inspector's men drove it away an hour ago,' Jacques said. 'I called you. The hotel said you were out.'

'That's right, I was.'

'The police said they were acting at your request. They even signed for it.' He pulled a paper out of a back pocket.

'All right, Jacques, I'll deal with this.'

I paid Jacques what I owed him out of the money in Bellon's envelope. 'Come on,' I said to Max, 'take me to the car and make it quick.'

It was clear that Jacques could scarcely believe his ears. The people of Paris live in an uneasy relationship with their various police forces. Some would call it symbiosis but to me it's more like a kind of dangerous bio-feedback in which each excess of the police encounters just enough resistance to prevent a more outrageous incursion into civil rights, with both sides having long ago mastered the dangerous game. But whichever way you played it, you did not tell an *Inspecteur* to make it quick.

'Monsieur William, I am sorry,' Jacques said. 'When you get her back, bring her to see me.'

We shook hands. 'I will.'

'Don't blame me,' Max said in the car. 'Orders.'

'How did you find the place? I lost your flatfoot every time.'

'What you call my flatfoot was there for you to lose. You never saw the man who was doing the real job.'

'No one followed me all the way.'

'Of course not. You were handed on. Our methods,' he said smugly, 'are sound.'

We crossed a branch of the river to the Ile de la Cité and turned left into the Rue de Lutèce, which runs alongside the great bulk of the *Préfecture de Police*. The driver turned into the courtyard and down a ramp to the underground garage. At one end was a workshop where mechanics were working on police cars and motorcycles. There were two armoured cars in a corner. Next to one of them stood my Bentley with a group of admiring mechanics rubbernecking round it. They dispersed as Max Boni alighted from our car, snapping and snarling.

'Where's Motta?'

'Working on a job.'

'Bring him here. Hurry!'

Motta proved to be a small, wizened man with a brush of iron-grey hair and a moustache to match. He was in grubby blue overalls, heavily grease-stained. He looked as if he never went up into the daylight above.

'Motta will be in charge of the job,' Max said. 'You will explain the problem to him.' He hadn't bothered to introduce us. 'We'll put as many men on the job as we need.' He turned to Motta. 'I want a report on my desk by three with a firm finishing date.' And he got back in his car and snapped an order to his driver. The atmosphere lightened as he drove back through the gloom of the great garage.

Motta shrugged at the retreating car and turned to me. '*Alors, Monsieur*, what can we do for you?'

'This car,' I said, 'is expected to carry one ton of metal, totally

54

concealed, plus a couple of passengers and modest luggage.' I explained the details.

'So let's take a look at her.'

They put the Bentley on a hoist and Motta inspected the underside. 'I thought we could strap the ingots to the chassis rails,' I said.

'No problem. We'll use metal strapping and weld the closures.'

'The coins will have to go behind the trim. They're in twenty-five-centimetre sticks.'

We brought the car down to ground level. Motta told two of his men to clean their hands and start removing the car's trim. The door panels and seats were carefully taken out. The wooden floor panel beneath the rear seat was unscrewed. Motta inspected the gap.

'We can build a metal container in there. It's nicely placed over the back axle. And we'll put another compartment behind the dashboard.'

'What about strength?'

Motta circled her, examined her wire wheels, paused reflectively at her rear. 'An extra leaf in the springs. I'll get the blacksmith on to it. And those fancy wheels will never take a ton – not on a long trip.'

'It is a long trip.'

'We'll need to re-spoke them with heavier-gauge wire. I'll get that started too. The four wheels plus your two spares – that's a week's job to be done in a couple of days.'

'Can you do it?'

'*Faut bien.* We've had our orders. I'll put half a dozen men on it and they won't be going home to their wives.'

'Then,' I said, 'there's the question of spares. I'll need fan belts, at least one set of clutch plates and a few inner tubes.'

'I'd take a spare petrol pump,' Motta said, 'and plugs of course.'

'Of course.'

'Who's the Bentley main dealer in Paris?'

I told him.

'We'll get after them.' He seemed to be a good man. He rummaged around under the bonnet. 'Has she been de-coked lately?'

'My man never had a chance. Your Inspector Boni snatched the car without warning us.'

'Oh, him? We'd better have the cylinder head off and de-coke her, just to be sure. We'll take a good look at the valves. If they need re-grinding we'll re-grind. Maybe I'll put in new valve springs and gaskets. Can't do any harm. Might as well do the job properly.' He was still peering into corners. 'These air inlet shutters on the radiator,' he said, 'I see they're thermostatically operated. Very neat.'

'Engine temperature controls the aperture.'

'It's obvious. But I don't approve of the idea. A few hours on a hot, dusty road and the whole thing can jam.'

'You can disconnect it,' I said. I showed him the pin to remove.

He grinned. 'You have a few good engineers over there.'

Before I left him he gave me a pass. 'Inspector Boni left this for you. Come in to see me any time you like. See how she's coming along.'

Clearly they'd had the whole thing planned before they even came to fetch me in Reims. All my discussions with Schlesser since then were so much chat. The Bentley was to do the job and that was that. But the question remained: what was Schlesser's angle?

Would Paris be defended? No one knew: neither her population, her government nor her attackers. General Hering, military governor of Paris, had received no orders. Roger Langeron, the Prefect of Police, had asked and received no reply. The fear of Hitler and of the French government was identical: Red Paris – a takeover by the people of the capital. It had happened in just such circumstances before. In 1870 another German army had crushed the French at Sedan. As the Uhlans approached Paris, the government had retreated to Versailles and the people of Paris had set up their Commune. To resist the Germans and to change society. They had failed; they were not to be given a second chance now.

Hitler was determined that his troops should not be pinned down in street fighting. And so his armies were ordered to advance to the west and east of the city in a giant pincer movement. On Monday and Tuesday, 10 and 11 June, the eastern arm of the pincer was pressing down through the French armies, crunching them to pieces as it raced towards the Seine.

The evacuation of ministries from Paris had been ordered on the sixth. Through the weekend fifty-nine special trains had been taking staff and archives south. There were trains full of criminals and lunatics. By midnight on the tenth the ministers themselves had started to leave. Earlier that day Premier Reynaud received a phone call from his ambassador in Rome: he was told that Italy had declared war on France.

Rommel to his wife: 'We'll soon reach the sea between the Somme and the Seine . . . We never dreamed the war in the west would go like this.'

Wrote de Gaulle later: 'Amid a prostrate and stupefied nation, behind an army without faith or hope, the machine of state was grinding on in utter confusion.'

Reynaud saw US Ambassador Bullitt and gave him a message for President Roosevelt, eloquent and quite without real purpose. At 7.30 on the tenth he broadcast to the nation: 'During a long and glorious history France has faced greater trials.' No one could recall any trial greater than this.

The Paris police force received an order of the day from the Prefect on the twelfth: 'We have been ordered to continue our task and maintain security and order in the capital.' During the day retreating French tanks were seen in the centre of the city. Confusion was turning to panic: the great exodus was getting under way.

Chapter 6

At midnight the telephone woke me. It was Marie Antoinette.
'My revenge,' she said. 'You woke me, I am waking you. I would like to talk.'

'I've been trying to reach you. It became very boring for the telephone operator here.' It was true: I had tried half a dozen times and both the operator and I had got tired of it.

'I have been out. But now I am at home, I feel lonely, and suddenly I thought it would be nice to talk to my English friend.'

'Let's go to the *Poisson d'Or*,' I said, repeating myself. 'We'll talk there.'

'It's closed.'

'How do you know?'

'It's the kind of thing I know about.'

'Well, somewhere else.'

'No, I have some good coffee here.'

'I will be with you very soon.'

'Mmmm,' she said, as if she were debating the idea in her mind. Then she rang off before I could start wheedling.

Forty minutes later I was in Francine's familiar apartment on the Chaillot hill, with its tall windows with the splendid view over the river to the Eiffel Tower. Only now they were closely curtained and the room itself was quite different. Francine's taste had been lush, aspiring to the fashionable, much given to Lalique glass and graphics by artists of the day. Her men didn't keep her but they gave her expensive baubles and she liked to festoon her place with them. It was the taste of a Paris demimondaine, vulgar in the quietest way. There were a lot of cushions about.

But all that had changed. The apartment had been completely done over in the classical style: a carefully random mix of the last two pre-Bastille Louis, complete with fine carpets and a tapestry on the wall which looked genuinely of the period. It was very much as if an interior decorator of the old school had been retained by a wealthy and ancient dame to fit up her apartment according to the style books. It must have cost a small fortune. In this totally inappropriate setting Marie Antoinette floated, infinitely delicate and puzzling, in a pale yellow thing which flowed over her tiny body and down to the ground. A very good aroma of coffee mixed wonderfully well with her perfume. The lights had been carefully set so that one could just see across the room, though not too clearly, and there were bottles and glasses on a table. As she opened the front door to me she had again offered the edge of her cheekbone to be kissed. I took her chin gently between two fingers and turned her head towards me. I encountered surprising resistance and my kiss fell no further towards her mouth than the centre of her cheek.

'Come in. The coffee is ready.'

We drank coffee and a good brandy, seated opposite each other in the uncomfortable Louix XV chairs. There was absolutely nothing that could be described as erotic about the setting, but everything about Marie Antoinette was at odds with the décor. Whereas I do not lust after every attractive woman I meet, I found that I was lusting after this girl with an intensity which astonished me. It was the effect of three years of prison, of her extraordinarily delicate beauty, her provocative and somehow dangerous personality, and the fact that she would invite me to her apartment after midnight and then tense herself against a kiss at the door.

'I have decided that I must leave Paris,' she said. 'I have been talking to my father on the phone and he wants me to come down there until Paris is out of danger.'

'Barbezieux, you said?'

'Yes, in the Charente department. You know, down in the south-west.'

'How will you get there?'

She shrugged. 'I've no idea, but I'm good at solving that kind of problem. You know – I smile, and then someone very kindly helps.' She smiled to show what she meant.

'Is that why you're smiling at me?'

'Certainly not. I don't see how you could get me down to Barbezieux.'

'But if I could?'

'Then I would smile again, I suppose. But meanwhile I'm asking around among friends. I know a lot of people. I have been pointing out that I am very small, wouldn't take up much room in a car, am a good navigator and delightful company.' The half-suppressed giggle again.

'But supposing I have plans to travel down to the south-west?' I said.

'You have a car?'

'I have a car.' No one said anything for a while and we drank our coffee. 'What's the Charente like?'

'Beautiful. You'd love the château and my parents are charming. The place is full of wonderful things, too. We have three very good Fragonards. You know, Sylvan glades and shepherdesses in *décolleté*.'

'And you'd like me to run you down there?'

'Of course,' she said. 'But isn't there a tiny problem?'

'What is the problem?'

'It goes like this. It is clear that you wish to go to bed with me. It is equally clear that your first, charmingly polite and very English gestures in that direction have not been encouraged. And now the possibility of your helping me to get away from Paris has arisen. So, if I decided I wanted to go to bed with you, it could only be taken as a way of bribing you to take me down to Barbezieux. That is the problem.'

'Let's take things in their proper order,' I said. 'First, does such an idea appeal to you at all?'

'Barbezieux?'

60

'The other.'

She nodded.

'Second, if I now say Barbezieux is off, will you come to bed with me?'

'But it will seem as if I hope to change your mind.'

'And what, for God's sake, is wrong with that?'

She thought for a while. 'I suppose . . . nothing.' Then she put her glass on the table, rose from her chair, took my glass and placed it beside the other one, and taking me most delicately by the hand led me into the bedroom. That room, too, I had known very well, and that, too, was completely transformed. It had the heavy and comfortless distinction of the late eighteenth century. None of which, a short while later, mattered to me in the slightest. Marie Antoinette, naked and smiling, a mixture of innocence and depravity, could have stepped straight out of one of the Fragonards at her father's château near Barbezieux in the south-west.

She was half asleep when I left her just after six, and as I kissed her mouth she opened her eyes, smiled and said: 'You may think otherwise but that really wasn't meant as payment for my ticket to Barbezieux.' Then she closed her eyes again and seemed to be sleeping. I don't usually feel bewitched just afterwards: if that is how it is going to be, the symptoms usually show up later. But by the time I had reached the hotel I was in a condition I recognized very well from the past. I would take her with me to Barbezieux.

At eight there was an air raid. This time they were coming in low over the main arteries into Paris and machine gunning the mass of humanity struggling to move southwards through the city. With the population of Paris itself now on the move the Place de la Concorde was transformed. From being unnaturally deserted it was to remain choked with people and vehicles from that Tuesday on as the population of the Right Bank pressed towards the Pont de la Concorde and the neighbouring bridges. At nine I set out for the *Préfecture*. For some reason the Metro was closed and I had to battle my way along the bank of the

61

Seine with crowds surging southwards across my path each time I came to a bridge. Air raid warnings went unheeded: there was nowhere for such vast crowds to shelter.

I found friend Motta had been as good as his word. The car was up on blocks again; all the wheels had disappeared to some other workshop and they were dismantling the suspension. Most of the interior trim, together with the seats, had been taken out and stashed away somewhere. Four men were working at what was little more than a chassis. Franay's master-coachbuilders would have wept.

'A spot of bother,' Motta said, ducking out from under the bonnet. 'We've had the cylinder head off, you see; thought we'd clean up her insides. But you must have driven this car like the devil. There's nothing we can do with the valves; it means new ones, and then they'll have to be ground in. So we were on to the Rolls-Bentley main agent in Paris first thing and he hasn't got a valve in the place to fit this engine. No spare pump either. I've told him to try his sub-agents anywhere the German armies haven't reached, and I got a friend upstairs to call Geneva to see what they've got there. When we locate them our men will get 'em here.'

While I was talking to him, Max appeared. I took him aside. 'I want a revolver,' I told him.

'I'll get you a standard police issue. If you press the muzzle firmly against the back of a man's neck and press the trigger you might just kill him. If the thing goes off, that is. Otherwise, you'll be lucky. We've complained for years.'

'Do I get some kind of escort?' I asked.

Max grunted. 'Don't be damn silly. You'll be a foreigner getting the hell out of it, like everyone else. An escort would show you had valuables on board. Or they might lynch you. We're expecting the Communists to attempt a rising any day now. Our men inside the party reckon it'll be within forty-eight hours.'

'I'd have thought they'd make straight for all the Bentleys anyway.'

'With luck, Motta will have you out of here before it

happens.' He turned to the little man. 'Christ, can't you get a move on?'

'*Oui, Monsieur l'Inspecteur.*' Motta's head ducked back into the bonnet. He wasn't going to discuss his problems with Max.

I made slow progress back to the hotel. It was clear now that those who were not tied down in Paris by work or duty were joining the milling throng of refugees. It was an odd mixture: whereas those coming through the city were mostly poor people – peasants, labourers and petty tradesmen – the Parisians joining them were mainly middle-class. Taxis were doing well. Limousines were interspersed with vans piled high with possessions. Outside the Ministry of Finance they were still loading boxes of papers on to lorries. Data for next year's budget? The figures for Franco–German trade? The current rumour was that Tours was now off as the new seat of government; it was to be Bordeaux. The ministers had already left. It was idiotic, but one felt abandoned.

'I have a good friend who is *Chef de Réception* at the Majestic,' the concierge told me. 'He gave me some very significant information on the telephone. It appears that a Swedish diplomat who is staying at the Majestic had some business at the Soviet Embassy yesterday afternoon and as he was leaving a car drew up outside and he distinctly saw Maurice Thorez get out and enter the embassy with two men. You will know that Thorez is supposed to be in Moscow. I ask you, Monsieur, what would the leader of the Communist Party be doing back in Paris, in secret and at the Soviet Embassy?' He didn't wait for an answer. 'To organize a rising, of course!' He looked at me carefully – a look which said he'd prefer the Germans.

'Rumours,' I said, 'are not helpful.'

'*Non, Monsieur.*' And he was once again the concierge of the Crillon, without opinions and all deference.

I called Marie Antoinette, not expecting her to be in. There was no reply. What did she do all day? An art gallery, she'd said. Were they still selling paintings, for God's sake, with all this going on?

63

I walked over to the Sporting Club, had my workout and felt more cheerful for it, though I couldn't detach my thoughts from one thing Marie Antoinette had said, her head next to mine on the pillow and her mouth an inch from my ear. 'That,' she said, 'was absolutely beautiful, but remember that the second occasion is always, always better.' I could still feel her hot breath in my ear. I made my last fruitless call to her at midnight and settled down to sleep as best I could. There had been five air raids during the day and bombs had dropped, they said, on army GHQ in the Château de Vincennes on the south-eastern edge of the city and on the Gare de l'Est.

You look back and you rack your brains to recognize the moment when the distant sound of alarm bells was first heard in your skull. Was it a loose word somewhere, an odd look, a couple of facts which should have added up and didn't? Or was there a hunch, dredged up from the unconscious? Then, having identified that first small moment of truth, you kick yourself and ask why you did not, *at the time*, draw those conclusions from it that were to appear so utterly self-evident later on. And you do not find the answer to the conundrum, though honesty would lead you to admit that you simply rationalized what seemed odd and ignored what you did not choose to contemplate.

Thus, when next morning I again presented my pass at the entrance to the *Préfecture de Police* and was told it was no longer valid, I failed to draw the appropriate conclusions. 'Bureaucracy,' I said to myself. I also said it to the polite but very firm duty sergeant.

'Please contact Inspector Boni. It is a mistake.'

But Inspector Boni was not to be found.

'Your man Motta in the workshops knows me. He is working on my car.'

The sergeant spent a little time on the phone. 'Motta confirms what you say, Monsieur, but he has no authority to issue a new pass.'

'Who said this one had expired?'

The sergeant shrugged. If he knew, he was not saying.

64

'May I use your phone?'

The sergeant pushed the instrument over and I called Schlesser's office. He was not there, someone said. Nor was he expected. Nor did they have another number where he could be reached. Then they rang off.

Whereas any fool can recognize a run-around of this kind when he encounters it, a wise man is required to guess *why* it is happening. I was not that wise. I left a message for Max Boni and stumped out into the brilliant sunshine and milling crowds pushing and cursing their way southwards across the island, over the Pont St Michel and down through the Latin Quarter to the southern exits of the city. When I reached the hotel again I called Marcel Bellon to see whether the bank had gone sour on me too. But that cheerful young man asked thoughtfully after my car, told me he had acquired many excellent maps and asked if he could give his brother-in-law a lift as far as Orléans. I told him no, both weight and space were lacking. Would we be ready to go by tomorrow, he asked. They said Rommel's advanced units were across the Seine and further east the front line had disappeared. 'The Germans will be here by the weekend,' he said. 'Also, we must get away before they unite their army groups south of Paris.'

'Yes,' I said. 'but we're in the hands of the police.'

'God help us.'

'For that,' I said, 'He will need to change sides.' I promised to keep in touch. Then I tried and failed to get through to Marie Antoinette.

Perhaps the telephone exchanges were playing tricks. On a hunch I decided to walk round to Marie Antoinette's apartment. As I made my way up the deserted Avenue d'Iéna a police car was coming towards me. I had seen it pull away from the kerb a hundred yards or so ahead, at a spot opposite Marie Antoinette's building. I glanced idly at the man sitting next to the driver. It was Max.

In the lift going up to Marie Antoinette's floor I cursed myself for my carelessness. They must have followed me here two nights ago.

65

Marie Antoinette answered my ring, a look of surprise on her face. 'Oh, you? Come in, Englishman. I was going to call you anyway.' She offered her mouth to be kissed in a rather absent way and did not part her lips.

'What was that policeman doing here?'

'He was asking about you.' She was leading me into the salon.

'What did he want to know?'

'Oh, how long we'd known each other, what you did in life, stuff like that.' She paced about, pretending to tidy the perfectly tidy room. 'He wanted to know who I was, too.'

'And what did you tell him about me?'

'Oh, all your secrets. Everything I know. Which is nothing at all. Why do you think he came?'

'They're very jumpy about foreigners just now,' I said, improvising. 'But I can't imagine why he'd come here, or how they even knew that we know each other. I'm sorry.'

She seemed to have been shaken by Max, who was after all a pretty frightening person with his small gimlet eyes, general foxiness and atrocious manners.

'I'll have a large Martini,' I said. 'With ice if you can find some.'

She busied herself with drinks, breaking off in the middle to bend over me, link her arms round my neck and kiss me fully on the mouth. 'Keep the police out of my apartment,' she said.

'I'll try. Anyway, I hope we'll be off by tomorrow, so keep a bag packed and listen for a very distinguished hooter which, I am told, sounds a chord of C sharp and G sharp.'

At 4.30 p.m. on Wednesday 12 June, German units were reported at Pierrefitte, 6½ miles north of the Paris ring road. During the evening they entered Drancy and Noisy-le-Sec. The French government had established itself at Tours and during the afternoon the Minister of the Interior phoned Roger Langeron, the Paris Prefect of Police. It was believed by the cabinet that Maurice Thorez was at the Elysée Palace and the Communist uprising had started. Langeron had difficulty in persuading him that there was no Thorez and no uprising (in fact, Thorez was to remain in Moscow until the end of the war).

66

During a long and stormy cabinet meeting Weygand, Pétain and two other ministers insisted that France must ask for an armistice. Meanwhile at Saint Valèry alone, 46,000 prisoners were being counted, including twelve generals. Rommel to his wife: 'Here the battle is over ... Marvellous moments.' And now the 5th Panzer Divison was driving south-west towards Dreux and Chartres, while to the east von Kleist's army was racing for Provins, seventy miles south-east of the capital. Von Rundstedt's infantry was across the Marne. The strategy of encirclement was succeeding.

'It is scarcely necessary to say,' Mussolini cabled to Hitler, 'that I shall prosecute the war with extreme energy.' Later that day he ordered raids on six towns in southern France. The Italian planes hit nothing of consequence, even at the Toulon naval base.

Chapter 7

But we were not off by the next day. I called the *Préfecture* soon after eight and they put me through to Max. No trouble this time.

'What the hell is this, Max?' I asked.

'What are you talking about?'

'Why didn't my pass work yesterday?'

'Didn't it?'

'You know damn well it didn't. I left a message for you.'

'I never got it. Things aren't normal here.'

'I bet you cancelled the pass yourself.'

'Don't be damn silly. Why would I do that?'

'Why would you call on Mlle de Bergemont?'

Max didn't sound surprised that I knew. 'She told you?'

'No, I saw you drive away.'

There was a pause. 'Routine precaution. My instructions are that you are an important person.'

'And the pass?'

'Must be a mistake somewhere.'

'Tell me it's bureaucracy.'

'It's bureaucracy.'

'I want to see that car this morning, Max.'

'No problem. I'll leave instructions to let you in.'

'All right.' I rang off.

When I got to the *Préfecture*, police cars and vans were being loaded and driven out of the courtyard. 'Some special services are leaving for Tours,' the duty sergeant said as he waved me inside. 'It looks like the end.'

'Don't tell me the police are leaving Paris.'

'Of course not. There are twenty-five thousand of us. Stands to reason we have to keep order when the Huns arrive. Anyway, didn't you hear the proclamation on the radio?'

'No.'

'Paris has been declared an open city. The army won't be allowed to fight here. We have to see the reds don't fight either.'

'Doing the Germans' work for 'em, eh?'

'*Ah, la vache!*' I could take it as I pleased.

Motta was haggard but seemed pleased with himself. 'We've worked all night,' he said. 'I haven't seen my wife since Tuesday. Here, take a look . . .'

The extra leaves of tempered steel in their leather jackets had been clamped into the rear suspension. The car was standing on its wheels again and the new wire spokes, thicker than the old ones, gleamed dully in the pale light of the workshop. 'They'll take the extra ton,' Motta said. 'The two spares will be ready in an hour or two.'

A couple of mechanics were replacing the trim and seats. 'When we strip her down again to load her you'll find the extra compartments we've built into her.'

'And the engine?'

We walked round to the front and Motta patted the cylinder head. 'We finally got the valves from Zurich,' he said. 'They went by motorcycle messenger to the French mission in Berne and a second secretary or whatever they're called drove to Paris with 'em yesterday and we finished grinding 'em in at seven this morning. He brought a spare fuel pump too. We got spare clutch plates and some fan belts and inner tubes here in Paris.' He wiped his sleeve wearily over his forehead, leaving a smear of oil. 'You'll find four cans of extra fuel in the boot, and there's a dozen spare plugs in a box.'

'When can I take her?' I asked.

'As soon as my men finish the wheels – say after lunch. I've been instructed to come with you to solder your load on to the chassis rails. I'll bring a couple of my men to help.'

I went up to Max's office at the end of a hundred yards

69

of corridor on the fifth floor. He was smoking and emitting irritable monosyllables into the telephone. He waved me to the solitary chair, and with a final 'So you will do as you're told or take the consequences' slammed the phone down and looked at me balefully.

'Have those lazy bastards downstairs done the job?'

I nodded.

'When will you load at the bank?'

'This afternoon. Perhaps you'd call young Bellon and tell him.'

Without answering he shoved the phone towards me across the table. 'The number is . . .' – he consulted a desk diary – 'Opera 07–07.'

I dialled and was put through to Marcel Bellon. 'We'll be with you by two or soon after,' I said.

'Terrific!' Bellon was bubbling at the other end of the line. There was nothing at all of the central banker about him.

'What about my gun?' I asked Max.

He pulled a drawer open, extracted a revolver in a hip holster and a box of cartridges and pushed them across the desk.

'Know how to use it?'

I shook my head. He leaned forward with a sigh, retrieved the gun, and spent ten minutes explaining its mechanism. 'It kicks,' he said. 'Grip it. It's all you need to know.'

'Shouldn't we have a gun for young Bellon?'

'I don't give police side-arms away as prizes,' Max said. 'If he wants a gun he'll have to buy himself one.' He opened another drawer, drew out a paper and passed it to me. 'Your Spanish *laissez-passer*. Equivalent to a visa. There's one for Bellon too. We couldn't get Portuguese visas in time so you'll have to do your best at the frontier. A handful of escudos . . .' He made the appropriate gesture. It was the kind of thing he knew about.

'What's the latest news?' I asked as I put the bit of paper in an inside pocket.

'There isn't any. Our wireless room is trying to pick up German transmissions. We expect some kind of meeting in the northern suburbs later today, which means they'll probably

70

march in tomorrow. So you'll have to be away tonight if you don't want a Panzer unit up your arse.'

We were in the courtyard of the *Banque de France* by three. The Bentley was driving beautifully and a kind of ancient joy seized me once again as I nosed her out of the *Préfecture*, across the bridge and along the Rue de Rivoli to the bank. Max had decided to ride with me. Motta and his men had set off in a police van.

'We've mapped a route for you,' Max said. 'You're to follow it precisely. It avoids some of the worst traffic jams, and police units between here and the outer suburbs have been told to clear a way for you if you need it. Then you're on your own, but you're to stay on our route all the way.'

'Who says so?'

'I say so.'

In the courtyard of the *Banque de France* the work of loading the car got under way. Motta had brought ramps and the car was raised enough for his men to climb under her with their reels of metal strapping and welding equipment. The bank's security men started bringing the ingots up on trolleys and with painful slowness pairs of ingots were tied on either side of each of the two chassis rails, the metal straps were wound round them and then welded together and spot-welded to the rails. The men cursed at the uncomfortable work. After the first pair had been fastened into position the indefatigable Motta climbed under the car to inspect what had been done.

'Not secure enough,' he pronounced. 'We'll need two straps instead of one. Have we got enough strapping?'

'Enough strapping all right, but we could use more men now you've doubled the job.'

'There's only room for two at a time under her, so get on with it. You'll never have another chance to get your hands on that much money.'

Motta busied himself dismantling the car's interior trim and I joined him. One by one the leather-clad panels were unfastened and removed, revealing the lattice of wooden struts

71

they'd built into the space between trim and body panels. We took the back seats out and unscrewed the floor panel. Underneath it, Motta had welded a roomy compartment. It lay immediately above the back axle. Under the front seat he'd constructed another space, and behind the dashboard more struts had been put in. The car was a false-bottomed suitcase on wheels.

'Brilliant!' I said.

'We do our best.'

With the trim removed, the cases containing the rods made up of closely packed coins wrapped in brown paper started to emerge from the vaults. Each rod had to be slotted into the latticework and secured by thin strips of wood that Motta had brought with him and which we now tacked carefully into place.

'You can reckon on a lot of bumping around,' he said. 'If any of this stuff breaks loose it's so heavy it'll smash the trim panels open.' He was packing the spaces between the coin rods with waste paper. He'd brought that with him too.

By nightfall the job was a little more than half done. The welding was taking longer than anyone had expected. Max had left at six and returned with Schlesser at ten.

'We've picked up a wireless message from the Germans at the *Préfecture*,' Max said. 'They're sending negotiators to meet our people at Sarcelles, north of Saint-Denis. It's the end. We'd better get a move on.'

I had slipped away earlier to call Marie Antoinette. 'It looks like early morning,' I told her. 'Get some sleep but I may call you before dawn.'

'Why the delay?'

'I'm working on the car. Goodbye.'

Clouds had come up during the evening and suddenly rain in torrents had descended on the dusty streets and parched public gardens of Paris. The Panzer divisions were not to be welcomed into Paris in brilliant sunshine after all. Schlesser was wearing a shiny black raincoat with a hat to match and looked like a bloated and dangerous beetle as he moved slowly round the car.

We had driven it under one of those glass and metal canopies they favour on public buildings in France.

'So you're staying?' I said.

'I am senator for a Paris district,' he said. 'The Germans do not frighten me.' He managed to make himself sound noble. 'In any case, there's no future in fighting Hitler any longer. He is our century's man of destiny, just as Napoleon was Europe's man of destiny in the nineteenth century.'

'So you believe he'll win the war?'

Schlesser looked at me steadily from under his black hat. 'Inevitably.'

'In that case,' I said, 'what the hell are we doing here with my Bentley and all the loot?' I waved a hand in the direction of the man loading the car. We had wandered across the courtyard. The rain had subsided.

Schlesser did not reply for a long while. I had the feeling he was running a moral tape measure over me, sizing up my willingness to undertake some squalid manoeuvre.

'This idea of Reynaud's that the war can be carried on from North Africa is insane,' he said. 'He has that Jew Mandel with him in the cabinet and no one else. A Jew at the Interior!' He grunted. 'The Germans can't be expected to deal with that sort of government. Some of us understand that hegemony in Europe has been earned by the German nation. We are the realists. Everything else . . .' – he made the familiar sweeping gesture with both arms – '*c'est du cinéma.*'

'And the platinum?'

He ignored me. 'Great Britain, you may say, what about Great Britain? I'll tell you. Six months maximum. And the Americans won't lift a finger. Roosevelt can never carry the Congress with him. It's Hitler's calculation and it's mine.' The beetle walked in silence by my side for a moment.

'Are you trying to tell me,' I asked, 'that the platinum and the rest are not to reach England?'

Schlesser stopped walking. We were in the middle of the courtyard. It was almost dark and the men round the car had lit storm lamps. The city around us was silent. I heard Motta say something to one of his men; I couldn't catch what it was but there was weariness in his voice.

'It is a matter for you, *cher ami*,' Schlesser said evenly. 'I can only advise you to think carefully about my assessment of the situation. I am sure you are a patriot. Well, the true patriot today is one who opposes the prolongation of a senseless war – the killing of innocent people – the mad attempt to halt the inexorable forward march of history. That is my political advice to you. My practical advice is simple: follow the route Max has given you.' He paused and tapped me on the arm. 'Exactly,' he added. 'It will be in your interest to do so.' Then, as he extended a delicate hand to bid me goodbye, he added quietly, 'Anything else will not. I speak as a friend.' Then he was gone.

Max, I found, had already disappeared, leaving his map with the route traced on it with Bellon.

'What did he say?' I asked.

'He just said we should wait for dawn to set off as we'd lose our way getting through the suburbs in the blackout. They don't expect the Germans to enter the city before daylight.'

'Is that all?'

'Yes. Then he just disappeared into the night. I think he had a car waiting for him outside in the road.'

'Did he give you your Spanish visa?'

'Yes.'

'Have you a gun?'

'No. I wouldn't know how to use it.'

'I'm going back to the hotel to get my stuff, and I shall sleep until three-thirty a.m. – that will give me four hours. I suggest you do the same. I'll be back here by four-thirty.'

'All right.'

I went and thanked Motta and his two men. 'Another hour's work,' he told me. They could hardly keep their eyes open.

'A great job,' I said.

'*C'est rien. Au revoir et bonne chance.*'

'You too,' I said. Then I was off.

At 11.25 that night the wireless room of the Police Municipale *picked*

74

up a message broadcast en clair by von Kuchler's 18th Army head-quarters. 'Will negotiate until 14th at 5 a.m. German time at Sarcelles. Transmit. Otherwise will order attack on Paris.' Then, at 2.40 a.m.: 'Military Governor of Paris to German High Command. Sending negotiator to Sarcelles, 5 a.m. French time.' In a roadside villa at Sarcelles, where the Paris–Calais and Paris–Dunkirk Routes Nationales separate north of the capital, the Germans laid down their conditions: end of French resistance in the sector; order and public services to be maintained in the city and suburbs; forty-eight hour curfew during German entry; no destruction of bridges. The conditions were accepted.

'The fate of Paris is sealed,' wrote Roger Langeron, Prefect of Police, in his diary. 'Tomorrow we will be cut off from the rest of the world.'

Chapter 8

From my room I called Marie Antoinette and told her to be ready by five. Then I set the alarm and slept for my four hours. I came downstairs with a suitcase and told the night porter to have my other cases stored until I got back – 'soon', I added hopefully. While he was getting someone to see to my bill I strolled towards the salon, but as I reached the entrance something made me stop. The sound of voices was coming from inside the room. I recognized the throaty voice of one of the Dutchmen. He was speaking German. I caught the end of a sentence, '. . . so we can expect the engineers during the morning.' Another voice asked: 'Has the time of entry been fixed yet?' I didn't catch the full reply, just the words *'auf gleicher Welle'* – on the same wavelength.

I toyed briefly with the idea of wishing them *auf Wiedersehen*; or maybe if I suddenly yelled *Heil Hitler!* they'd all jump to their feet and shove their right hands out. But I thought better of it. My bill settled, I shook hands with the night porter. 'Tell your colleague the concierge when you see him that he was wrong about Rotterdam. It was more probably Hamburg.'

'*Oui, Monsieur, Hambourg*.' He didn't know what I was talking about.

It took us twenty minutes to stow our gear and the cans of petrol in the car and raise and fasten the roof. Bellon had loaded a hamper of food and had got some hot coffee from somewhere. We drank it, acrid and steaming, from tin mugs. He split a *petit pain* and we dipped it in the coffee. Like anyone else, I feel lousy just before dawn and the coffee improved matters. We didn't speak until we were climbing into the car. He had Max's map of greater Paris on his lap with the route marked out. He offered to navigate. Then I told him we had a passenger to pick up in the Avenue d'Ièna. 'A lady,' I said. 'It's why I couldn't take your brother-in-law. I'd already promised. You'll like her.' He seemed to take it in good part.

The car's transmission coped nobly with the extra weight. We would have to see how things would be on the open road. She responded briskly as we emerged from the Rue de Rivoli and swept round the Place de la Concorde. Ten minutes later we were outside Marie Antoinette's apartment and I sounded the town horn. A few minutes after that she appeared, carrying a very small case. She was dressed as if we were off to the races at Longchamps – a clinging summer dress and a large picture hat. She had a coat over her arm. In the dawn light she looked fragile and entirely out of place. It was a little after five-thirty as I turned left towards the river and the Pont d'Ièna.

'We're to leave by the Porte Didot,' Bellon said. 'Then according to this map we follow quite a tricky route through the back streets of Malakoff. We'll be running more or less parallel to *Route Nationale 20*.'

'Makes sense if RN 20 is choked with people.'

Bellon was peering at the map. 'I can see a simple way to go without touching RN 20. My grandmother lives in Bagneux and I know the area. I visit her every summer. We can stay with Inspector Boni's route as far as the Bagneux cemetery. Then I can do better.'

I recalled Schlesser's words: 'Follow the route Max has given you . . . exactly.' He'd put a lot of emphasis into that final adverb.

'I'm in your hands,' I said to Bellon. We were passing the Invalides. Someone had told me they'd sent Napoleon's grey trenchcoat and famous hat, together with some German standards he'd captured at Austerlitz and Ièna, into hiding somewhere in the south. I glanced behind me: Marie Antoinette was asleep, her hat on her knees and her head resting on an arm.

Just after 5 a.m. the first feldgrau *uniforms were seen in the northern streets of Paris. Motorcycle units of General von Briesen's Silesian tank division had entered the city through the Porte de la Villette and were driving down the Rue de Flandres towards the Gare du Nord. They were followed by one or two light tanks. One of the first Germans into Paris wrote later: 'The population watched as if they were paralysed with fear and astonishment. Then they took to their heels. Mothers seized their children and retreated into their houses. Doors and windows were shut . . . In the square at the Hotel de Ville, the 2nd company set up a battery of anti-tank guns to protect the bridges. Then the French flag was hauled down and a German flag was run up on the Hotel de Ville.'*

There is a long, dead straight stretch of the Rue Didot between the Rue d'Alésia and the Boulevard Brune. That was where I first realized we were being followed. My rear-view mirror showed a car some two hundred yards behind us. I slowed down: the car got no closer. Yet Max had said there would be no escort. So if it was not Max's men, who would it be?

'Could anyone from the bank be escorting us discreetly?' I asked Bellon.

'Definitely not.'

'Well, there's a car on our tail and we'd better find out what it is.'

We were approaching the Boulevard Brune, which forms part of the Paris ring road. There was a side turning just before the Boulevard and I took the car into it and stopped beyond the corner.

'Would you like me to investigate?' Bellon asked.

'Go and have a look. I'd best stay with the car.'

Marie Antoinette had woken up. 'Where on earth are we?' she demanded. The spot where I'd stopped was admittedly unpromising: factory wall on one side of the road with *Croix de Feu!* scrawled on it, and a vacant lot on the other.

'Just a precaution. Friend Bellon is checking.'

'Checking what?'

'There was a car behind us.'

'The police?'

'I've no idea.'

I heard a car pulling up a short distance away. Then the sound of a car door slamming. Then I distinctly heard a shout which seemed to be cut short suddenly. Then the door again and a car engine accelerating away. I jumped out and ran to the corner. I could see a car disappearing at speed across the Boulevard towards the suburb of Malakoff. Bellon had been wearing a motoring cap. I picked it up from the pavement and brought it back to the car. I had no idea what to do, nor what to say to Marie Antoinette. I improvised.

'I think we are in some kind of trouble.'

'Where is Monsieur Bellon?'

'Gone.'

'Gone where?'

'I've no idea. His cap was on the pavement. You heard that car drive away; he must have been in it.'

'Why would he do that?'

'Perhaps he changed his mind about the trip.'

'That's absurd. His bag is still here.'

It was absurd. I shrugged.

'Do you think he was kidnapped?' she asked.

I nodded.

'But why?'

I shrugged again. I was not doing well.

'Are we in some kind of danger?' She asked the question as one might ask the name of the district.

'I don't know,' I said, 'but my instinct tells me to get moving. I'll try to explain later.'

Bellon had left Max's route map on the front passenger seat. I spent a moment finding where we were, then I turned the car back into the Rue Didot and took her across Boulevard Brune and so into the winding back streets of industrial Malakoff. It was after six and a few pedestrians were about. There was no sign of the exodus here: that must be choking RN 20 half a mile to the east. I passed the map to Marie Antoinette.

'Can you navigate?'

'Of course.'

She led me southwards through Malakoff and then, surprisingly, westwards past the old fort which makes up part of the city's ancient defences.

'Are you sure?' I asked her. 'I'd have thought we'd bear left, not right.'

'It's what it says here.' She seemed perfectly happy.

We were heading for Clamart, further to the west. I wondered when we were to turn south and start putting some useful ground between ourselves and the city. The car was running beautifully, a little headstrong on the curves but generally obedient, eager and responsive. We were touching sixty along the deserted Avenue de Verdun, heading for the old village of Meudon, when I first picked up another car in my rear-view mirror. It was gaining on us, and there was maybe a hundred yards between us when the driver activated his siren. It was a police Citroen.

The Avenue de Verdun was cobbled – the notorious French *pavé*. It did not seem politic to take my extra ton of freight over that kind of surface at over sixty. And so I held my speed and allowed myself to be overtaken and signalled down by the police car.

There were three men in plain clothes inside. One of them got out and walked back towards us. As he did so, another Citroen pulled up behind. 'Don't worry,' I said to Marie Antoinette as the man came level with us, 'it has to be a mistake unless you are a fugitive from justice.'

'Not me. What about you?'

By the standards of the Paris police, the whole thing was courtesy itself. The man was beefy and dark and there was no expression of any kind on his face. He pulled an identity card from a breast pocket, opened it out and held it up for me to see.

'Police, Inspector Rossi.' He snapped the card wallet shut. 'Your papers.' His accent was heavily Corsican.

I showed him my passport.

'The car's papers.'

I showed him those. He glanced at them without apparent interest. He opened the door.

80

'*Descendez.*'

I obliged. Then he walked round to the back of the car, pointed a finger at the boot, then crooked his finger upwards. He was not talkative. I opened the boot. One of his men joined him and started rummaging among our things.

'May I ask what this is about?'

'A stolen car has been reported.'

'This is not a stolen car. It is my car.'

'Where are you going?'

'Barbezieux,' I said.

'Why?'

'Half Paris is on the move and you ask me why?'

This was not the way to treat this man, but nor was it the way to treat me. 'May I have my papers back?' I suggested politely.

He handed them back. 'You will accompany us to the nearest *poste de police.*' He called off his man, who was lifting bags and cans to see what was underneath, and regained his car. Then we set off in procession, a police car fore and aft.

At 8 a.m. a military band struck up at the Arc de Triomphe and General von Breisen, mounted on a charger, took the salute as the men of his 30th Division marched past and on down the deserted Champs Elysées. When they reached the Concorde, a specialist detachment from general head-quarters peeled off and entered the Hotel Crillon, which was to become for the next four years the army of occupation's GHQ in Paris. At 9.10 a.m. a German unit occupied the headquarters of the postal and telegraph services. At 9.27 the German flag was raised on the Air Ministry. At about this time a middle-aged German major drove up to the Elysée Palace and had the following conversation with the concierge:

'Bonjour, Monsieur.'

'Bonjour, Monsieur.'

'Is President Lebrun in?'

'He didn't wait for you.'

'Where is he?'

'He didn't leave a forwarding address.'

A few more words were exchanged, then:

'Au revoir, Monsieur.'

'Au revoir, Monsieur.'

Von Briesen was killed on the Russian steppes while serving with Hitler's 52nd Army corps nineteen months later.

Chapter 9

We all turned left out of the Avenue de Verdun into a narrow road and stopped outside a solitary two-storeyed house with a brief unkempt front garden in which geraniums were wilting. The rest of the road was bounded by high brick walls and a few yards away a police van or something very much like one was parked.

Whatever it was, this was no *poste de police*; from which I concluded these were no honest policemen, however much their appearance bespoke that clearly definable species, the plain-clothes man from the *Police Judiciaire*. As I got out of the car, the bully-boy who alleged he was Inspector Rossi waited, his palm outstretched.

'The car keys.'

I handed them over.

'*Allez, avancez!*' He nodded towards the front door of the house, which stood ajar, and I started walking. Marie Antoinette had alighted and, absurdly, had put on her picture hat. Beneath it one could just see her beautiful little face. She seemed entirely self-composed.

'I'm sorry – this looks bad,' I muttered as we mounted the few steps to the door.

Her hand stretched out, caught one of my fingers and squeezed it briefly. She said nothing.

The door was pushed open. I noticed a key sticking out of the lock on the outside. Someone had apparently just opened the place up for the present purpose. Then we were inside, Rossi in the lead, then Marie Antoinette and myself, and two others behind. As far as I could tell they'd left a man outside to keep an eye on the cars.

Inside the narrow hall with its echoing tiles we advanced a few paces, then Rossi opened a door to our left and jerked his head: we were to go in. I normally defer to ladies but it seemed to me that gallantry in this case dictated otherwise and I advanced into the room. Marie Antoinette, hat still elegantly in place, followed close behind.

The room was devoid of furniture save for a trestle table and three chairs. Seated on one of them at the far side of the table was Max, his hat on the table before him, a look of quite astonishing insolence on his face. He had the usual yellow *maïs* hanging from his lower lip.

'Sit down,' he said. 'No problems?' The question was addressed to Marie Antoinette. She shook her head.

I stretched out a hand and carefully removed her hat so that I could see her eyes. She tried to grab it but failed. 'I see,' I said. A kind of pleading look stole into her eyes – the look of a child caught at the sweet jar. 'I can explain,' it said. I shook my head and sat down. 'I should have realized – you didn't react yesterday like someone who'd had an unexpected visit from the police. Most people throw up in the toilet after Max makes one of his calls.'

She sat down and said nothing.

'What is that riff-raff outside?' I asked.

'Police officers,' Max said.

'Scum.'

'I'm sorry if their methods are lacking in tact. They aren't ballet dancers.'

'And this young lady?'

'We had to be sure – in case we missed you here and you got among the crowds going south.'

'She was to contact you?'

'I'm not here to answer questions,' Max said. 'I'm here to tell you where you stand.'

His cigarette was burning low, wreathing his face in grey smoke. He slowly extracted a pack from his pocket, tapped one

84

out and lit it from the stub, which then went on to the floor. The lengthy performance gave me time to think – time which I used to precious little effect. Marie Antoinette was absolutely motionless beside me, the sexual arrogance all drained away, her eyes not meeting mine.

'The Germans are in Paris,' Max said. 'They'll have the rest of the country before the month's out. Then I'd give England what – six months? That'd be tops. *Et voilà!* . . . the whole of Europe in Hitler's pocket – what he calls the New Order. He says a thousand years. I'll settle for a hundred – fifty even. So what's the point of pretending? All that shit – Blum, Mandel and the Jews, and Reynaud and all the political bandits – done for, *Kaput!*' He spat out the last word as if he were practising for the future.

'Cut the geopolitics, Max,' I said. 'You haven't got the intellect for it and I've heard it put more delicately by Schlesser.'

He ignored my remark. 'Where do you stand in all this?' he asked.

'You were going to tell *me* where I stand.'

'Old man Schlesser has understood,' Max said. 'He knows which side his bread's buttered, and he knows the Germans have all the butter now. It stands to reason, this bloody nonsense with the bank's loot going down south – it's not on. *C'est con, quoi!*'

Marie Antoinette was still motionless beside me. Noises were coming from the next room; presumably Rossi and his lads had settled in there. I had a ridiculous hunch, based entirely upon what in my foolishness I thought I knew about women.

'I'm not prepared to talk to you in front of her.'

'You can.'

'I can but I won't. She'd better go back to the car.'

Max nodded and Marie Antoinette got up. 'Here,' I said, and handed her the hat. She took it without looking at me and left the room. A few moments later the car door slammed.

'What happened to that chap Bellon?' I asked.

Max shrugged. 'Never mind Bellon, let's talk about you.' He

stretched his legs out under the table and tilted his chair back. 'Schlesser says all that cash . . .' – he nodded towards the window – 'is to stay here. There'll be plenty of constructive uses for it once the German occupation has settled down. Maybe he's thinking of a new political party – something clean and realistic which will give the country a clear lead.'

'A firm hand,' I said.

'That's right.'

'With Nazi approval.'

'How the hell else will anyone be able to organize political parties?'

'Also,' I said lightly, 'Schlesser is entitled to some material reward for all his trouble.'

'Of course.'

'So are you.'

'And you,' Max said, sensing a 180-degree turn on my part, induced by the wind of political realism blowing through the room.

'Naturally.' I paused and stretched out my own legs and tilted my chair in imitation of Max. We were two buddies about to divide the loot.

'You can keep the car,' Max was saying, 'and take your chance on getting out of the country.'

'What if I tell 'em what I know in London?'

'What if we tell 'em otherwise? Senator Jean Paul Schlesser versus one William Quinton, jailbird. Come on. *Faut être con!*'

'If I accept, what's the deal?'

'We unload here. The van will take the stuff. You get a hundred thousand in cash.' He patted a side pocket. 'I'll leave a man to keep a friendly eye on you and an hour after we've left he'll give you your car keys and you're on your way. Simple.'

'Don't insult me, Max,' I said. 'Two hundred thousand.'

'Schlesser said he's not bargaining. A hundred.'

'You always were a liar, Max.'

Max spread his hands in what he imagined was a deprecatory gesture. Perhaps he thought I'd paid him a compliment.

86

'I don't know why you don't like me. I've been a good friend to you.'

'Two hundred, Max.'

I was talking a language he understood.

'I'll go to a hundred and twenty and take the roasting from Schlesser.'

'It's a steal, but O.K.' I gave in with good grace. Max looked pleased; he had to be making something on the side. 'By the way,' I said, 'does all this mean that Monsieur Fresnoy at the bank is one of us?'

'Of course not. That's why we had to lose his man Bellon.'

'What time will I be away from here?'

'I don't know – midday or so.'

That was when I realized they had no intention of giving me the chance to get away, let alone 120,000 francs to take with me. I looked at my watch; it was close to 10.30. Stripping and unloading the car had to be a four or five-hour job. Assuming they started right away, the Germans would be swarming over the neighbourhood long before I could get going. And a 3½-litre Bentley coupé was going to stand out against the surrounding scenery like a good deed in a naughty world.

'It sounds all right,' I said. 'I don't exactly subscribe to Schlesser's reach-me-down political philosophy but I can see the thing from his angle. Also yours; you always were a bloody opportunist.' I tried to make it sound like a compliment.

'Not an opportunist,' Max said delicately. 'Let's say I have a sense of opportunity. And this one is the mother of them all.' He allowed himself a brief grin in which he showed a row of uneven yellow teeth.

I got slowly to my feet and stretched. 'And when do I, er, get the cash?'

'When we leave.'

'I think I could use the loo,' I said. 'Where is it?'

Max went to the door, opened it and yelled. One of the men from the next room appeared.

'Take him to the bog.'

'There's a window in there.'

87

'Then you'd better go in with him, hadn't you?'

'I object,' I said.

'Then don't go,' Max said.

I shrugged and went out into the corridor, Max's man close behind me.

'End door on the right.'

We entered the evil-smelling lavatory together and the man stood behind me as I went through the unnecessary routine of relieving myself. As I stood there, racking my brains, I noticed that there was a window all right, though you would need to be an agile dwarf to get through it. I also noticed the wall tiles. They were unusually large and rising damp had loosened them so that several were standing away from the wall and looked as if they'd come away easily enough if one grabbed hold of them.

I finished what I had to do and, being a gentleman, adjusted my dress. My guard was leaning against the door behind me, which put about two feet of space between us. Having selected the tile which looked most likely to come away from the wall, I moved fast. I leaned forward, grabbed the tile and yanked it loose: it came easily. I swung round, the tile in my right hand, my arm outstretched. I'd got the distance just right. The flat of the tile caught him smack on the forehead. I'd put all my strength behind the blow and it was enough to daze him. Then, as his head dropped forward, I hit him again, this time on the back of the skull. He went down without a murmur. I had to heave him away from the door in order to get out and into the corridor. Then I sprinted for the front door and managed to do it on tiptoe. The doors of the rooms occupied by Max and his gang were ajar, but not enough for me to be seen.

I was through the front door and locking it behind me in a couple of seconds. As I ran the few yards through the garden and over to the car I took the police revolver from its hip holster. There was a man sitting in one of the cars; he had been reading a newspaper and looked up as he heard me coming. He was about to open the car door when he saw the gun.

'Stay there,' I yelled at him, 'or I shoot.' The thought that I sounded ridiculous crossed my mind: I'd never fired a shot in anger in my life. The man didn't know it. He stayed where he was.

I ran for the Bentley. Marie Antoinette was in the passenger seat. I'd formed no idea in my mind of what I would do if she struggled and tried to stop me driving away. Throw her out on to the road? Or hit her and drive away with her next to me? Or again, was my earlier hunch about women – this woman – any good at all?

It was. I saw her lean across to open the driver's door for me. By now there was a hullabaloo inside the house as Max and his men hammered on the locked front door and the glass of the ground-floor window was smashed by someone inside.

'The keys!' Marie Antoinette was shouting. 'They have the car keys.'

I held up the spare set; they'd been in my pocket. And now I was in the car, her engine hummed into life, she was in gear and I was away, pulling out hard to get round the car parked ahead of me. As I did so, the thug in the second car started shooting. I heard one bullet whistle past and there was a spurt of dust as another hit the road to our left. Nothing hit us. Then the other car started up behind me.

The road we were in offered little joy. It simply looped back into the Avenue de Verdun with its damned *pavé*. 'Find me a straight stretch, macadamized, say ten kilometres or so. Our only hope is that we're faster, but it has to be a good surface, or we'll shake ourselves to bits.'

There was still only a solitary car behind us but the others must have set out soon after.

Marie Antoinette was studying the map. 'If we can hold on till we're through Meudon we can get on to D181 through the forest. It's only five kilometres but it's straight and there are tracks leading off it. If you can get far enough ahead you'll be able to turn off without them seeing.'

'Good thinking. Later you must tell me why you're doing this.'

'I will.'

I was not shaking off the Citroen. The outskirts of Meudon

89

slowed both of us down: on balance, I was doing better through the patchy traffic than he was. And then an astonishing thing happened. There was a crossroads ahead, and as we approached I could see a couple of cars halted ahead of me as a convoy of trucks crossed from right to left. If this was a French unit in retreat we were in deep trouble. But as I started to lose speed the last truck passed. Standing in the middle of the intersection was a motorbike and sidecar, and directing the traffic with a circular disc on the end of a stick was a tall figure in grey-green uniform: the *Feldgendarmerie!* The Germans were in Meudon, guiding their motorized infantry southwards through the French traffic! A few pedestrians stood gawping, and as the German military policeman waved me placidly through, I heard Marie Antoinette next to me stifle a scream.

'Things are not normal,' I said.

We came to a fork. 'Bear left,' she shouted, 'this is it.'

We were on D181, the dense Meudon forest with its geometrical pattern of rides and *promenades* enclosing us on either side. The Citroen was still on our tail.

At kilometre 2 on D181 the speedometer needle flickered a little above eighty-five. The Bentley was holding the road beautifully, pinned down as she was by her all-up weight of some 3½ tons. This was fine, but what would she do at this speed in the curves, and what about the inertial effect of the extra weight when I used my brakes on the monstrous projectile that the car had become?

By kilometre 3 we were touching ninety. Revs were satisfactory, there was no engine strain and response to finger-touch on the steering was immediate. The Citroen was now a half-kilometre behind us and falling away.

'Not enough,' I said. 'To lose him I need another kilometre at least before I slow for a turn.' We were passing the openings to tracks through the forest on either side of the road.

'Two kilometres to the end of the straight stretch,' Marie Antoinette said, studying the map. 'About one and a half from here there's a likely turning to the left. It should give us another four kilometres through the forest in a straight line.'

'We'll go for that.'

At kilometre 4 the car was touching ninety-five and the Citroen, which must have been nearly a kilometre behind us, was out of sight below the brow of a shallow hill.

'I reckon the track's some four hundred metres ahead,' Marie Antoinette said.

I took my foot off the accelerator and stroked the brake pedal gingerly. I had visions of the brake linings going up in smoke as they encountered the enormous pull of our 3½ tons. I even had the idea that they might fade completely as we hurtled onwards in a straight line, unstoppable and doomed. But they didn't; the car responded as I pressed on the pedal, and I managed to get her down to twenty or so in the space of three hundred metres. We were in luck: the turning appeared on our left exactly when I needed it, I pulled her round on to the track. A short distance ahead there was a break in the densely packed trees: I pulled in among them and switched off the engine. As I did so I heard the sound of the Citroen racing past on D181. The ruse had worked.

Marie Antoinette was studying the map. 'If we go down this track,' she said, 'we can get out of the forest at the far end and then on to D53 going south. I don't think we ought to stop here even though I'm ravenous.'

I started up the car. 'If you can reach the hamper on the back seat there should be food in it. You could pass me something, too.'

Soon she had extracted a couple of rolls with ham and sharp pickle. 'That nice young man from the bank provided the basket,' I said. 'What do you think they did with him?'

'They're killers,' Marie Antoinette said drily. 'There's a vast fortune at stake and the bank mustn't know.'

'The coins aren't marketable. Any dealer will know their origin at once.'

'You forget,' Marie Antoinette said, 'the Nazis are here. The days of professional integrity are probably over.' She no longer sounded like the girl who had announced she'd be the one in the red dress. If she'd been a kind of sexual enigma before, now she was something else: devious, complicated and changing sides a shade too easily. I didn't know whether to be angry at her duplicity or pleased that she appeared to have ended up on my side. It must be how controllers feel about their double agents, never knowing whose side, ultimately, they're on. But it would have to keep.

When we got out of the forest she guided me expertly along country roads, nosing gradually round to a southwards course. At one point we could see RN446 to our right as it followed a ridge. It was solid with vehicles which were scarcely moving at all.

'Can we avoid crossing it?' I asked.

'I think so. But if we move too far to the east we'll be in worse trouble with RN20. We're in a corridor between the two and it gets narrower.'

I drove on for half an hour, making good progress and persuading myself that we'd shaken off Max Boni and his friends. But, as I say, I am extremely cautious. I asked Marie Antoinette if the second car could have skirted round the eastern side of the forest and so ended up on D53 ahead of us.

'Yes,' she said, her head bowed over the map, 'and we're reaching it now, so we'll soon know.'

I could see a crossing ahead with a few houses clustered round it. I stopped the car, got out and walked to the corner. Carefully, I peered round. A hundred yards ahead, where the road narrowed between two houses, the police van was parked broadside-on. It blocked the road. I retreated to the car and gave Marie Antoinette my news.

'You know,' she said, 'I honestly didn't do it on purpose.'

'No?'

'I swear it on the head of my mother.'

I had no way of knowing how readily good Catholics consign their mothers to perdition, so I took the map. 'If we can get on to D53 south of that van we're probably out of their net.' But we couldn't – the map made that perfectly clear.

'I got you into this,' Marie Antoinette said, 'so I must get you out. It will prove whose side I'm on.' She took the map from me and studied it. 'A pencil, quick.' I handed her mine. She was

92

making marks on the map. 'I get off here,' she said. 'You'll find me again in one of these places.' She showed me the map. 'Either in Gometz on RN188 – that's about twenty-five kilometres south of here – or in St Cheron on D116 – say twenty-five kilometres further on. Wait for me until five-thirty tonight at the local *bistro* in Gometz or tomorrow morning in St Cheron. If I don't come by then you must move on or the Germans will get you. That swine Schlesser will find a way of letting them know.'

'Can't we arrange a third chance, further south? What about Barbezieux?'

She laughed. 'I wouldn't know how to get there. I've never been in the Charente in my life.' She leant over, took my face gently between her fingers, and kissed me slowly on the lips.

'What are you going to do?'

'Never mind and do as I say.'

There was a farm on our left which appeared deserted. A short dirt track led off behind the farm buildings. 'Drive in there,' Marie Antoinette said, 'so that you can't be seen from the road. When you see the van drive past, you can turn left on to D53 and head south.'

'And you?'

'Oh, I'll be in the van.'

'Why are you doing this?' I asked.

'I told you – they are killers. Tomorrow, or one fine day soon, I want to be with you again. Perhaps you've forgotten what I said about the second time being even better.'

With that she was out of the car and walking jauntily towards the crossroads, leaving her suitcase and ridiculous hat behind.

I called after her: 'Outside the post office at Chateaudun at midday on Sunday – just in case we miss each other.' She waved and blew a kiss. She scooped up two handfuls of dust from the roadside and rubbed it over her dress. Then she was gone.

I drove the car out of sight behind the farm buildings and waited, wondering if I'd driven into yet another trap. A few minutes later I heard the van approaching at speed. There was a screaming of tyres as it slowed suddenly to take the corner; then it was past my hiding place and picking up speed, back along the route we had just taken. I gave it a minute or so and nosed out on to the road and up to the crossing. I turned left, feeling very lonely, and headed down a deserted country road – Marie Antoinette's chosen D53 – down into the valley of the Chevreuse. I had never seen the French countryside look more beautiful.

Throughout Friday 14 June the army of Paris was retiring southwards as best it could, with the Germans streaming through the city from the Porte de la Villette in the north-west to the exits in the south-east and south-west. But every road to the south was blocked by civilians and the French units had no opportunity to regroup in order to turn and fight. To the west the port of Le Havre was taken during the day. In the early hours of the morning Premier Reynaud had drafted a final appeal to President Roosevelt. During the morning he told the US Ambassador: 'The French Army is in pieces and in Cabinet yesterday it was only with the greatest difficulty that I persuaded my colleagues to continue the struggle.' If the US would not declare war, France would have to seek an armistice. 'Absolute despair,' was how the Ambassador described the atmosphere in his cable to the President as the members of the French government climbed wearily into their limousines in Tours. Their destination was Bordeaux, further to the south.

Chapter 10

Gometz turned out to be a featureless huddle of grey stone houses set astride the road to a place called St Arnoult that I'd never heard of. I reached it at four-thirty, having run into a column of slow-moving cars, lorries and carts. I drove the Bentley off the main road and stopped her a hundred yards along a lane leading up a thickly wooded hill. I had an hour to wait for Marie Antoinette. I devoted twenty minutes to a cat-nap and a further ten to a snack from poor Bellon's nicely stocked hamper. It occurred to me that I had never practised with my police revolver and it seemed a good idea to fire it at least once. I took it from its holster, released the safety catch, and holding the damn thing as instructed, aimed through the open window of the car at the nearest tree. Max had loaded it for me. I fired. Nothing hit the tree. Amateur I may be, but it seemed unlikely that I'd miss the massive trunk of an elm at twenty feet. I fired again and did no better. Then it dawned on me. I broke the breech and shook the cartridges into my palm. They were blanks.

I wondered what else had been faked in Max's careful preparations for my journey. I got out of the car, opened the boot, lifted out one of the petrol cans and unscrewed the stopper. There was no smell of petrol. I was carrying four cans of water.

I felt I'd uncovered enough unpleasant truths for one summer afternoon. It was close to five. I turned the car and ran it down to the main road and climbed out. A heavy stream of traffic was travelling south. Standing outside the *bistro*, I scanned every vehicle for Marie Antoinette. A man on a farm waggon offered me a lift for a hundred francs. Someone shouted: 'The *Boches* are in Palaiseau; we saw them shoot a crazy fellow who tried to block their way with his van.' Then came a convoy of French troops, trying to clear a way through the mass of refugees. They looked exhausted and fed up. 'Some army!' someone shouted. The soldiers paid no attention.

At five-thirty I decided I couldn't wait any longer. And then it occurred to me to ask why I was waiting at all. This girl had made a fool of me, had been working with as *louche* a bunch of cowboys as you'd find in all Paris, had lied and was probably still lying – so why was I bothering, losing valuable time, running absurd risks? Lust, merely? Nothing but the old Adam? Come, now; I may be very fond of women and I had certainly been living like a monk for far too long, but I wasn't dolt enough to risk my life and those untold millions simply because there was an extraordinary sexual aura around this strange creature. Having contemplated my own folly for a while as the sad procession passed before me on the road, I decided that Marie Antoinette could be defined as a calculated risk and a risk which, all things considered, I intended to take. That is, if I could find her again at the second rendezvous at St Cheron.

I nosed the Bentley into the stream of traffic and found myself following a crowded bus with a number plate denoting Lille, far to the north. Behind me was a Paris taxi with six people in it, the roof piled high with luggage. We were travelling at eight miles or so an hour with occasional stops which could last as long as fifteen minutes. There was no hope of overtaking and no point in turning back.

It took us over an hour to cover the four miles from Gometz to a slightly larger place called Limours, by which time I had decided that I'd best take my chances along the country lanes. My map was a bit vague about a crossing of a river called the Remarde that seemed essential to me, and the prospect of trying to navigate as night fell was not attractive. On the other hand the funereal pace of our procession, with Max and Hitler both on my tail, was not to be endured. Soon after Limours I picked a likely turning to my left and took it. The Bentley positively throbbed with pleasure as I let her move up into the fifties.

At Gometz, with the news of my cans of water fresh in my mind, I'd done some arithmetic. I'd covered some sixty miles. I had started out with a full tank of eighteen gallons and she couldn't have been giving me much above ten to the gallon. So a third of my petrol had gone. Now my thoughts were increasingly fixed on fuel and how to acquire it in a virtually deserted countryside. I'd have swapped a forestful of splendid trees for one shabby petrol pump.

By ten-thirty I'd successfully negotiated the crossing of the Remarde. It wasn't much of a bridge, but then it was not much of a stream either. The light had gone and I no longer had any hope of finding my way. I ran the car on to the verge and settled down to sleep. Behind the friendly night-sounds of the countryside I began to sense – it was little more at first – a distant boom. I thought it must be a thunderstorm brewing in the overcharged summer heat. Only slowly did it dawn on me that I was listening to an artillery duel far to the east of Paris. A duel? It was only too likely to be a solo effort by the German heavy guns.

My last waking thought was that this waiting around for a girl whose duplicity was the only fact about her that had been established beyond reasonable doubt was a prize piece of idiocy.

With which, I slept.

I woke to a rapid succession of alarming impressions. First of all, I had no idea where I was. Then I became aware of having a very stiff neck and no feeling at all in my left foot. I moved slightly and my elbow hit a sharp edge. Then I realized I was in the car, slumped down in the driving seat. I opened my eyes: it was daylight. My watch revealed the time at 6.05 a.m. I was just about to impose myself on my habitat when I became aware of a gentle tapping sound. Something or someone was hitting the door panel at my side. It didn't sound hostile, but what the hell was it? Woodpeckers don't peck at the lacquered sheet metalwork of 3½-litre Bentleys.

I hoisted myself up in my seat and peered over the ledge of the window. My gaze met the steady blue-eyed stare of a small and very solemn boy. For quite a long time we stayed like that, trying to outstare each other – a game which a determined child will always win. Then, to break the social log-jam, I offered a smile. The child simply stared. Then he started again, tapping gently on the door with a bit of stick, as if he wanted to be let in.

I lowered the window.

'*Bonjour.*'

No answer; just the steady stare. I noticed that his face was streaked with dirt. He'd been crying.

I tried again: '*Bonjour.*'

'*M'sieu.*'

He was about six. Very small and thin, with a big head and the unblinking blue eyes. A country lad, to judge by the way he handled his stick and rubbed his foot round and round in the dust.

'What's your name?'

'Jules.'

'What are you doing here?'

'I'm lost.'

'Where do you live?'

He nodded in the direction of the river. 'The farm at Machery. We left to go to my aunty's place. My mum and dad lost me on the road. They didn't lose my sister.' His lip quivered at this favouritism.

Question and answer elicited the fact that they'd set out on their cart for aunty's and he'd jumped off for some reason which wasn't clear, and then the cart wasn't there and he'd searched in the column of vehicles and people and now he was lost.

At this point in our conversation his manliness abandoned him and he burst into tears.

This, I thought, was all I needed, as I fed him on bread and cheese and coffee from the hamper. Lost: one difficult woman. Found: one mislaid child. And bearing down on me were people who wished me ill.

'Can you show me the way to Machery?' I asked.

He nodded. 'Can I drive the car?'

'No, but you can be my navigator.' I had to explain what navigators do before he decided he'd take the job. All the way, he chattered about his mum and dad and his aunty.

He was a good navigator and the farm was where he said it was. When we arrived he jumped out of the car and played the host with efficiency and charm. He produced a key from behind a water butt and handed it to me. 'I can't,' he said, 'but I'll be able to after I'm six.'

When we got inside he took hold of my hand and led me into the living room and over to a dresser. 'There,' he said, 'my mum and dad.' He pointed to a photo in a metal frame. 'And that's my aunty.'

I had an idea. 'What's your aunty's name?'

'*Tante Marthe.*'

'And her family name?'

He shrugged.

'I don't suppose,' I said, 'you know where she lives?'

He looked at me with a touch of contempt. 'Of course I do. She lives at Patay, doesn't she?'

'That's right,' I said, 'of course she does. Let's take the photos with us, shall we, and go and find your aunty and mum and dad at Patay?'

'And my sister. She's only three.'

We went out of the house and locked up. I had an idea. 'Does your dad have a tractor?' I asked.

'Of course. Ours is the biggest farm so we need a tractor.'

'Show me.'

He took me by the hand and we found the tractor in a shed at the end of the yard. 'We'll take some petrol,' I said, 'so that we can get to Patay.'

He nodded solemnly. 'Over there. My dad keeps it in those cans.'

I managed to fill my tank and my four cans and added a couple belonging to the farmer. In all, I now had about three hundred miles of fuel, given fair road conditions.

'Thank you,' I said to Jules, 'let's go.' It was about 9 a.m. and likely to be another scorching day. The sound of the artillery barrage seemed louder but it may have been a shift in the wind.

St Cheron, where I was to try again to find Marie Antoinette, proved to be a delightful village sitting quietly in the valley of the Orge. Jules and I arrived there at lunchtime and I found a yard in which to conceal the car. The place seemed largely deserted and both *bistros* were shuttered.

'Why have we stopped?' Jules wanted to know.

'We'll meet a lady here and take her with us.'

'Why?'

'She's a friend.'

'Is she your wife?'

'No, just a friend.'

'Do you let her drive your car?'

'No, I don't.'

We were walking hand-in-hand towards the first *bistro*. Hammering on the door brought no response. We crossed the road. We had more luck at the second place. The *patron* opened the door. Could he give us something to eat? The wife would see what she could do. We went in and were offered the use of a tap and sink out at the back. While madame was preparing an omelette I shaved and persuaded Jules to have his face washed. Then we ate the omelette and a salad while madame apologized because the bread wasn't fresh. Her husband opened a bottle of wine and poured me a glass.

'I have water in mine,' Jules said. 'When I'm six in August I'll not let them put in water any more.'

The *patron* asked where we were headed. Patay, I told him, to find Jules' parents. I left it at that. Then I told him about my meeting with Marie Antoinette and how Jules and I couldn't wait any longer, and if she turned up later would they remind her of our next meeting place because I'd definitely be there as promised. I reckoned it was a bit over a hundred miles by secondary roads. If my luck held, I'd make it by nightfall, always provided the hunt for aunty in Patay didn't hold us up. Marie Antoinette, on the other hand, wasn't likely to be travel-

100

ling as fast as us. 'I'll wait there until lunchtime tomorrow,' I told the *patron*.

'All right. These are terrible times, with people lost on the roads of France.'

'And you're staying here?'

'My parents were driven from their house in St Quentin in the north,' madame said, 'and that was in 1915. I've told my husband I'm not budging this time.'

'We've family in Provence,' the *patron* said. 'I tried to persuade her . . .' He shrugged.

I topped up the hamper and took a few bottles of wine aboard, and paid for what we'd had. The *patron* added a bottle of cognac 'for the journey' and would take no money. We set out, waving vigorously, and barely a moment later Jules was fast asleep, his head against my arm.

Patay, according to my map, lay within my rural corridor between the chaos on RN20 to the east and RN10 to the west. It was in the Loiret department, some seventy miles by zig-zagging country roads. I drove past orchards heavy with fruit and field after field of cereals, promising a bumper harvest. But every time my route approached either of the two main roads which hemmed me in, I caught above the purr of the Bentley a dull roar – the confused and angry sound of a nation in flight. Twice, on distant hills, I saw the blackish line of vehicles silhouetted against the sky.

Stukas flew over, and once I heard the rattle of machine-gun fire. It must have been one of Goering's pilots having a little sport along the near-motionless column of humanity: there was chaos enough for the German high command's purposes without wasting ammunition. The Stuka attacks accounted for the mattresses on the roofs of many cars: they provided a semblance of protection against machine-gun bullets. After an hour Jules woke up and entertained me with anecdotes about the farm dog and some geese.

It was getting on for four o'clock when we reached Patay. A unit of Senegalese with a couple of anti-tank guns had bivouacked in the place and most of the men were squatting against the walls in the neat village square, their faces expressionless, as I drove carefully to the shade of a row of plane trees and stopped the car.

A white lieutenant came up and saluted. '*Bonjour, Monsieur.*' '*Bonjour.*'

'Where have you come from?'

I told him as best I could.

'Do you know where the advanced German units are?'

'I've no idea.'

'You see,' he said hopelessly, 'we've lost contact with our company. I tried telephoning from here. The telephone exchanges at Dreux and Rambouillet have closed down, so I imagine the Germans are in the towns. We're part of the 2nd Light Colonials, attached to the Second Army. We've been up on the Seine.' There was a plan to set up a new defensive line north of Patay, he said, but he'd had no orders since the day before and his men weren't properly fed. He seemed near to tears.

'I'm sorry I can't help,' I said. 'I have to find this boy's aunt.' He was talking of armies and I was talking of a farm boy's aunt: it sounded ridiculous.

'Good luck, *Monsieur*,' the young lieutenant said, and saluted again.

'You, too.'

It took us a half-hour of showing *tante Marthe's* photo around the village to learn that her husband farmed out towards Villardu, four miles away. 'Can I drive there?' Jules asked.

'You can be the lookout man and shout when you see your aunty.'

We found the farm and as we climbed out of the car Jules kept saying, 'I shall shout!' The door was opened by a very good likeness of the photograph and Jules started shouting. Beyond, in the stone-flagged hallway of the farm, were his parents. I am not at my best in tear-stained scenes of reunion and joy but we had a nice time trying to explain to each other what had happened, with Jules tugging at his father to come and inspect the Bentley.

I explained about the petrol and payment was refused. When I left, after some rapid drinking and much kissing of cheeks, I was loaded down further – this time with a basket of peaches and half a ham. 'When I'm six,' Jules shouted after me, 'I'll have a birthday and you'll bring me a present.'

'That's right,' I said, 'in August.'

'In August.' And they were behind me, hidden by the dust storm thrown up by my rear wheels.

Patay to Chateaudun is twenty miles, but in the wrong direction; Jules had taken me out of my way. Put another way, Marie Antoinette was now taking me out of my way, since I was travelling due west to meet her, whereas it would have made more sense to race southwards to the Loire in the hope of getting across before Max, studying a map, had decided which bridge I was likely to choose.

Chateaudun on that Saturday evening was a scene of almost total chaos. Its narrow streets were acting as a tight bottleneck on the endless stream of vehicles and humanity pressing down from the north along RN20 while others tried to force their way through the town along D927 from the north-east. There was no food left in the place and no petrol. There were no vacant beds and what goodwill there had been towards the invaders had long since been exhausted. Everything was barred and shuttered, and while the bulk of the refugees struggled through and continued their trek to the Loire, thousands were settling down as best they could for a night's sleep on the pavements and benches. The central square was packed. Here and there scuffles broke out, but in general the crowd was listless and defeated. And, as always, among them were soldiers alone or in groups, with or without their officers.

I had parked the Bentley as near to the square as I could get with any hope of moving it again when I wanted to, and leaving my vast fortune on wheels for as long as I dared, I elbowed my way forward and located the post office on the square's eastern side. If you wanted to post a letter it was no doubt an excellent place to do so, but as a rendezvous it was currently a failure:

Marie Antoinette was not to be found. We had said Sunday morning anyway, and this was still Saturday. I returned to the car to eat from my hamper and settle down for the night. I made a tolerable meal of ham, tomatoes and Gruyère, washed down with some of the wine from St Cheron. If I tucked the Bentley away in some courtyard or dark alleyway it would be a sitting duck for marauders during the night. I chose a street which was almost full of parked vehicles and their passengers and found a space. Then I settled down to sleep, the centre of a tight little circle of admirers.

During the day Premier Reynaud heard from Washington: the USA would not enter the war. He also received a complaint from the British Ambassador about 'the wave of anglophobia which seems to have engulfed certain French circles'. When politicians in Bordeaux suggested that Parliament might be recalled, its president Edouard Herriot threw up his hands: 'Good God! Whatever for? What a spectacle we'd make of ourselves!' During the afternoon, premier and commander-in-chief quarrelled over how to get an armistice. At four the cabinet met: at 7.55 the meeting ended. Another row, this time between the commander-in-chief and The President of the Republic, led Weygand to storm back to his headquarters in a fury. Later that night, Reynaud cabled Churchill: could he agree to France seeking the German conditions for an armistice? All night the phone and telegraph lines between Bordeaux and London were kept busy. Meanwhile, in the world of brute force — and thus of reality — Rommel was writing to his wife: 'Today we cross the Seine . . .' To the west the remnants of the French Xth Army were driven into Brittany while the VIth and VIIth were scrambling back towards the Loire in almost total confusion. With fewer refugees on the roads to the east, the German Panzer divisions moved even faster. Guderian's tanks were approaching Dijon, deep in the French heartland.

Chapter 11

I woke next morning with a cold breeze blowing on the back of my neck. I looked back and saw sky through a slit in the canvas of the hood. Someone in the night had managed to extract my hamper through the torn roof without waking me. When they take food and leave suitcases one is getting down to the basic data of civilization. In the dark they'd missed the peaches, ham and a couple of bottles of wine. It would be an unbalanced diet from now on. The car which had been parked ahead of me had gone, presumably with my hamper aboard. With me asleep in the car they hadn't had the nerve to force the boot.

A family from Rouen was in the car behind; a couple and two polite teenage boys who were mesmerized by the Bentley. We did a little trading: ham for bread and butter. 'We aren't setting out till later,' the father said. 'We're waiting here for my brother.'

'I'm also waiting for someone.'

He offered to guard the car while I mounted my vigil at the post office. 'My boys will sit in it. And I think I can do something about the tear in your hood. I've some twine on board.'

At eight I was outside the post office, watching for Marie Antoinette in the densely packed stream of humanity passing slowly through the square. I never saw her approaching, and the first I knew was when two arms were flung round my neck from behind. Then she was clinging to me, sobbing and laughing. All she could say was, 'Oh, my God . . . Oh, my God!' Then came the tears and her slender body shuddered and trembled in my arms.

'I got away from them!' She kept gasping the words, as if she couldn't believe them, and so had to persuade herself that I would believe them.

'I don't want to know anything now. Let's get away from here.'

My friend from Rouen had done a neat first-aid job on the hood and the boys were sitting entranced in the car as if they owned it. I thanked everyone, kissed madame, shook all available hands, and with Marie Antoinette by my side, pulled out into the traffic and out of the crowded centre of the town. I had rescued her hat from the back seat and tenderly put it back on her head. She rewarded me with one of her smiles.

We stopped in a deserted street in the south of the town and I gave her breakfast. She ate ravenously.

'When was your last meal?'

'This time yesterday. Bread and cold coffee. God, I'm hungry.'

There was a purple bruise on her cheek.

'How did you get that?'

'I jumped while the car was moving. Look . . .' She lifted her dress, which was stained and torn. There were two angry welts on her thigh. 'Now we have to move fast,' she said.

'I've got a route to the Loire and a good place to cross.'

She shook her head vigorously. 'Not south of here. They'll be watching the bridges.'

'There's about thirty of them between Nevers and the sea; I've counted.'

'They've alerted the police in Orléans, and they'll be watching all along the river. We'll never get across.'

'I thought – a country bridge or a ferry . . .'

She shook her head again. 'Believe me, it can't work.'

I thought about it. 'Why should I believe you?' I asked.

'You have every right not to, but I am telling the truth.'

'If they wanted to catch me on the Loire they'd send you back to me, wouldn't they, with precisely such a story?'

'They would.'

'And they'd rough you up a bit, just to make it stick.'

106

She nodded miserably. 'I was afraid that was what you'd say and I can't stop you heading for the nearest bridge. I can only say that if you do, they'll catch you, and that means they'll catch me.'

'What then?'

She sat silent for a moment. 'You must make your decision now', she said. 'If you decide for the Orléans area I will wish you all the luck in the world and leave you now. If I stay with you and we're caught, my life is in danger – as much danger as yours. According to your theory, they'll reward me for delivering you and the car. I know better. So I'll leave now. You must choose.'

'Where will you go?'

She gave me a thin smile. 'You should realize by now that I know how to look after myself.'

'In this madhouse?'

She nodded. There was a long silence. 'Have you decided?'

'I've decided. I'll trust you. I don't know why, but I actually think you've been telling the truth this time. So what do we do?'

'We travel due east from here and get over the Loire as far upstream as we can. They believe you'll be racing for the nearest crossing point. Max Boni thinks you'll reckon he won't dare to bring in other police forces.'

'What I don't understand is why they didn't sabotage the car while they were busy providing fake cans of petrol and a gun full of blanks.'

'Schlesser forbade it because I was with you. He laid it down: no accidents.' I looked at her and she put on an elaborate performance of peeling a peach, her eyes carefully averted from mine. 'Anyway' – between mouthfuls of peach – 'I can tell you the spare fan belts don't fit this car; nor does the petrol pump. And they never sent to Zurich for valves. In fact, I don't think they did anything to the engine at all. It was all an elaborate charade to make their scenario look right. All except strengthening her, of course.' She had finished eating and was licking the tips of her fingers delicately – a kitten again. What she had said reminded me of the strange episode of my cancelled pass to the police garage.

'Is that why I was suddenly barred while Boni's men were working on the car?'

She ventured a laugh. 'That was because I was there.'

'You?'

'They wanted me to be familiar with the Bentley in case anything happened to you and I had to drive it.'

I digested that piece of intelligence. I had started the car while we talked and was heading east out of the town. Now she took hold of the map and for a few minutes was silent while she studied it.

'We can go east on D955,' she said, 'and then the tricky thing will be to get across RN20 somehow, just north of Orléans. It's about fifty kilometres from here. Then we've a long run mainly eastwards before we dare turn south towards the river – maybe two hundred and fifty kilometres or more.'

'I know,' I said, 'don't tell me: the inner tubes on my spare wheels have tiny holes in them.'

She nodded. 'Quite big ones.'

If the road through Chateaudun was chaotic, RN20 when we reached it was bloody hell itself. Before, the prevailing mood had been apathy, punctuated by brief outbursts of panic. But here, on the main route of retreat from Paris, the mood was bitter, angry and dangerous, with army units thrusting civilians off the crown of the road and vehicles which had run out of petrol being tipped into the ditches by those held up behind, while their occupants stood by in impotent fury or in tears. It was each for themself – a sickening show of what happens when fear rips through the thin surface of civilization.

I nosed the car up to the main road and waited for someone to let me cross. With everything moving at a crawl, no one had anything to lose by giving way. But no one would.

'*C'est des sales Anglais!*' a man on a bicycle shouted, and I thought we might well be lynched there and then. But Marie Antoinette reacted like a fury, leaping from the car and screaming: '*Nous sommes aussi Français que vous!*' Being infinitely French,

108

her furious claim that we both were seemed to quell this localized outbreak of anglophobia. And finally she got us across the stream of vehicles by planting herself, frail but utterly immovable, legs apart and arms outstretched, in the path of an oncoming truck full of troops. I steered the Bentley over and as Marie Antoinette darted after me the traffic closed up behind us.

The Loire is the most beautiful of Europe's rivers. Rising in the stark granite hills of the Massif Central, it flows roughly due north as far as Nevers and then turns towards the west, gaining fullness and character as it describes a series of sweeping curves with Joan's Orléans at the apex of the greatest of them, and so, ever swelling and broadening, flows on to pour its waters into the Atlantic at St Nazaire. With a little help from the warm air brought in by the Gulf Stream, the river has created a veritable garden along its broad valley; asparagus and peaches, soft fruit and vines all grow there in abundance amid the fairy castles – Chenonceaux and Blois, Chambord, Amboise and Villandry. 'A countryside of grace, moderation and gentleness,' the guidebook says. None of which was it to be my pleasure to see on that dazzling Sunday in June. If we were to get over the river it must be in the upper reaches where the Loire runs from its source in the south, up towards Nevers. Between Nevers and Roanne, 120 miles upstream, are nine bridges. It would have to be one of those.

As we drove eastward in the blazing heat Marie Antoinette was busy with the map. 'A place called Decize looks good,' she said. 'It's thirty-four kilometres south of Nevers and there are no main roads.' We'd been working our way round the outside of the river's great Orléans curve, keeping to secondary roads, of which a number were abominable, and covering maybe three miles for every one flown by the bird. We'd had to cross RN7, which was almost as bad as RN20, and soon afterwards the steering wheel wrenched in my hand and I felt the grinding vibration which told me we had a puncture. I tramped a mile back to the main road, found a garage which had no stock of anything, and bought from the proprietor the remains of his own repair kit for the price of three new tyres. A couple of hours later we were rolling again, having used our last two bottles of wine to test my makeshift repair for telltale air bubbles.

I thought the time for explanations had come. 'And now,' I said, 'I'm listening. How did you get away?'

'Well, I ran to the van which was blocking the D53, looking as dishevelled and distressed as I could. I told them you'd pulled up at the crossroads, saw the van when you reconnoitred, concluded I'd led you into a trap, threw me out of the car and drove back the way you'd just come.'

'They bought it?'

'I'm good at stories.'

'You are.'

She smiled. 'Then we drove back – you must have seen us go by – and met Max and the others. Max would have hit me, but he's afraid of Schlesser, so he screamed at the others instead.'

'Some day,' I said, 'you must tell me what role Schlesser plays in your life.'

'You won't want to listen.' Her voice was flat.

'Go on with your tale of cops and robbers.'

'They questioned me about your plans, of course. I told them you were aiming for the Loire between Tours and Orléans. That's the corridor of countryside between RN10 and 20. Max said, of course, that you'd remember that I knew as much and now you might go for one of the bridges on either side of that stretch. He spent half an hour on the phone to the police chief in Orléans, who seemed to be a pal of his. The man promised to have the bridges watched along the big curve of the river. And there you are.'

'And how did you get away? Didn't you say you jumped from a moving car?'

There was a long silence which I didn't care to break. Then, in a small voice: 'I didn't jump from a car. I stole away during the night, got lucky with a couple of lifts, reached Chateaudun and here we are.' She tried one of her giggles on me, but it was unhappy and forced.

110

'And the bruises?'

Another pause. Then: 'Max did hit me.'

'Despite Schlesser?'

'Max is a very violent man. He was positively livid with fury at the thought of all that money getting away from him.'

'I suppose,' I said, 'I have to accept your latest version for want of anything better.'

'I *am* telling you the truth. I swear I am.'

'You find it difficult, don't you?'

'Yes.'

I allowed her a longish silence because she seemed to want it. 'Would you like to tell me about Schlesser?'

'No.'

'All right.'

We drove on in silence through the Nièvre department with its flourishing farms untouched by the war. 'What will Max do now, chase southwards after us?'

'I don't know. He'll have to report to Schlesser and do what he's told.'

'Perhaps we're rid of him.'

She laughed. 'One is never rid of the Max Bonis.'

By nightfall at ten we found ourselves in a hamlet outside Decize, maybe half a mile from the river. 'And here we stay while I sleep,' I said.

'Is it wise?'

'Is it wise to drive through the night with the driver dozing?'

'I can drive her.'

'Not on these crazy roads at night. And if we have another puncture you're not strong enough to keep her out of the ditch. She's as heavy as a London bus.'

We scrounged water and some bread from a farmer who told us we could run the car under a raised loft where the dry hay was deep enough to make a tolerably comfortable bed. 'Better than the car,' I said. 'We need to stretch out.' We ate some of our precious ham with the bread, washed as best we could at a pump and climbed into the loft. Later she was lying in my arms, the pent-up emotions of the day released in a fit of sobbing

111

which shook her entire body and went on until – fumbling and awkward in the dark – I made love to her.

'You were right.' I was wiping the tears from her face, which had tasted salty as I kissed her.

'About the second time?'

'Yes, even in a barn like a couple of kids.'

'And do you trust me yet?'

'I trust you.'

A few moments later she was asleep and did not wake up when I lifted her head off my chest as gently as I could and settled down myself, exhausted and soon asleep.

On Sunday 16 June the French government met three times. At its last session it had before it a proposal by Winston Churchill that there should be a Union of Great Britain and France to prosecute the war. The government turned it down and went on to agree to ask Hitler for armistice terms. Paul Reynaud resigned and the President called on Marshal Pétain to form a new government. Reynaud emerged from the meeting at midnight, exhausted and finally driven out by those who were determined to come to terms with Germany. The day had been an unmitigated disaster for the French armies as they fell back to the Loire. All day the Germans, and now the Italians, flew sorties to bomb the Loire bridges and machine gun the approaches which were choked with a struggling mass of humanity, desperate to cross the river. At Gien and Orléans thousands were killed and wounded. By five p.m. advanced units of Hoth's Panzers were fighting in the northern suburbs of Orléans, their advance slowed down by the chaos on the roads. Von Kleist's armoured corps had cut through the French IVth Army under General Requin further east and had reached the river at Nevers during the day. By nightfall spearheads had been put across on bridges which should have been blown but were not. The remnants of General Touchon's VIth and General Frère's VIIth Armies had managed to scramble across and form a thin and largely useless defensive line on the left bank, with units and stragglers distributed ad hoc. Two Czech regiments extricated themselves for later transfer to England, donating their transport to a French infantry regiment. 'A complete picture of breakdown,' commented General von Bock when he visited Orléans the following day.

Chapter 12

I woke to a finger of light falling across my face from a slit in the wall – to that and the sound of men shouting. I could also hear the revving of heavy engines and the rumble of traffic. I looked at Marie Antoinette beside me: she lay with her head turned my way, her eyes wide open, frightened.

'I hear voices,' I said.

'They are not French voices.'

'I thought not.'

'They are German.'

'I'm afraid so.'

'What do we do?'

'We take a look.'

'Perhaps we should pray.'

'If you like, but I've never found that it helped.'

We crawled over the straw to an unglazed window giving on to the road.

'Oh, my God!' Marie Antoinette dug her nails into the back of my hand.

Below us a steady stream of trucks was moving slowly south towards the river, and the trucks were full of men in the *feldgrau* uniforms of Hitler's infantry. As we watched, the trucks gave way to a column of transporters, each with a tank aboard. Motorcyclists overtook the convoy from time to time. A staff car loaded with officers drove by at speed. And above the racket below us we could hear the heavy thump of explosions to the south. We had wandered stupidly into Hitler's *Blitzkrieg* simply because I had wanted a good night's sleep. The Germans had got to the Loire first.

'You were right: we should have pushed on.'

'Never mind who was right. What do we *do*?'

As we watched, a truck pulled into the roadside and the driver leaned out. The farmer must have been standing below us. A shouted exchange took place; it sounded relaxed. Then the driver gave the thumbs up and pulled back into the convoy.

'If they can be so damn friendly with the locals,' I said, 'I see no reason why we shouldn't take our chances, always provided we're both French. Come on.'

We scrambled down the ladder and joined the farmer by the roadside.

'They're behaving themselves,' he said.

'But what are they doing on the Loire?' Marie Antoinette asked. 'If they want to behave, let them behave at home.'

The farmer looked at her. 'Don't you know why they're here? We've been sold, that's why. Our politicians sold us. And our generals. Idiots. I was in the last round and I can tell you – idiots one and all!' He spat in the dust. 'One and all.'

Suddenly, I felt a fool, standing there watching Hitler's invasion of France as if it were the Lord Mayor's Show. 'Come on,' I said, 'I've seen enough of the *Herrenvolk* for the time being.'

The farmer grunted and walked back into the yard with us. 'At least,' he said, 'they've not had to fight their way into my living room.'

I heard a vehicle pull up outside the yard and the sound of shouting.

'*Bleiben wir hier?*'

'*Jawohl.*'

'*Gut. Aussteigen!*'

A soldier with two stripes up stamped into the yard, his automatic rifle slung on his back. He could hardly be far out of his teens – a strapping youth with carroty hair, and badly in need of a wash and shave. Someone had told him the way to communicate with the population of France was to shout at them, first in German and then in pidgin French. Every inch the noble conqueror he now barked at the farmer: 'This place is requisitioned. We need this yard. *Schnell!*'

The farmer, possibly recalling similar scenes of conquest in
'14–'18, shrugged as only the rural French can shrug. 'It's all
yours, my lad. I'm only the owner, aren't I?'

'We're a motor transport company. I want food for twelve
men.'

'I've no food.'

'We'll soon see!'

'I can't stop you.'

'Where's the water?'

The farmer nodded towards the pump.

'Who are they?' The corporal jerked his head in our direction.

'Friends on their way south.'

We were favoured with a brief inspection, then the corporal
turned on his heel and marched towards the road, beckoning
his men in much the same tone of voice. It was warfare and
leadership as he understood the terms.

'I suppose he too has a mother,' the farmer said. 'Poor
woman.'

Two towing trucks and what looked like a mobile workshop
pulled off the roadside and into the yard. The corporal's dozen
men jumped down from their vehicles and started nosing
around, waiting for further orders. The corporal himself had
followed the farmer into the house and could be heard stamping
and cursing about the place, looking for food. Soon a small,
admiring group formed round the Bentley.

'*Französisch?*'

'*Nein, Englisch mit Französischer carosserie.*'

'*Zehr schön.*'

'*Jawohl.*'

One of them spoke a little French. 'What will she do?'

'About one-fifty kilometres an hour.'

'Show us her engine.'

I lifted the bonnet and there were more grunts of approval.

'You French?'

'Of course.'

'You've lost the war. Our radio told us you've asked for armistice terms.'

'When was that?'

'I don't know – during the night. They say the Spaniards are intermediaries. We licked you, eh?'

'You licked us.'

'No one can beat us, eh?'

'Be careful,' I said, 'it's what Napoleon and Alexander the Great said, and they were wrong. So was your Kaiser.'

'The hell with them. We have Adolf Hitler.'

'Aren't you lucky,' I said.

Marie Antoinette tugged gently on my sleeve and I shut up. She bestowed one of her most melting smiles on the young German. 'Do you think we can continue our journey? We have to get to my family in Vichy. That's south of here, across the river.'

The soldier shook his head. 'No civilian vehicles allowed on the roads. We've orders to throw 'em into the ditches. The Fourth Panzer Division is crossing the river here. That's part of General von Kleist's army group. You can hear 'em out there.' He nodded in the direction of the road, where the roar of truck engines was now unceasing. 'We're a transport regiment.'

'If there's an armistice I suppose you'll stop your advance,' Marie Antoinette said, 'then maybe . . .'

'Don't ask me. I'm just a bloody private. And don't ask our corporal; he'll have you shot for insubordination.' The soldier grinned without much enthusiasm. 'A lousy pig!'

'We'll see.' The murmur from Marie Antoinette was barely audible.

As we turned away I said, 'I am the last one to encourage you to seduce the disgusting German soldiery, but maybe that famous smile of yours . . .'

'Leave the corporal to me. I've known worse.'

The corporal emerged, scowling, from the house. Behind him the farmer was inscrutable. If there was food in the house, none had been found. A peasant youth from Pomerania, or wherever this one had come from, was not going to get the better of a peasant of the Nièvre.

116

'Could you immobilize the car so that they can't get it going again?' Marie Antoinette asked.

'Sure, if the audience of Krauts will kindly go elsewhere for a couple of minutes.'

At that moment the corporal barked some orders and the men dispersed to their vehicles. A staff car pulled into the yard and the corporal went rigid while an officer snapped at him and drove off. Then he went out to the road.

'Do it now,' Marie Antoinette said.

'You wouldn't care to tell me what you have in mind?'

'Simple. We plead a breakdown and get them to tow us across.' She said it with a perfectly straight face. Was it black humour or did the girl live entirely in a fantasy world?

'For that,' I said, 'you'd have to go to bed with the entire IVth Panzer Division.'

'I will go to bed with no one but you. I do not sleep with the enemies of France.' She seemed quite cross at the suggestion.

'All right, all right, but the Germans are not running a breakdown service.'

'Oh yes they are. That soldier said so. My plan is simply to persuade them to include us.'

'And I am to put this beautiful car of mine out of action for a lunatic scheme like that?'

She nodded. 'But you've got to be able to get her running again in a flash. We may need speed at the other end.'

'Now you're pushing an open door. I am all for speed. Absolutely. Never more so.'

'All right, Englishman, get going please, while the corporal is out of the way. But whatever you do to the car, it has to be something they can't spot in a hurry.'

'I'd thought of that. All I need is a pencil.'

'I have a little one with my diary.'

'A little one will do, provided it's a lead pencil.'

She fetched it and it was.

'You will please mount the watch,' I said, 'and scream if any of them come back. I need one minute.'

The bonnet lifted, I drew a straight pencilled line from top to

117

bottom of two of the plugs. The current would flow down the graphite of the pencil mark and the plugs would not spark. Result: two cylinders out of action. It was something Jacques had taught me in Paris in the old days though I couldn't remember why. The whole thing took me under the minute and I had the bonnet back in place without being disturbed.

'The car won't start,' I said, 'and I defy your corporal to find the fault.'

'Good, because I'm going to ask him to try.'

Her opportunity came an hour later. A tank transporter had been towed into the yard with a pain in its guts. The corporal put a couple of his men to work on it. 'Go away and leave this disgusting oaf to me,' Marie Antoinette said. I gave her the ignition key and retreated to the far side of the yard. Then I saw her go up to the corporal, switching on her smile as she went. From where I stood it was impossible to tell how the conversation was going, but they walked over to the car and the corporal lifted the bonnet and peered inside. Then he climbed into the driving seat, turned the key and pressed the starter. When nothing happened he shook his head. And then, to my astonishment, Marie Antoinette burst into tears.

The corporal seemed embarrassed. He was saying something to her and she was replying through her sobs. Bravely, she tried to smile, laying a delicate hand on the corporal's sleeve. It was a touching and appalling performance. When the corporal had marched off to supervise what they were doing to the transporter, Marie Antoinette sidled over to me. 'He's putting a man on it to find the fault. Are you sure he won't find it?'

'Pretty sure, unless he takes the thing apart. And if he hits on the idea of new plugs he'll be unlucky because the spares are in my pocket.'

'What did you think of my performance?'

'Horrifying.'

'You haven't seen the end of it yet.'

The corporal's man spent a miserable half-hour on the Bentley while I looked on sympathetically and diverted his attention into mechanical blind alleys from time to time. Then

118

he reported failure and the corporal, having forgotten that this was not a German staff car but one of the civilian vehicles they'd been overturning and smashing up on their way through France, bawled him out.

'Time now for act two,' Marie Antoinette said. 'Please go away.'

I did as I was told and soon she was again deep in conversation with the unspeakable youth. From where I stood it looked first of all like an argument, then there was a passage of wheedling, much decorated with the smile, then what could be taken for a conspiracy. The corporal allowed himself a grin and Marie Antoinette rewarded him with another dazzling smile and a hand which lingered longer this time on his sleeve. Then he moved away and she joined me at the far side of the yard.

'He'll do it,' she said simply.

'Do what?'

'Tow us over, of course.'

'Don't make jokes in bad taste. This is the Nazi soldiery, the scourge of Europe. They kill people; they don't tow Bentleys as a favour.'

'Oh yes they do, if you know how to go about it.'

'So how did you go about it?'

'I told him my mother is dying in Vichy and that she'll die heartbroken if she doesn't see her only daughter before the end. I added that it was my understanding that the National Socialists under their great leader Adolf Hitler were chivalrous, brave and devoted to a pure Aryan womanhood of which I was a pretty fair specimen. All this rubbish he took seriously. Then I said that I didn't expect him to run risks on my behalf without some fitting reward, but that unfortunately we had no ready money. On the other hand, there was always . . . me.' She smiled sweetly.

'You mean to say you told him he could . . .' I had a little difficulty with the words.

'Oh, yes. I said if he towed us through Decize to the far side of the river, where I knew there was a big garage, he could have me.'

119

'Just like that?'

'Just like that. I reckoned after fighting his way through Holland, Belgium and most of France he needed a woman. In any case, it would be a nice thing to brag about among his mates. He was easy.'

'And do you plan to honour your promise?'

'Not if I can help it.'

'I regard that as an equivocal answer.'

She smiled. 'I am in an equivocal situation. And anyway, if you have a better plan, I'll drop mine and we can adopt yours.'

I ignored it. 'When is this lunatic scheme to take place?'

'This evening. He says it'll be easier then. He'll hitch us behind one of their towing trucks and we'll look like a staff car in the dark. You and I will have to conceal ourselves.'

'And what role am I supposed to be playing in all this?'

'Oh, you're just someone I cadged a lift from and you're making yourself a thorough sexual nuisance. I shall be delighted to show you that I prefer a younger, more vigorous man from the glorious super-race. I think he rather liked that.'

'Thank you.'

While Rommel's VIIth Panzers raced for Cherbourg in the north-west, trying to cut off the retreat of General Marshall-Cornwall's British force, the Vth Panzers reached the Loire at Saumur and further east Guderian's tanks were driving hard through central France. The French general staff had now lost overall control of its armies: telegrams were sent and remained unacknowledged and the telephone network was virtually useless. Thousands of miles of roads were choked with humanity and littered with smashed or abandoned vehicles. At 3 a.m. the French request for armistice terms had reached Berlin via the Spanish Embassy. From the German headquarters at Sedan in eastern France, Hitler called Mussolini to a meeting. At 9.30 p.m. Mussolini and his advisors left Rome for Munich, where he was to meet the German leader on the following day. During the morning General de Gaulle had left Bordeaux for London and at his refuelling stop in Jersey he asked for a cup of coffee and was given tea. 'His martyrdom had started,' observed General Spears, who was with him. Later, someone realized that no armistice request had gone to the

120

Italians and the Vatican's nuncio was asked to act for the French. At 12.30 p.m. Marshal Pétain broadcast to the nation: 'I give to France the gift of my person to mitigate her distress . . .' His speech produced total confusion in the army; whole regiments took it as authority to surrender.

Chapter 13

At ten the corporal announced that he was ready. The dusk had softened the edges of the landscape and the traffic on the road had thinned down since the morning. There was an unremitting rumble in the distance, as of thunder, but it was the German guns beyond Nevers wasting shells on the remnants of French units north of the river.

'The unit moves forward at midnight,' the corporal said. 'There's time to get to the river and back before then. I'll drive myself.' He offered Marie Antoinette a sickly grin. From the expression of his men who stood around watching us I guessed he'd told them he was off to have this classy woman. He'd had a shave and I noticed he'd scrubbed some of the grime off his hands. He still smelt bad.

We were pushing the Bentley to the centre of the yard to be hitched to the breakdown truck.

'Christ, she's heavy!'

'That's right,' I said, 'too much metal in her. Lousy engineering.' The disloyalty broke my heart.

We got her into position and the corporal secured a chain from the truck to the car's front axle.

'Get in and cover yourselves, and if we're stopped you don't make a sound, right?'

We did as we were told. The hood was down and we pulled the canvas cover over our heads. The corporal secured it.

Then we felt the front of the car rising into the air as it was winched up behind the truck. We crouched on the floor in positions of extreme discomfort.

'Do you have your gun?'

'I do. Also some blank cartridges which make a very frightening noise.'

'You may have to bluff with it,' Marie Antoinette said.

'I rather like the idea of taking on the IVth Panzer Division with a revolver full of blanks.'

'I haven't even got that.'

'True. How do you plan to survive a fate worse than death when we get to the other end?'

'It isn't worse than death.' That was all she would say but when I took her hand I noticed her palm was wet and she wouldn't let my hand go. We were moving and I felt the jolt as we left the yard and pulled on to the road.

We had been running for what seemed like half an hour but must have been all of three minutes when the truck's brakes screamed and we came to a halt. There were sounds of shouting and I could hear army boots stamping on paving stones.

'This must be Decize,' I whispered to Marie Antoinette. 'Sounds as if the place is full of troops.' I felt her shiver as she tightened her grip on my hand.

The voices were clearer now.

'Who are you?'

'Corporal Sauer, 125th motor, attached to IVth Panzers.'

'Where are you going?'

'Taking this load across the river. There's a repair unit of ours on the other side.'

'Get on with it, then.'

We were moving again, slowly, with changes of direction as if the road wound uncertainly through the town. Then it appeared to straighten.

'I think we're on the bridge.'

'Thank God!'

'You told him there's a garage on the other side, but is there?'

'I've no idea. But if there isn't he'll stop anyway for his reward, won't he?'

'I reckon I'll have to jump him somehow before the prize-giving has to start. Did you notice how he's armed?'

123

'The usual: a revolver and dagger in his belt. I didn't see the rifle.'

I lifted a corner of the canvas and undid the row of fasteners. Then I pushed my head through cautiously. We were doing about fifteen and were approaching the other side of the Loire. We seemed to be alone on the bridge. The truck was driving on its side lights and they did nothing to illuminate the darkness. If there was to be a moon it hadn't put in an appearance yet.

Ahead of us I could just see the darker outline of buildings against the sky. It looked as if the little town sat astride the river. The corporal would drive on until he came to a garage or to the end of the built-up area. Then he'd stop and that was when I would have to become a hero. It seemed to me that the smart way to do it was to attack him before he climbed out of the driver's seat.

'I'm going up front,' I told Marie Antoinette. 'You stay there. When he stops I'll try to knock him out.'

Clambering aboard the truck wasn't difficult: there were only a couple of feet between the Bentley's nose and the truck's tailboard. The truck had wing mirrors but the driver couldn't see what was happening directly behind his head unless he turned round. I crept forward, releasing my revolver from its holster and gripping it by the barrel. I had no idea whether a blow on the back of the head from the butt would put a man out. Fortunately, the corporal was wearing a forage cap; a German army helmet with its long neckpiece would have defeated me. We had crossed the river and were moving slowly between houses; he must be watching for a garage in the darkness. But there was no garage and soon the houses had thinned out and we were out of the town. So now he must be looking for a likely place to stop, take payment, and bring his little adventure to an end before a nosy officer took a closer look at the car and handed him over to the *Feldgendarmerie*. Ahead the road forked. There were no German units in sight; presumably the spearhead of the division had pushed on. I felt the truck slow down. I was crouching immediately behind the driving seat, gripping my revolver and sweating freely. Then, as he brought the truck to a standstill on the verge, I leaned forward, swept his cap off his head with my left hand and brought the butt of the revolver down on his skull with all the strength I could muster.

The heavy butt made a nasty sound as it thudded into the bone. It was followed by a kind of strangled curse. Then the corporal slumped forward and his head hit the upper edge of the steering wheel.

'Come on, I've dealt with your friend.' My voice sounded hoarse and I realized that I was trembling. Perhaps I'd get used to this sort of thing and stop reacting like a girl of refined sensibilities.

Marie Antoinette scrambled out of the car and joined me. We dragged him clear and deposited him behind a bush by the roadside. He seemed to be in poor shape but alive. I had no special desire to see him dead.

I found the handle of the winch, lowered the car to the ground and unfastened the chain. Then I opened the bonnet and did what could have been the fastest job of changing two plugs in the dark that the world had ever seen. (N.B.: after the little trick with the lead pencil the plug is done for, though I don't know why.) I switched on the ignition and pressed the starter: she sang like an angel and settled into her familiar purr. Marie Antoinette had wandered off and now she returned with a dagger in one hand and a German service revolver in the other. 'Could come in handy,' she said, passing them to me. As she spoke, the sound of a vehicle reached us from the town. Two points of light were moving along the road and moving fast.

'Right, we're off.'

Marie Antoinette jumped in beside me and as we headed down the lesser of the two prongs of the fork, something fast and heavy reached the intersection. It took the other prong.

I risked switching on my headlights and revved the Bentley up into the sixties along the straight country road, trees flashing by on either side and nothing in sight. 'The interesting question,' I said, 'must be whether the forward units are ahead of us or over to our right along the other road. That other fellow just now was a good sign: he must have been heading for the

German positions. On the other hand, where on earth are we going?'

'We're going to Moulins: that's about thirty kilometres. Then Vichy, another fifty or so. And there you can take the waters and do your liver a lot of good.'

Cured of my earlier tendency to sleep in hay lofts, I drove all night, headlights on and Marie Antoinette keeping me awake. For this, she sang – with a thin, sweet voice and a repertoire of French country songs interspersed with hits from American musical films. These she delivered in fractured English. At one point she showed she was word-perfect in three of Edith Piaf's street songs but entirely without Piaf's street-wise despair. We passed through Vichy and the industrial haze of Clermont Ferrand. Then up among the crags and ravines of the Massif Central, with sheer drops, hairpins, one-in-sixes – everything to avoid in a 3½-ton car travelling too fast at two, then three, then four in the morning. By five we were at Aurillac in the Cantal and soon after six we dropped exhausted into bed at the Hotel de la Poste in Figeac.

'Please wake us at ten,' I asked the *patronne*.

'Nine,' Marie Antoinette said.

'Ten.'

The *patronne* said, 'Make up your minds.'

I compromised. 'Nine, and we'd like coffee and rolls.'

We woke to thumps on the door, blazing sun through the window and the rich aroma of coffee. An hour later, breakfasted and bathed, we were down the road at a garage, filling the tank and cans with petrol. At the grocer's we took food and drink aboard. There were no shortages in this rural backwater. Marie Antoinette looked as if she had just stepped from her apartment in the Avenue d'Iéna – immaculate and beautiful. In her honour, I spent ten minutes wiping grime from the Bentley. Then we took D922 to Villefranche, sprawling around its famous church, followed the road as it meandered down past Cordes, perched high on its hill as if the Middle Ages had never come to an end, and so, in the airless midday heat to Albi. The

126

ancient town seemed to have escaped the onslaught of the refugees: no doubt there were better ways of getting to Toulouse and Carcassone in the south if that was where one wanted to go. I parked in the shadow of the immense brick cathedral that the local bishop had built to put the fear of God into any Cathar dissidents who, by sheer agility, had escaped his torture squads. That was late in the thirteenth century. It struck me that we were on the run in much the same way from a cruder and later despotism, and Hitler would build not cathedrals but triumphal arches all over Europe if he got the chance. At that time I had no idea that his chosen monuments would be gas chambers.

We sat in the car and ate local garlic sausage, washed it down with a very fruity red wine from a neighbouring hillside, and concluded with a fine goat cheese. We set off again at two and after skirting Toulouse an hour or so later, pushed on southwards on secondary roads. By late afternoon we were in the foothills of the Pyrenees at Foix. We sat outside a café in the shadow of Gaston de Foix's great castle perched high above the valley of the Ariège. We drank beer and pored over our maps. The Bentley was parked across the square, comfortably within view.

'We can cross the frontier at Pas de la Case or Bourg-Madame,' I said. 'About seventy or a hundred kilometres from here.'

'Oh, my God!' Marie Antoinette said, 'I don't know how I could have forgotten such a thing.'

'What thing?'

'I'm stupid – hopelessly stupid.'

'You'll have to explain.'

'Your Spanish visa,' she said miserably.

'What about my visa?'

'And mine.'

'So what about our visas?'

'Yours is no good.'

'It hardly surprises me.'

'And I haven't got one.'

127

'That isn't exactly surprising either.'

'And the Spanish consulates aren't issuing them unless one has an onward visa to somewhere like Portugal.'

'And we haven't.'

She shook her head. 'We haven't.'

'And I'm not having you offering to seduce the Spanish frontier police.'

'Perhaps you could buy them?'

'I intend to try. What do you think it would cost?'

She shrugged. 'Schlesser always said people usually cost about half what you'd think.'

'You still haven't explained about Schlesser.'

'I will.'

There was a silence. 'In any case . . .' I said.

Marie Antoinette finished the sentence for me. '. . . we probably won't get past the French frontier post. Max will have sent messages.'

'Do you think, amid all this chaos . . .?'

'I think Max will have warned them. I heard him muttering about a colonel something in Perpignan. I think that's their headquarters.'

'Do you think we could buy the French *and* the Spaniards? I have a lot of money.'

'Risky. And if you fail, they have you. I can't see you getting out of it with the butt end of your silly revolver.'

'Or the dagger.'

'Or even my corporal's gun. He was disgusting, wasn't he?'

We sat in silence and an ancient waiter offered us more beer. Behind the battlements of the castle the setting sun was throwing up an attractive pink glow. The beer was light and cool, the place was peaceful and there was a fascinating woman on the other side of the little table. Perfect! It was only the context which was wrong.

'I know,' Marie Antoinette said, slipping into the midstream of my thoughts again. 'It could have been marvellous here . . . both of us.'

128

'It is pretty marvellous. It's just that we have one of the great mountain ranges of Europe to get over with a car weighing three and a half tons, with a posse of villains on our tail.'

'My Englishman will do it. You say "for King and country" – right?'

A small group of locals had gathered round the car. I could see them peering in at the dashboard and exchanging opinions. Among them was the local *flic* in the dark blue uniform of the *Gendarmerie*.

'You were going to tell me about Schlesser.'

'It will spoil things.'

'I want to know.'

'Then first you have to understand about me.'

'Tell me.'

She was twisting her beer mug between her long fingers, looking into the golden liquid as if some kind of absolution were to be found there. Then she looked up at me and there were tears in her eyes. 'Please don't sympathize,' she said. 'You can see I am crying, but it's only self-pity and that's unworthy and doesn't deserve sympathy.'

'Why are you sorry for yourself?'

'My life has not been what I wanted. None of it has been like the dreams I used to have.'

'Dreams of being Marie Antoinette de Bergemont whose father had a place near Barbezieux?'

'Something like that.' She took a long draught of beer. 'Actually my father was a drunkard who could never hold down a job. When he was drunk he would get violent. Once he nearly killed my mother with a mallet. She was in hospital for six weeks and I ran away from home. But they brought me back and he . . .' She shook her head as if she were trying to dislodge the memory. 'He had a heavy leather belt. And then there were other things. I don't talk about them. Maybe one day I can tell you, but not now. I've never told anyone.'

'When did you leave home?'

'I was sixteen. We lived in Mantes; that's near Paris. A lousy dump. I had a cousin in Paris who took me in, but one thing led to another and I got into trouble. That's when I met Max. In his official capacity, I'm afraid.'

There was still a group round the car but the *flic* had disappeared. Much later I convinced myself that I'd seen him make a note of the car's registration number, but it made no impression at the time as I listened to Marie Antoinette's story.

'And Max passed you on to Schlesser?'

'Among other things I suppose you could say he was a kind of pimp for Schlesser. That old monster has a particular taste for young girls. I was a little over sixteen. Not as innocent and untouched as Schlesser would have liked, but I knew how to pretend. He was crazy about me – an old man's obsession. He set me up in an apartment in Montparnasse, and later, when your Francine left for Rome, he took her place, redecorated it abominably and put me in there.'

'So it was Rome and not America.'

She nodded. 'Sorry about that, but it was what I was told to say.'

'And why,' I asked, 'did you go along with all this if you didn't like it?'

'I never said I hated it. After all, I was a girl from nowhere and here was a famous man – a member of the government at the time – spending money on me, teaching me how to stand up to waiters in great restaurants and how to buy clothes. All that isn't distasteful, you know. And as for the sex . . .' The slender fingers were flicked gracefully in the space between us: 'There is worse. I've *known* worse. In any case, his appetites were pretty minimal. Even rather pathetic in a certain way.'

She had painted a pretty banal picture: the Parisian tart, complete with unhappy childhood as justification. I wondered whether she realized what it all sounded like. Perhaps she noticed, with her very acute perceptiveness, a trace of dismay in my expression.

'I am sure you don't approve of all this, and I only tell you because you ask me repeatedly. But it is the truth about me, and if you wish to judge, then you must judge. But what was the difference between your Francine and me? I will tell you:

130

eighteen centimetres. If I had been taller, I too could have been a mannequin, and what would have been the difference then? Men would have regarded me as the working girl who also accepted valuable gifts. As it is, I accept the gifts and only work occasionally. The art gallery is true: I worked in the Avenue Montaigne all of last year.'

'I wasn't judging.'

'You were. All men judge. They don't consider what life in Paris can be for a girl on her own, with weaknesses – plenty of weaknesses, no doubt – who absolutely refuses to work from nine till six at the Galleries Lafayette until her ankles swell and she has varicose veins at twenty-five.'

'I repeat, I wasn't judging.'

'And you, how did you earn your living? Schlesser told me about your sentence.'

'That's why I wasn't judging. That, and the fact that in earlier times I earned my living playing cards.'

She laughed. 'I suppose neither of us could be considered as productive and socially desirable people.'

'I suppose not.'

'But I like to think what we are doing now redeems us just a little. It is useful, isn't it?'

'I think so.'

She put her hand in mine across the table. 'I suppose it's silly, really, but if I have one wish in the world now it's that you should think well of me. Do you think that is possible?'

'Altogether possible.'

'Thank you.'

'Now tell me how they drew you into this little conspiracy of theirs.'

'I was frightened,' she said simply. 'Max is a bigger brute than you know. I could tell you things . . .' She trailed off again. 'And as I said, I had been in trouble.' She finished her beer, taking her time over it. 'I am not a crook,' she said finally. 'You must believe that I am not a crook.'

'Who am I to judge a thing like that?'

'Don't abandon me, please,' she said. 'Promise to take me

with you to Portugal, to England, wherever.'

'I don't abandon my friends.'

'People don't abandon their friends, but they often abandon their lovers, and we are lovers.'

'Then let's be friends as well.'

She gave me a very sweet smile. 'Let's stay in this beautiful little place tonight and I will make love to you. The frontier will still be there tomorrow.'

I nodded and called the waiter. For some reason I couldn't define I'd hardly believed a word of her story about her family. 'By the way,' I said, 'you've never told me your real name.'

She looked up at me and I thought she was actually frightened for a moment. Then her eyes wandered down to the table and then beyond me to the far side of the street.

'My real name? Oh, its Catherine.' A slight pause. 'Catherine Bourg. But I prefer Marie Antoinette.'

'Let's stay with that, then.'

As we got up to go, I put a tip on the table. To be exact, on the beer mat. *Bières to Sarrebourg*, it said in fancy gothic script.

The German advance continued unchecked throughout Tuesday 18 June, with a new bridgehead won on the left bank of the Loire and the encirclement of the French IInd Army group in the east completed. All centres of population of more than 20,000 people were declared open cities and the French units which still had arms, ammunition and leadership were urged to continue fighting. The two conflicting decisions produced confusion almost everywhere. During the day, furious arguments raged around the new government in Bordeaux. Unsuccessful efforts were made to persuade Marshal Pétain to go to North Africa and continue the war from there. In Munich, Hitler was conferring with Mussolini. 'As for the French fleet,' he declared, 'the best thing from our point of view is that they should scuttle it. The worst, that it should sail for England.' In fact, the scuttling of most of the fleet started on that day: the government decided that the fleet should not join the British despite strong pleas by the British and American governments. At 3 p.m. General de Gaulle arrived at Broadcasting House in London. 'I, General de Gaulle, presently in London, invite the officers and soldiers of France who are in Britain or

132

may come to find themselves there . . . to get in touch with me. Whatever happens, the flame of resistance must not and will not be extinguished.'

Chapter 14

The road from Foix south to Ax-les-Thermes follows the right bank of the Ariège along its valley, past such engagingly named places as the Pont du Diable, Bompas and Tarascon. As the road climbs steadily into the mountain range, the river gets younger and fiercer, the valley becomes a gorge and the hills turn into peaks. The bed of the Ariège was gouged out of the rock by glaciers and at Tarascon, where the ancient ice was 1,300 feet thick, the rock still bears its grievous scars. This is myth and legend country where untold atrocities were perpetrated in the name of divine revelation and ecclesiastical purity and demons ruled the minds of the mountain folk and for all I know rule them still. We hardly spoke as the car laboured up the flanks of the mountains, valley breaking into valley and gorge into gorge. It was raining, at first gently and then brutally in driving sheets as we travelled steadily up to meet the heavy clouds. We were shipping a good deal of water through the ill-repaired rent in the hood. I expected the weather, the gradients and the thin air at that height to combine in some obscure fashion to defeat the Bentley. But she held out nobly.

It was as we approached the village of Luzenac, which sits in the valley of the Ariège on the river's left bank, that I became aware of a car on our tail. The rain and mist made it impossible to tell what sort of car it was, and it could well have been someone just like us who had chosen this route to the frontier. But for a fugitive from the war it would be a pretty eccentric route. Maybe a local? Why not? And yet I felt decidedly apprehensive. The other car was travelling fast and was certainly closing the gap between us.

This stretch of the road had been chiselled out of the flank of the mountain, and where height was to be won or lost the engineers had built hairpin bends. As we kept doubling back on our tracks, gaining height, I could see the other car below us. When I had first noticed it, the distance between us might have been a mile or more: it was little more than a crawling speck down below in the valley. But as we passed from one mountain-side to the next and the hairpins eased down the flank of the mountain, the car reappeared above us and could not have been more than half a mile away. Were we really being followed or was I flogging the Bentley on in order to escape from a local farmer in a hurry to buy a pig?

'You've noticed it too,' Marie Antoinette said. 'I saw it way back. I didn't like to say anything in case it was just paranoia.'

'Paranoia doesn't do eighty on wet mountain roads.'

'What did you think of that *gendarme* back in Foix? Do you think perhaps he was too interested in our car?'

'Maybe. But I don't see how Max could alert the local *Gendarmerie* in a Godforsaken place like Foix.'

'You mustn't underestimate Max. They could have put out a general alert in the frontier area for a stolen Bentley.'

'Are you telling me they can do things like that with the Germans smashing through the country and half the population on the run?'

'I don't know. Maybe bits of the bureaucracy are still working as if nothing had happened. If the police telephone network is still functioning in these parts, I suppose the thing would be possible.'

We had passed through Luzenac and crossed the river. Here the road stays down in the valley for a few miles, following the twisting course of the river itself. The car behind us had reduced the half mile to maybe five hundred yards. It hadn't stopped at Luzenac, it hadn't slackened its speed over a difficult stretch, it was closing fast.

'For all practical purposes,' I said, 'we have to treat it as the enemy.'

And now the road started to clamber up the mountainside

135

again and I prayed the gradient wouldn't get too steep. I reckoned our weight would tell against us if it came to a long-drawn climbing contest. On the flat I could move faster if I was willing to take idiotic risks which, perforce, I was.

'Oh God!' Marie Antoinette was peering up into the mist above us. My own gaze was fixed on the glistening road immediately ahead.

'What is it?'

'In a few moments we will reach a waggon piled high with logs. It looks about as wide as the road.'

'You reckon we won't get past it?'

'Not unless there's a lay-by, and we've not seen many of them.'

I had been taking the bends in a thoroughly unprofessional manner, forcing the car round much faster than the road conditions allowed, and getting into a rear-wheel skid almost every time as the rear of the car broke away. Then, as I regained control when she straightened up, and thrust down on the accelerator again, wheelspin would force me to ease off. But I'd got used to that hazard: this was far worse.

'I am praying for us,' Marie Antoinette said.

The country horn on a Bentley offers a commanding sound – a blend of imperious impatience and a dire warning to anything which fails to get out of the way. I now started to sound the horn, hoping it would signal the waggoner ahead of me that I proposed to drive him off the road if he failed to flatten himself somehow against the mountainside and let me by. Fifty yards below us the pursuing car flashed past, heading for the hairpin we had just negotiated. I reckoned a couple of hundred yards between us. Our extra weight was telling against us.

'A Peugeot,' Marie Antoinette said. 'Two men inside. I couldn't see if they were in uniform.'

And now the waggon came clearly into view just ahead. Marie Antoinette had been right; there wasn't room for both of us abreast on the road. Its load was balanced precariously between upright planks and it swayed drunkenly on the uneven road surface. It was drawn by two sturdy horses, the driver

136

completely hidden by his load.

'They'll be armed if they're policemen,' Marie Antoinette said. 'What do we do?'

'You get down on the floor and stay there.'

'I want to help.'

'That's the best way to help.'

She did as she was told.

It was now clear that we had been incredibly unlucky. If we had reached the waggon a few moments earlier it would have been on a widened stretch of road and we'd have been able to squeeze past. As it was, the driver had ignored my horn, no doubt as a bone-headed mountain gesture against all outsiders, and he was twenty yards beyond the wide stretch as I reached it. I reckoned there was only one option left and I took it. I slowed to a crawl at a point where the road was still wide enough for the pursuing car to pass me, calculating that if they were policemen they'd be doing exactly what the manual says – in this case under the heading: Fugitive Vehicles – How to Stop Them. And what the manual no doubt says is overtake and stop, thus forcing the fugitive to stop behind you. The Peugeot duly overtook us, braked sharply and came to a halt just where the road narrowed again.

Two men jumped out. One was the *gendarme* from the square in Foix; the other was in plain clothes. Neither had drawn a gun as they walked back towards us with the self-conscious swagger that policemen adopt on such occasions.

'*Vos papiers.*' One stood on either side of the car.

'You'd better sit up again,' I said to Marie Antoinette. 'It looks as if there's to be no mayhem after all.'

She got back into her seat with perfect dignity and treated the man on her side of the car to a smile.

We handed over our papers, which were scrutinized in the approved fashion. While my man was trying to make head or tail of my passport I was busy working out some simple logistics of my own which included an appraisal of the distance between the Bentley and the Peugeot and the Peugeot and the sheer drop down the mountainside.

137

The papers were handed back.

'Where are you going?'

'To Ax-les-Thermes.'

'Why?'

'We are on our way south.'

'To Andorra,' Marie Antoinette added. She lied readily and always with style.

'Show the car's papers.' I complied. 'You claim to be the owner of this vehicle?'

'I *am* the owner.'

'We have information that this car is stolen. There is also a matter of a crime of violence committed against the owner of the vehicle.'

'Ridiculous! This car was made specially for me in 1933.'

'You will return to Foix with us. Get out of the car. My colleague will drive.'

The fellow had his hand on the handle of the door and a foot on the running board. It seemed to me we could tarry no longer.

I had kept the engine running. Now I slipped her into gear, took my left foot off the brake pedal and stepped as hard as I dared on the accelerator. The Bentley leaped forward like a nervous horse which had felt the spurs on its flanks. The policeman staggered and nearly fell as the handle was whipped out of his hand and the running board moved suddenly from beneath his foot.

At that point the Bentley was some ten yards from the Peugeot, which in turn was barely a yard from the edge of the road. Beyond the edge was a dead drop down the rock-strewn side of the mountain. I aimed the car at the back of the Peugeot and slightly to its near side. I had no idea if my 3½-ton projectile would carry enough inertial force to shift the other car despite its brakes. Nor did I know whether I'd be doing my car some fatal damage in the process – maybe puncturing the radiator or driving one of the wings back on to the wheel.

The Bentley, as I say, leapt forward and covered the space separating it from the Peugeot in a second or two. Then came the crunch of metal as we hit the rear of the other car. I felt a moment of absolutely dead resistance as the Peugeot absorbed the initial shock. Then it lurched forward and seemed to bounce its way a few yards up the road, veering as it did so towards the edge on its right. I was in second gear, which seemed to give me the maximum driving power, and I could hear the engine whining in protest at the unaccustomed resistance.

Then it was all over. The offside wheels of the Peugeot went over the edge and the car seemed to hesitate for a moment before plunging sideways into the void. As it disappeared from view I heard the sound of buckling metal and the snapping of tree branches.

'Hold on,' I yelled to Marie Antoinette, 'and duck down – they may decide to shoot.'

I kept the Bentley going, up towards the waggon which was now out of sight round the next bend. As I did so, the crack of a hand gun reached us. The shots were following each other pretty fast but it sounded like only one gun in action. I fancied I also heard a metallic snap at the rear of the car. At least one shot had found us.

'You all right?'

'Fine. That was brilliant.'

'We aren't out of it yet.'

But we were very nearly out of it. As I pulled the Bentley round the bend ahead the waggon was maybe ten yards or so further on. And there was just room to get past. The waggon was on my left, against the mountain wall, and I slowed down to pass it. But I was too close to it and we touched the projecting end of an axle as we went past. There was the sound of cracking wood and I could see in my rear-view mirror that the wheel had fallen outwards and the waggon was toppling crazily to the right. At that point the uprights gave way and it started to shed its great load of logs. The last we saw was a mass of logs blocking the road as the waggoner scrambled to safety.

'How careless of me!'

'You did it on purpose.'

'I hated doing it but I thought it might be wise to block the road. Who knows, there may be a second car behind.'

139

I didn't stop to inspect the car until we'd put another five miles between ourselves and the policemen. But I noticed that the petrol gauge was showing a rapid depletion in the tank. When we pulled up and got out we found a neat hole in the bodywork at the back of the car. Lying flat on the road beneath it, I traced the leak: there was a small round hole in the tank.

Fortunately it was a few inches up from the base; had it been lower, we'd have run dry long since.

I found a slender branch, cut off a short length, trimmed it and managed to plug the hole tightly.

'It'll last until we find a decent garage.'

'We'd better not stop at Ax.'

'Right.'

The front of the car bore some scars: the bumper would need a lot of attention and there was a nasty dent in the nearside wing. I felt like apologizing.

We drove on through the rain.

Ax-les-Thermes proved to be a dated sort of place at the confluence of three rivers. A notice at the entrance to the town said there were eighty natural springs, all of them good for you. In the main square, steam was rising from a kind of trough. Aged persons with stiff joints wandered about under umbrellas, presumably on their way to the thermal establishments. We kept moving through the centre, resisting the powerful tempt- ation to stop for something to eat, and so on towards Bourg- Madame, following the river eastwards up towards its source and then gradually descending into the great plain of the Cerdagne. As we did so, the rain ceased, a brilliant sun appeared and we were driving among willow-bordered streams, rich farmlands and trim villages, all of it framed in a ring of mountains. By three we were in Bourg-Madame and up the road to our right was Puigcerda – the one in France, the other in Spain. We had reached the frontier.

Chapter 15

What in God's name do you do?

You are at a frontier post without a visa with which to placate your host country and you nurse a strong belief that the frontier police on your side have had instructions to arrest you. Your car is carrying a ton of gold and platinum which any customs officer will tell you is contraband, and as if that were not enough there's a war on and the Spanish dictator has placed his money on Adolf Hitler.

So what in God's name do you do?

'The one thing we cannot do,' Marie Antoinette said, 'is present ourselves at the frontier post. The risk of finding a policeman who is too stupid to accept a bribe is too great.'

'Agreed.'

'Also, we dare not stop here. If they knew about us at Foix they'll know about us here as well.'

'Agreed.'

'So?'

'I'm working on it.'

'Does the map show other roads across the frontier?'

We looked. There was a nearby road, but it seemed to lose confidence half way up a mountain and simply give up. That, or there was something the cartographer didn't know.

'There must be smugglers,' I muttered. 'No one is going to tell me smuggling isn't a going concern in mountains like these. They used to mine gold not far from here. People always smuggle gold. *We* are smuggling gold, for heaven's sake.'

'I don't want to sound defeatist,' Marie Antoinette said, 'but smugglers don't usually have 3½-ton Bentleys. These mountain tracks . . .' She shrugged.

'I think we should go up there . . .' – I nodded towards the mountainside – 'and take a good look. We may meet someone who knows about these things.'

The road led out of Bourg-Madame parallel to the frontier, skirted a hill and then headed towards a valley. Soon it left the farms behind. We were in meadowland, with flocks of sheep tended by long-haired dogs and stocky men whose faces had been so beaten by sun and wind that they resembled walnuts. Then the pastures fell away and we were among the pines. The road was fair enough, though each hairpin bend was crazier than the last.

Marie Antoinette was reading the map. 'About a kilometre from here,' she said, 'this road simply stops with no reason given.'

But when we had covered another kilometre we found that the road became an unsurfaced track through the pine forest. 'It must lead somewhere,' I said. 'Someone has kept it clear of fallen branches. We'll try it.'

A further kilometre and the track reached a clearing in the woods. A stone house stood at the edge of the clearing, complete with kitchen garden, a pile of roughly stacked logs and barking dog tethered to a post. As we stopped a short, wiry man appeared at the door and looked at us. Marie Antoinette tried a *bonjour* and the man stayed where he was, still looking, expressionless. We were getting more human responses from the dog.

'Where does the track lead?' I shouted at him.

'Into the mountain.'

'Into Spain?'

The man shrugged. I thought I'd try something different.

'Can we buy something to eat?'

'I've some cheese.'

Perhaps this could be built on. We got out of the car and walked over. The dog was frantic but out of range. The man turned and cursed it in Catalan *patois* and it shut up as if it expected a beating if it failed to do so. Then he turned on his

heel, beckoning with a flick of his head. We weren't worth a lot
of muscular effort. The interior of the house was filthy and smelt
of mildew and garlic. We were in the kitchen – a sombre room
with an open stove unlit and a weird accumulation of unwashed
dishes, garden equipment and miscellaneous clothing. The
man had gone to a cupboard and was banging things about
inside it.

'You live here alone?'

He shook his head without turning round.

Discouraged, I waited for the cheese to appear. It proved to
be a dubious off-white mass, sweating at the edges.

'Goat?'

'Ewe.'

He was searching for a knife, found one and wiped it on a
cloth. Then he cut a corner off the cheese.

'Do you have paper?'

Marie Antoinette ran out to the car and returned with
wrapping paper from the remains of our own cheese. The man
scraped the piece on to the paper and while he was doing so I
searched for an excuse for staying a bit longer.

'Any fruit?'

Without a word he returned to the cupboard and produced
four apples.

'We are interested,' I said, 'in reaching the frontier.' An
interest in actually crossing the frontier seemed indelicate at
this stage in our acquaintance.

The man shrugged. 'You cross at Bourg-Madame.'

'I know, but there are great crowds there – people without
visas. We would like to cross somewhere else.' It was true.
Bourg-Madame had been choked with cars, trucks, bicycles,
people . . . The frontier post was under siege. 'We may have visa
trouble ourselves,' I added carefully.

The man looked at me for quite a while before he answered.
He had very small, unblinking eyes beneath heavy brows. Eyes
and face were sullen. The effect produced was one of discomfort, even alarm. I still preferred the dog.

'With that?' He jerked his head towards the car outside.

Perhaps we talked altogether too much for this solitary creature. I nodded.

'I don't know – there may be a way.'

'I have money.' I was getting used to the meagre use of words.

'They ask a lot.'

'Who?'

'The ones who can see you over.' He still had his mistrustful eyes fixed on me. 'And those on the other side.'

'I understand. Can you organize it?'

He wrapped the cheese and shoved it towards me with the apples. There was no reply to my question.

'How much for this?'

'Forty *sous*.'

I dug out the money and handed it over. He counted the coins carefully and dropped them into a pocket.

'And how much for the other?'

'How much have you got?'

'Probably enough.'

So the price was geared to the customer and not to the service rendered. We were dishevelled enough but beneath the grime the Bentley still looked expensive. This man must carry in his head the accumulated guile, mistrust and greed of generations of his forebears who had needed these things and more to gouge an existence from the inhospitable mountains. He was probably descended from those Cathars of the Languedoc who had fled south to escape slaughter and worse. Did he live off forestry or off trade of the kind we offered? Probably a bit of both. And now he was assessing our ability to pay and fixing his price. He must have done this kind of thing pretty often.

'It costs a lot.'

'How much?'

'How much do you have?'

'How much?'

He seemed to make up his mind. 'Fifty thousand.'

The hollow laugh I produced was perfectly genuine. 'You're joking.'

144

'Fifty thousand.'

'We haven't got that sort of money.'

'You wouldn't say how much you have. Fifty's the price.'

'Tell me what happens.'

'I go away to fix things. You stay here. I come back tomorrow and lead you to the others. We do it at night.'

'On tracks which will take a heavy car?'

He nodded. 'The carts use them to fetch the logs.'

'How far is it?'

'You'll be over by early morning.'

'How do I know you'll get me over?'

'You don't. For this sort of thing you have to trust.'

'And when do I pay?'

'Half in advance, half when I hand you over.'

'You could take me into the wilderness.'

He shrugged. 'It's up to you.'

'I ought to tell you we are armed.'

'It doesn't interest me. I honour my bargains.'

There was the sound of footsteps outside and a brief shout. The dog did not bark.

'My brother. He has sheep lower down.'

They could have been twins. The brother nodded to us, threw off his cloak and dropped a canvas bag to the floor. They talked in *patois*. Marie Antoinette's gently raised eyebrows told me she didn't understand a word. It sounded like a row.

'My brother says fifty is too low.'

Was this to be a Chinese auction, with the price going up as bargaining proceeded?

'I say it's too high. I offer twenty-five.'

More *patois*. 'My brother says sixty is the price, but I will do it for fifty. There are heavy expenses.'

'Twenty now and ten when we part.'

'Twenty and twenty.'

Why was I bargaining like this? It wasn't my money. And I had no doubt that wealthy refugees were spending a good deal more to get out of France. On the other hand, if I were too easy this sinister pair would suspect us of carrying vast treasure; they

145

probably had a well-prepared scenario for robbing people like us.

'Twenty and fifteen.'

'No.'

I gave in with ill grace. 'All right. It's robbery.'

The brothers consulted again, and again it wasn't brotherly.

'In an hour I'll be off up the valley. You'll see me again at midday tomorrow. Now, the money.'

I counted out twenty thousand-franc notes. They were so crisp and clean I thought he might refuse them as fakes, but he counted them a second time and pocketed them without a word. Then he asked: 'Does anyone know you came this way?'

'We passed a farm cart as we left the main road to head up here.' It wasn't true but it could do no harm for him to think we could be traced.

He went into the house and the brother took a cloak and some food and set off down the track. An hour later, as he was preparing to leave, our man said: 'You can sleep in the house.'

'We'll sleep in the car.'

Without a word he took a cloak from a hook on the wall, put a hunk of bread and a piece of sausage in a bag which he slung over a shoulder, and filled a bottle with water. Then he locked the door of the house and set off to the right up the valley, the dog at his heels. I watched him go, wondering why on earth men like these should bother to honour a bargain with people like us.

'We have no choice,' Marie Antoinette said.

We slept in the car and woke in the early hours, stiff and miserable with cold. Soon the birdsong was almost deafening. There was heavy dew on everything.

'What honour I have left I would sell this instant for one mug of hot coffee,' Marie Antoinette said. Her teeth were chattering and her face was pinched with cold. Her hand was icy when she put it in mine.

We ate miserably from our small stock and to get warm I busied myself with the car. Two tyres looked dangerously thin; I went through the tedious business of repairing the inner tubes of the two spares and changing them over. It was as much an exercise to get warm as a piece of careful foresight. Marie Antoinette had found a pump and was washing off the caked mud. Then she made some improvements in the repair to the hood. I wiped the dust out of the ventilator flaps and cleaned the plugs. The engine had coughed a bit on the way up from Bourg-Madame; I cleaned grit out of the petrol filter. Then I filled her up from our four cans. I reckoned that would give us another hundred miles.

'Try the German gun, just in case,' Marie Antoinette said.

I tried it and found it kicked unpleasantly, but the bullet hit a tree with a satisfactory smack. The explosion echoed through the woods and created immense alarm among the birds.

'That leaves five.'

We had the gun, the French police revolver in its holster with its useless blanks, and the corporal's dagger with no sheath. We also had a stroke of luck: fiddling around with our armoury, I tried the German ammunition in the French weapon: it fitted. I put three bullets in the French gun, followed by three blanks, and left two in the German, followed by the remaining blank, feeling pretty pleased with myself. I explained it all to Marie Antoinette. Then the German gun went into the car's glove compartment and I donned the French gun in its holster.

Marie Antoinette wrapped the dagger in a duster and nestled it between her breasts, secured beneath her bra.

At twelve the brother came up the track, nodded to us and went into the house. A moment later he came out carrying bread and sausage, sat himself on a log and ate his lunch, carving hunks of bread and sausage alternately with a penknife and washing them down with draughts of red wine from a bottle.

'So you're crossing over?'

I nodded.

'It's a tough journey.'

'D'you think the car will make it?'

He looked across at it. 'If it doesn't rain and you keep out of the ditches. Also, there are some dangerous bits – sheer drops.

147

But if it rains, forget it.' He attended to his food.

'Your brother knows the way?' A nod. 'And these people we're passed on to – they're all right?' Another nod. Then a long draught of wine. 'He's a hard man, my brother.'

'You and he . . .?'

'A man to be wary of. He had a woman here once. A decent woman. She had to leave – couldn't stand him. A man without feelings. A brute. We don't get on.'

'Had others here lately . . . to cross over?'

'A family a couple of days back. Said they were Jews. Apparently the Germans kill the Jews. They paid plenty.'

'And they got over?'

A shrug. 'As far as I know.'

Half an hour later the other brother appeared. 'We leave at nine,' he said. 'You'll get no sleep.'

At 6.25 a.m. on 19 June the French government received the German reply to their request for armistice talks: send the names of your delegates. A meeting at seven at Pétain's residence decided on the composition of the delegation and had it transmitted. During the morning Mussolini was persuaded with some difficulty by his associates not to order the Italian 1st Army into action against the remnants of the French forces. What would Fascist Italy look like if it failed to win against an already ruined enemy? The Italian generals didn't judge the military task sufficiently easy. In the government in Bordeaux weary argument continued on the pros and cons of removing to North Africa; they decided instead to prepare a removal to Perpignan in the south-west. During the day a deputation flew in from London to seek assurances that the French fleet would not fall into German hands. The assurances were given. A British move to enlist the support of the governors of the French colonies on the African continent failed and in London there was no sign yet of anyone of importance rallying to de Gaulle. In France fighting continued on four limited fronts. At Saumur the 2,200 cadets of the military academy decided to fight pour l'honneur. Armed with five Hotchkiss tanks, three machine gun carriers, fourteen medium guns, a few howitzers and their side-arms, they were to hold a twenty-five-kilometre front for forty-eight hours against the German infantry and tanks. Honour satisfied, they surrendered. In the north,

Rommel was in Cherbourg and in the centre the Germans lay to the south of Lyons and Clermont Ferrand. Bordeaux itself, seat of government, was now threatened.

Chapter 16

We set out in the first chill of the mountain night. Our guide refused to get in the car. Instead, he led out a donkey from behind the house and mounted it. The animal sagged under his weight but moved forward when he talked to it and whacked its flank. Dirty grey clouds had been piling up since late afternoon and now they were scudding across the sky above the mountains and I recalled the brother's warning: 'If it rains, forget it.'

'Do you expect rain?' I shouted as we laboured up the track.

'Maybe.' It was all I could get out of him.

The donkey's pace wasn't at all what the Bentley liked and I had visions of her sinking in up to her axles if we came across a soft patch. Within a short while the night was pitch black. The man took a torch from his pocket and we followed the thin pencil of yellow light, unable to see the edges of the track. Soon the trees thinned out and we were advancing along the steep flank of a mountain. Marie Antoinette leaned over the side, shouting instructions whenever we came too close to the edge – my only insurance against toppling into the ravine below. Then the track divided, one arm going down towards the river that could be heard rushing and churning beneath us, the other climbing steadily upwards. We travelled up and it started to rain. Just a drizzle, but rain. The tyres were still gripping but if the drizzle turned into a typical mountain downpour I had no doubt that we'd be stuck. As we drove on, the drizzle grew up into a strapping rainstorm. Still we gripped the track, though now ominous squelching sounds came from beneath us and on a short, sharp incline I felt the rear wheels churning mud. I prayed for level ground; then minutes later we found it and the car was plainly as relieved as I was. We had been running for over an hour.

Soon we came to another incline where the dust of the track had been turned into viscous mud with rivulets of rainwater threading through it. And here we ran into the trouble I had feared all along. First there was the familiar thrashing sound from the rear wheels as we advanced slowly, and then they were spinning in troughs they had dug for themselves and the car stopped altogether.

'We're stuck.'

'It's what the man said would happen if it rained.'

I yelled at our guide and the light of the torch wavered and then moved back towards us.

'The car won't move. We'd better see what happens when we push it.'

But the three of us could achieve nothing at all. Then we tried with Marie Antoinette at the wheel. Then we tried pushing the Bentley back to try to get a better grip on the track further down the slope. We shifted her a yard or two and I got back in and tried to rush her past the bad patch. It didn't work: the wheels spun round again in the grooves they'd made the first time. And meanwhile the rain beat down on us and on the car and the track.

'If I can get her down the hill, is there another route?'

'No.' Our guide was still saving his words.

'The donkey!' Marie Antoinette shouted suddenly. 'Why should we do all the work? Can't the donkey help?'

'Have you got a rope?' I asked our guide.

Without a word, he took a coil of rope which had been tied to the donkey's saddle and handed it to me. We tethered the wretched animal to the car's bumper and then we tried again, the guide and I shoving from behind and Marie Antoinette at the wheel under close instructions as to acceleration, steering and the like – all this in pitch blackness save for the dim cone of yellow light from the torch.

But the donkey had other ideas. It stood stock still, ignoring

151

the distant curses from its master behind the car. It would strain forward when lashed with a stick, but once the lashes stopped the effort stopped too. We were swapping the man's strength for the donkey's, and though there was doubtless some gain in the transaction, there clearly wasn't much.

I took the torch and reconnoitred the areas on either side of the track, hoping we might make a modest detour. But the ground was too broken to run the car over it. And now I was beginning to fear that the dead weight of the car was driving it so far into the mud that no amount of pulling or pushing would shift it. We couldn't dig it out because we had no spades and we couldn't run it out over sacks or even over bits of our clothing because there wasn't anything available. I felt near to tears.

Then, spurred on by the prospect of losing the second half of his money, our guide made a whole speech.

'We can tie the donkey to the rear of the car on a short rope. Then, as we pull the car back we can encourage the donkey. The lady can drive. After that, we can see about covering the bad patch with branches.'

We tried it, tying the donkey so close to the rear bumper that his master could hit him with the switch with one hand while he tugged at the car with the other. Marie Antoinette was at the wheel with the car in reverse. I was pushing and shouting instructions.

The donkey must have been stronger than he looked. With the rear wheels still spinning wildly, the Bentley finally emerged from the deep ruts and moved down the incline. We stopped her after five yards or so on a stretch which appeared to be firmer and would afford us a smooth take-off. Now our guide took command, leading us to undergrowth where dead branches could be yanked out without too much effort. It took us half an hour to lay a thick carpet of branches across the track for a distance of ten yards or so. At the spot where we'd come to grief, we rolled a lot of heavy stuff into place, the guide directing operations, choosing the branches and deploying them.

'Sometimes the carts get stuck,' he said.

Eventually he expressed himself satisfied. 'The car must go over at a good speed,' he said. 'I will stand ahead with the torch and you will direct the car at the light. Don't slow down to watch for the edge. Just drive for the light.'

Marie Antoinette went ahead with him, I climbed back into the car, put her in gear and drove for the small yellow light ahead. The sound of cracking wood beneath me was odd. There was no thrashing of mud.

It was all over in a matter of seconds: the car was over the liquid mud and up to the light, where the ground was firmer. Marie Antoinette climbed in.

'Thanks,' I said. The guide said nothing, turned and cursed his donkey and plodded ahead. Once again we were running along the top of a ridge.

Soon we were on a gentle incline, losing height on open ground which seemed to be covered in bushes or large boulders. Still the thin yellow glow ahead of us kept moving forward and still it rained.

'Do you think he's really taking us to the frontier, or is it a clever way of getting money for nothing?'

'I'd say the frontier. If he just planned to lose us he didn't need to ride for hours through the rain.'

'For someone like him this is just an evening outing.'

'Anyway, I have the gun,' I said, rather stupidly. If the man couldn't lead us over the frontier, waving a gun at him or even shooting him wasn't going to get us into Spain.

It was close to midnight when the light ahead of us stopped. We had lost a lot of height and were once again among trees, but we seemed to have come to some sort of clearing. The rain had reverted to fine drizzle.

'We're there.' The man's voice reached us as he rode back to the car.

'Where?'

'The rendezvous. The others will take you on from here.'

'And the frontier?'

'You're on the frontier.'

'How do we know?'

'If you knew that sort of thing you wouldn't need me, would you?'

For him it was a long speech, and it made sense. But the brother had said he was a hard man, a brute. Why would a hard man play this thing straight?

'So what do we do?'

'Wait.'

He dismounted and walked away from us and we could follow his path by the yellow light of the torch. He was walking forward and over to the right. Then, maybe twenty yards away, the light stopped and was waved three times from side to side.

'I don't like it at all,' Marie Antoinette said.

'That makes two of us.'

Beyond the spot where we had seen the signal, a whiter light appeared. It didn't move. Perhaps a storm lamp. The yellow torch was returning to us.

'You go up there,' the man said when he was beside the car. 'They'll be in the hut.'

I had switched off the engine. Now I got out of the car. Something told me to play safe: I removed the key from the ignition and slipped it under the carpet beneath the driver's seat. 'Stay there,' I said to Marie Antoinette.

'The other half,' the man said.

'You'll get the other half when I've seen who's in that hut. You can wait here with Mademoiselle. I have no plans to run away.'

'I'm frightened,' Marie Antoinette said.

'So am I.' Then I started walking towards the point of light, stumbling over roots and large stones as I went. I freed the French gun from its holster, released the catch and still holding on to it, slipped it into the pocket of my jacket. As I got nearer I could see that the light belonged to a lamp and the lamp was standing in the window of what looked like a square wooden hut. There was enough light from the lamp to make out a door next to the window. I took my gun from my pocket and with my left hand gave the door a shove. It yielded at once as someone on the other side drew it full back. The pale glow from the lamp revealed a man standing immediately in front of me on the far

154

side of the bare hut. Someone else was behind the door.

Why hadn't these characters come down to the car with our guide? Why the business with the door? I don't know whether the brain decides to look sharp on these tricky occasions, to work a bit faster; or maybe the central nervous system does something to your reasoning faculties even as it's organizing the extra delivery of adrenalin to give you more muscle. Whatever it was, in the second or so between the moment when I felt the door being pulled away from my hand and the realization that a trap of some kind had been sprung, I achieved the following piece of deductive reasoning:

Our man had set off up the mountain yesterday. Fine.

His brother had set off down the mountain, back to his sheep. Also fine.

On the following day, the brother had returned before our man. He ate his lunch. In order to cut his bread and sausage he had taken a jack-knife from his pocket. And as he did so I had distinctly seen the edges of new banknotes. It had struck me as a bit odd at the time, but clearly it wasn't all that odd: our man had already shared the half-loot with his brother.

But they hadn't been alone at the house since I'd paid the money on the previous day. *Ergo*, they must have met since.

Where? Down towards Bourg-Madame, surely. Furthermore, if he used a donkey to cover the distance tonight, why no donkey last night? Clearly our man had only gone a short distance up the mountain and had come down by another route, seen his brother, and instead of arranging a mountain rendezvous had nipped into Bourg-Madame to tell the frontier police he had another present for them. Who knew what deals were made by these mountain people? And who knew whether fools like us were ever taken down the mountain again, police or no police?

That, I was convinced, was the scenario, and it took all of one second to imprint itself on my mind.

I was alone in a hut in the high Pyrenees with a couple of policemen who might or might not be gangsters on their day off. Either way, it was bad news.

My eyes took a moment or two to adjust to the pale light in the hut. Before me stood a man wearing a raincoat and soft hat. The brim was down and shadowed his face. I stayed on the threshold: if I advanced into the hut the other man would be behind me. I said the first thing that came into my head. 'Who the hell are you?'

'I am Inspector Max Boni of the *Police Judiciaire* in Paris.' He removed his hat and there was a disgusting grin on his face. He had his hands back in his pockets. He appeared to be enjoying himself hugely. He looked down at my gun and shook his head. 'Put that away, Quinton.'

The other man came from behind the door. He was some kind of policeman. 'This,' said Max, 'is Sergeant Couiza of the frontier police and I am arresting you on a charge of attempting an illegal passage of the frontier without presenting the appropriate papers at our frontier post. Also, you have a stolen car. Now put that gun down.'

I saw the sergeant's hand creeping down towards his holster. 'You had better put your hands up,' I said. I tried to make my voice sound steady but it didn't really work.

'Don't worry about his gun,' Max said to his colleague. 'It's full of blanks.'

I thought I'd be smart and decided to adopt what I hoped was a puzzled expression. This didn't seem the best time to tell them I'd acquired an altogether better type of ammunition. Max appeared to have overlooked the possibility that Marie Antoinette had told me about his blanks. And so I stood there in the doorway, waving my gun at them while Max grinned and the local sergeant looked edgy. It gave me time to decide that it really would be unwise to shoot two French policemen on my way out of France, war or no war.

'How did you find me, Max?'

'We have an alert system at the frontiers. I put one out for you and then I came south and waited for you in Perpignan. You got away along the Ariège but here your peasant friend reported you – *voilà!*'

'And what do you intend to do?'

156

'I intend to accompany you to the nearest Spanish town and then we'll see.'

So we were in Spain after all.

'I would have thought your duty required you to go back into France.'

Max cast a rapid glance at the sergeant. 'You are on Spanish territory. And the route down the mountain is easier.'

'So are you, and that's pretty dubious for a start.'

'I know international law. And I know the extradition agreement between France and Spain.'

'And what if I won't budge?'

'You will get hurt, you and the girl.' For the first time there was a hint of interest in his eyes. 'Mainly the girl.'

'We could do a deal, Max,' I said.

'We've done all the deals we are ever going to do.' Again he looked at the sergeant. In the gloom of the hut it was impossible to tell whether the other man was venal or stupid. I couldn't see Max picking up an honest policeman to follow him into the mountains.

'We could do a deal,' I persisted. 'Maybe just this once you could be a gentleman.'

Max's laugh was very brief, very humourless. I had used the English word gentleman: the French have no term for it. 'I don't speak English,' he said.

I had had enough. 'I changed the ammunition, Max,' I said quietly.

I couldn't see his eyes all that clearly but I saw him frown. Then he shouted, 'Henri!' and a second later a foot crunched the gravel behind me and I felt my arms being wrenched back and down to my sides in a very powerful grip. The gun fell from my right hand. A foot came from behind and kicked it into the room and Max bent and picked it up. The thug holding me was breathing unpleasantly into the back of my neck and creating a good deal of pain in my arms. He smelt of stale tobacco.

Max looked reflectively at the gun, then at me, then back to the gun. Then he took three steps towards me, holding the gun by the barrel. The first blow caught me on the cheekbone and it hurt like hell. I remember no more: the second blow must have been to my head.

The first sound I was aware of was the dry, uncontrollable choking of a woman who had been sobbing for a long time. Then I became aware of my own condition: dreadful pain in my head, seemingly in the whole of my head, and waves of nausea coming up from my stomach. When I tried to move I realized my hands were secured very tightly behind my back and were hurting me. Then I regained full consciousness as a mass of cold water hit me in the face and a heavy boot landed in the small of my back. I gasped for breath and produced a quite involuntary groan.

'He's with us,' a voice said. Then I heard steps and a door was slammed.

I was lying in a corner of the hut and Marie Antoinette was next to me. The lamp was on the floor in front of us and I could see her clearly. There were nasty cuts and bruises on her legs and a bruise on the side of her face where someone had hit her. On the cold night air I detected the familiar smell of Max's *maïs* cigarettes. Then I noticed the even more familiar contents of my own pockets strewn across the floor. But they had overlooked the body belt in which I carried most of my money. It wasn't small change they were after, and everything was small change compared with the contents of the car. There was no one else in the room.

Marie Antoinette's sobbing subsided as I shifted painfully and tried to prop myself up against the wall.

'What happened?'

'Soon after you reached the hut I heard noises and concluded you'd been ambushed in some way. I decided it would be best to immobilize the car, just in case they had a way of starting it and getting away. So I repeated your trick with the pencil.'

'Which valves?'

'The front two on the driver's side. Our guide just watched while I tinkered under the bonnet but he didn't seem to be very technically minded. I said the engine needed adjusting.'

'Then what?'

'Then they came for me. But first Max gave our guide some money and he and the policeman set off with the donkey. I suppose they were going back the way we came. Then Max said they wanted the car keys and started to beat me up out there by torchlight. Then he said they'd get better results if they made you watch them do it. They reckoned you'd tell them rather than have me knocked about. Would you?'

I nodded and it hurt like hell. The nausea was abating but my head seemed to crack open every time I blinked.

'Did you tell them where I'd put the keys?'

She shook her head. 'I didn't see you and you never told me.'

'I'm sorry.'

'I think I'd have told them. I hate pain.'

'I expect they're searching the car,' I said.

'Do you think they'll find the keys?'

'I doubt it.'

'So they'll be back.'

'That's about it.'

She burst into tears again. 'Please don't let them do things to me. You've no idea the things they do. Max said . . .' She trailed off.

'Nothing will be done to you, I promise.'

'So this is the end of the road. They'll take the car and then they'll kill us both and leave us here where no one will ever find us.'

'It isn't Max's style,' I told her, though I didn't believe a word I was saying. 'He'd be leaving two witnesses: there's the local sergeant and our friend from the woods. Both ugly customers, and they could get ugly with Max.'

'So what is going to happen?'

'Max reckons he'll come with us into Spain and perform the next act of his little drama there. That gets rid of the witnesses. I suppose the fellow who jumped me, a character by the name of Henri, is a mate of Max's from Paris. So he'll probably come along too. It means we have some sort of opportunity to deal with the two of them between here and wherever we're heading for in Spain.'

'Where?'

'Who knows?'

My own guess was pretty simple. Max and Henri would take us as short a distance into Spain as possible and then dump us with bullets in the nape of the neck, which is the spot favoured by the *milieu* on such occasions. Then Max would drive back into France by a safer and more orthodox route. I had little doubt about his ability to manoeuvre his way across at Bourg-Madame. What story he'd handed to the sergeant I had no idea, but he was an inspector in a very senior police service in Paris and sergeants don't go looking for trouble.

These were the idle thoughts which were interrupted when the door was shoved open. Max and his sidekick came into the room. It was my first sight of Henri. He turned out to be the Inspector Rossi who had stopped me on the road near Meudon and delivered me to Max. By way of greeting he kicked me violently in the thigh.

'You've given us altogether too damn much trouble,' he said.

'All right Henri, leave them to me.' Max squatted down in front of us to give a friendly air to our conversation. 'I want the car keys,' he said. His voice was matter of fact, very relaxed.

'Fuck you.'

'That is no way to talk to me, Quinton. I propose to hit you in the mouth once for each impertinence. You can have that one on the house. Now let us start again. I want the car keys.'

'Without wishing to be impertinent, Max,' I said carefully, 'I'm afraid you'll have to find them yourself. I don't remember where I put them.'

He leaned forward quite slowly and suddenly shot his fist out. A heavy signet ring caught me on the lip and blood spurted into my mouth. The jolt made my head explode again.

'I have what I think is a quicker way,' Max said. Slowly he took a pack of cigarettes from his pocket and lit one and hung it on his lower lip. 'Perhaps I should explain.'

I waited while he puffed reflectively. The cigarette appeared to be a prop in the drama. I heard Marie Antoinette catch her breath.

'Henri here will kindly pull her clothes off when I ask him to in a moment and then I will stub out my cigarette carefully and thoroughly, since I am known for my tidiness. If that does not produce the keys I will light another cigarette, these being my favourite brand, and I will stub that one out too.' He paused, still perfectly amiable. 'Would you like me to tell you precisely where on her splendid body my cigarettes will land? No, I thought not.' He puffed on the *maïs* as a kind of demonstration. Ash fell down his coat.

'Try doing it on me instead,' I said, in a gesture of hopeless bravado.

Max grinned. 'Less effective.' He paused. 'And I would get less satisfaction. If we have to deal with you we will simply kick you and hit you about the head until you change your stupid mind.' He grinned again. 'But I don't think it will be needed.' He turned to Henri and gestured towards Marie Antoinette.

'Wait, wait,' I said. 'Untie my hands. I'll show you where the keys are.'

My hands were untied and then they untied Marie Antoinette. We led them back to the car by the light of the storm lamp. They had made a fair mess of the car's interior but though the carpet had been displaced, they had failed in the dark to spot the keys. Also, the glove compartment containing the revolver remained locked. Anyone could have told you that locking it in the first place was a pretty stupid thing to do, but clearly they would have been wrong.

I retrieved the keys and handed them to Max. 'Your turn,' I said.

'You will drive. Now get on with it.'

I got into the driving seat and Max got in beside me. Marie Antoinette and Henri were in the back. Max had drawn a gun from somewhere inside his raincoat and was holding it loosely on his lap. I had absolutely no idea how we were going to get out of this appalling mess.

I turned the key in the ignition and pressed the starter.

Nothing happened. For good effect I tried several times. The Bentley remained impervious. Marie Antionette's pencil marks were performing nicely.

'We'll have to see,' I said. 'Two hours crawling up the mountain hasn't done her any good.'

'What do you think it is?' Max asked.

'Feels like petrol starvation. If there's trouble with the pump we'll be stuck, thanks to you and your fake spares.' I stopped myself from adding anything about it serving him right.

'Well, get on with it.'

Max, as I had hoped, got out of the car. I lifted the bonnet and messed around for as long as I dared, Max holding the lamp for me. The messing was to give me time to think and I was finding it difficult. My head was still splitting, for one thing. For another, I had no clear idea how I was to get to the German gun, use it if necessary, and avoid damage to Marie Antoinette and myself. I assumed Henri was armed and would shoot us as soon as spit at us.

Max was getting impatient. I felt it was time to move on. 'Must be a plug,' I said, 'I've got some in the car.'

I walked round to the passenger side. Max remained at the bonnet. Marie Antoinette had sensed what was about to happen and casually got out and joined me.

'You,' Max said to her, 'don't move away.'

I unlocked the glove compartment and rummaged around inside. The plugs were there. I picked up the gun instead and eased the safety catch before taking it out. My hand was trembling but that was something I could do nothing about. I had decided that if murder was what I now had to commit, then murder it would be. Or could I reasonably call it killing instead? Wasn't there a war on, and weren't people murdering each other all over the place and calling it killing? And wasn't I trying to save a substantial treasure for the allied cause? I was, and killing it would therefore become.

The lighting situation was as follows. I was in near-darkness inside the car and Henri just behind me was only a shadow in the rear seat. What light there was reached us from the storm lamp which Max had stood on the bonnet. It lit him up in clear silhouette. As for logistics, I had just two live bullets, followed by the blank, whereas there were probably twelve shots available to the other two if they managed to get at their guns. The whole thing was crazy and should never have been attempted.

I decided to shoot Max first, partly because I disliked him and partly because I knew his gun was in his coat pocket and thus easy to get at. It was not the right decision, I grant you, since it gave Henri behind me time to interfere. But who makes perfect decisions at such moments? And if I go into all this now, it is the better to clarify what happened next and why. I was standing by the open door, still leaning in towards the dashboard. 'Got 'em,' I said, by way of steadying everyone's nerves.

Then my hand emerged, still trembling, from the glove compartment, and it was holding the gun. I brought it up level with my eyes, held my right wrist in my left hand in the way I had seen them do it on the movies, aimed at Max's heart and pulled the trigger. I did it all pretty fast for an amateur.

The explosion jerked the gun upwards and almost out of my hand, but I had the presence of mind to duck as I turned towards Henri. Again I took what I thought was careful aim and pressed the trigger again. But as I did so, there was a harsh whistle in my ear and a roar from the car. Henri had also had his gun handy and had shot at me before I had had a chance to shoot at him. Shot and missed.

My own shot lost itself somewhere in the dark and it did not seem to have damaged Henri. A second shot from his direction underlined the point. From Max there was no sound. For some reason the lamp had fallen inside the engine space and hardly any light was reaching us now. The fact that I was still alive could reasonably be attributed to that.

I thought it expedient to fire the blank, as a kind of signal to Henri not to get too adventurous. And there matters rested for a moment. There was no ammunition left in my gun.

Henri was the first to speak. 'Put your hands up and stand up. You have no chance of getting away.'

'Nor have you. The car won't move and if you get out of that seat I shall shoot your head off.'

I heard a twig crack near me and suddenly remembered Marie Antoinette. It seemed expedient to keep the dialogue going.

'If you shoot me you can't move the car. It's a special engine. Also, the plugs are not where I've been looking.'

There was a rather long silence. 'What are you after, Quinton?'

'I propose to take the car to Lisbon exactly as instructed by the bank. And in view of the fact that you kicked me in the ribs and the thigh, both times very painfully, I don't propose to offer you a lift.' Again a twig snapping, this time behind the car.

'It is always possible to make a deal,' Henri said. His voice carried little conviction.

'What kind of deal?'

'We would let you go with a suitable portion of the gold.'

'We? I think your friend Max is probably dead. If you throw me your gun you can get out and see how he is.'

'I'm not that much of a fool.'

Then there was a most extraordinary noise from the interior of the car – a cross between a choking sound and a long sigh which ended in a high-pitched scream. The sound was so inhuman that I felt the hairs stand up on the back of my neck. I dared not move until, suddenly, another scream, followed by the sound of wild sobbing told me that whatever had happened inside the car, Marie Antoinette was a part of it. I got to my feet and tried to see something in the gloom.

'Marie Antoinette, what the hell is going on?'

All I got in reply was more hysteria.

I rushed to the far side of the car. She had sunk down to the ground and was leaning against the rear wheel, unable to speak. There was no sound from Henri.

'What happened? What did you do?'

'The dagger . . . I . . . the dagger . . . his throat or, or . . . his chest . . . it felt terrible, terrible.'

I got the lamp and shone it inside the car, hoping somehow not to see what I knew was there. Henri Rossi lay back, covered in blood which must have spurted from his jugular vein or whatever crucial organ Marie Antoinette's German dagger had reached. He was staring quite horribly at me, unseeing, dead. Blood was everywhere. The nausea returned and I retched repeatedly as I turned away.

At 2.30 p.m. on the twentieth the French armistice delegation set out from Bordeaux by car and after endless difficulties reached the German lines at midnight. They motored on to Paris and arrived there early the following morning after seventeen hours of continuous travel. At 1.30 p.m. on the twenty-first they set out under German escort for Rethondes in the forest of Compiègne. This was where the French armistice terms had been imposed on the Kaiser's defeated armies in 1918. Hitler was waiting — in the same railway carriage that had been used twenty-two years before. At 3.30 p.m. the armistice conditions were read out. They were to be signed after long and largely fruitless argument at 6.50 p.m. on the following day. Meanwhile, the Italians had made a last attempt to achieve something — anything. Mussolini's Ist Army launched an attack with nineteen divisions at dawn on the twenty-first. They made no progress at all. 'The Duce was humiliated,' his Foreign Minister wrote in his diary. In Bordeaux there was confusion, anger and deep divisions in government circles, and a flaming row between the British ambassador and the Foreign Minister. Anglo-French hostility and mistrust was now total and on full public display, led by a vigorous attack on the armistice terms by Churchill. Britain's arch-enemy in France, Pierre Laval, was brought into the government to become the key figure in Franco-German collaboration, and eventually to die after the liberation before an execution squad. On the twenty-third the Pétain government stripped General de Gaulle of his rank. On the twenty-fourth an Italian armistice was signed. Then, at thirty-five minutes past midnight on 25 June buglers along the whole length of the front sounded the cease-fire. France had ceased to fight.

There had been over ten million refugees on the roads of France. There had been a lack of will at the top and a total failure of military leadership. Now there would be an absurd belief that Nazi Germany could be an honourable conqueror, willing to allow the French to lead a national existence in dignity. The Germans were to bleed the country white, to hunt down and murder the Jews, to use France as a base for their attacks on

Britain, and to let loose in every French locality the Gestapo with its system of informers and torture chambers.

'It has all been wonderful,' wrote Rommel to his wife.

Chapter 17

The two days we took to cover the five hundred miles across northern Spain to what I thought would be a clever place on the Portuguese frontier are not all that clear in my mind. I remember the descent from the high Pyrenees into the valley of the Segre in the chill of the early morning. No doubt in more auspicious times we'd have enjoyed our first view of Catalonia. As it was, Marie Antoinette had curled up miserably in her seat, turned in on herself, uncommunicative. She stared into some kind of middle distance and refused to look at the map or anything else. That much I remember. Then we reached the road which heads south to Lerida, left it after fifty miles or so past the orchards and olive groves to start moving westwards over the foothills of the mountain range. We passed through Barbastro and Hucsca and no doubt other places too.

At Huesca we turned south towards the valley of the Ebro and Saragossa, and there we found a seedy hotel in the suburbs of the town where I reckoned papers might not be called for. Wherever we had stopped on the way, small knots of locals had formed to inspect the Bentley. On one occasion a *Garda Civil*, splendid in his Napoleonic hat, had shown a lot of interest. We had no language in common but by signs and noises we had communication of a sort. Fortunately, he never thought of shifting his attention from the car to ourselves and our civic status; the car was too interesting.

The hotel in Saragossa was passably clean, passably friendly in a somewhat distant Spanish fashion, and capable of producing a highly indifferent meal in which oil and garlic predominated. We picked unhappily at our food, Marie Antoinette still morose and withdrawn. Afterwards, as we lay in bed, the cathartic storm broke at last and she wept and trembled for a long while.

'I killed someone!' It was all she would say. 'I killed . . .'

At last, well after midnight, she fell asleep. And next morning she managed a thin smile for the first time since we'd left France.

The country itself was somehow even more derelict than France had been. The ravages of the recently ended civil war lay about us, and sullen misery seemed a fair description of the populace. Saragossa, sitting proudly on the Ebro, had remained loyal to the Republic, and Franco and his Falange had made her pay for it, just as a hundred and thirty years earlier she had defied Napoleon and to the French call for surrender the governor of the town had replied; 'After you have killed me, we'll talk.' It had cost fifty thousand lives among the townspeople. Now the town was again a victim – battered, hungry and defeated.

It was clear that by current Spanish standards the hotel's kitchen had done us proud. When I found a garage close by, three mechanics were put to work on the Bentley for what seemed to me a very small fistful of pesetas. I had everything done to the car that I could think of, including the repairs to the petrol tank and bumper from our little adventure on the road to Ax. No one could understand why I insisted on hanging around while the perfectly competent men got on with it. In the end we even gave her a coat of polish. Then on eastwards, crossing from Aragon into the rich greenery of the Asturias. Soon we passed through Soria on the banks of the Duero, and reached Valladolid, where we found a *pension* of great squalor, though undeniably discreet.

'The *whole* night?' the proprietress inquired. She was an exhausted and discouraged woman, without any kind of expression, who was clearly more accustomed to letting her rooms by the hour, with use of towel.

'Sorry about this,' I said to Marie Antoinette as we tried to secure the door of our bedroom.

'I feel like a ten-franc whore,' she said.

'What do I get if I make it twenty?'

'For twenty you can stay the night. But I don't kiss.'

We rustled up a smile between us and went out in search of soup and wine. When we got back to our room later someone was having hysterics on the floor above and whoever had been through our gear had a very heavy touch. A bar of soap – very precious in Spain at that time – had been taken. Nothing else. But our clothes had been spilled all over the place.

And so, next morning, we set out for the frontier – still eastwards to Zamora and then on to a side road to reach the frontier itself at the village of Fermoselle on the Spanish side of the river Douro. This, I had reckoned, would be the kind of frontier post where they were used to processing the local peasantry who worked on one side of the line and lived on the other. In such a place, surely, the waving of pesetas would produce results, and with very few onlookers to make the thing difficult.

'What on earth is all that?' Marie Antoinette exclaimed. We were rolling easily down the shallow incline leading to the village, and as we took a turn in the road we came in view of an almighty traffic jam. The village itself seemed to be packed with vehicles of all kinds – the line stretching up towards us, so that half a mile or so before the houses started we were brought to a halt behind a long line of cars and lorries. The one immediately ahead of us had a Brussels number plate.

'Wrong again. And I thought I was being smart.'

I stopped, got out and walked forward. The Belgian car had six people aboard. I grinned at the driver. 'Is the queue moving at all?'

'From time to time.'

'D'you think all these people have visas?'

'No.'

'But they're getting across?'

'Maybe.'

'Have you been down to have a look?'

169

The driver shook his head. He was some kind of fatalist who didn't believe in trying to influence events.

'Which of us is to go down there to find out?' I asked Marie Antoinette.

'I'll go. I've already proved my capacity to persuade people.'

I gave her some money – a great deal of money, to be more precise – and she set off, striding jauntily down the road past the solid mass of vehicles. She had picked up her big hat and was trailing it behind her by its ribbon, like a kite. I sat in the car and allowed the midday sun to make me uncomfortable. We were not moving, and soon there was plenty of traffic piled up behind me.

It was nearly three hours before I caught sight of Marie Antoinette making her way up the incline, her hat still trailing. There was a small but triumphant smile on her face.

'No problem,' she said as she got into the car.

'Good girl. How did you do it?'

'The Spaniards were easy. They'd pay *us* to leave the country.'

'And the Portuguese?'

'The man said "*A su disposicion.*" He was very charming.'

'What did you say?'

'I said "two thousand", and I added "*muchas gracias*" because that's all the Portuguese I know.'

'You mean to say you've done a deal to get us over for two thousand?'

'I think so. Unless the man was having me on.'

A suspicion weaseled its way into my mind. 'What else did you promise him?'

'What do you mean?'

'When you say that, you're playing for time to prepare a lie. Come on, the truth.'

Marie Antoinette smiled sweetly. 'Well, perhaps I allowed it to be inferred that I found him not altogether . . .' Her fingers fluttered.

'What was he like?'

'I do believe you're jealous, Englishman.' She laughed. 'My

170

Englishman is jealous of a fat Portuguese frontier guard.'

'Don't be damn silly. It's just that if you go offering your person around Europe in this way, sooner or later you'll have to deliver. This kind of international cock-teasing is not very nice.'

'Okay, so we stay here in our traffic jam, growing old graciously and spending our evenings getting the bats out of our hair. I don't mind. I think I'd love to grow old with you in a Bentley. We could grow honeysuckle over it.'

'Anyway, how do we reach your Portuguese friend? Nothing's moving. Since you started out I've achieved maybe a hundred yards.'

We studied the map. Five miles back a track led off to the left through farmlands. I had noticed it as we drove past. According to the map it led via a couple of farms and a hamlet to the river, where a road of sorts followed the bank to the point where the bridge linked Spain and Portugal.

'It's worth a try.'

I turned the car, drove back the way we had come, and turned off the road on to the track. The surface was fair and there appeared to be no hazards. We were driving through parched farmland with peasants working here and there in the fields. The hamlet was clearly poverty-stricken, with scraggy chickens and a couple of dogs nosing about in the dust. Then the track dipped down towards the river and we were on the road into Fermoselle. We had jumped the long queue of vehicles.

I stopped the car at the approach to the bridge and Marie Antoinette got out. She still had the money I had given her.

'Wait here. I'm going to find my Portuguese.'

Soon she returned. 'It's all fixed. We just drive on.'

I threaded my way into the queue over the bridge, and as we reached the frontier post Marie Antoinette waved to one of the guards. He sauntered over, smiled broadly at her and ignored me completely. He was fat.

'Your passport.'

I showed it. Marie Antoinette just smiled. The guard took it away and returned minutes later and handed it back. It was

171

stamped but still bore no visa. He seemed uninterested in the fact that Marie Antoinette had no passport at all.

'Very good. You may go through. Good day, *senhorita*.'

'Good day. *Muito obrigado.*'

'You said you only knew *muchas gracias*.'

'You know I find it hard to tell the truth. It's because I had to tell lies as a child. Now I suppose lying just a little is what comes easiest.'

As we drove into Portugal a great wave of relief engulfed me. 'I don't care what it cost, it was a brilliant piece of work.'

'Only two thousand. It's a bit less than most of the others are paying. He'd have charged you three thousand.'

Night was falling, we were five hundred kilometres from Lisbon and about two hundred from the nearest town. I had no confidence in our ability to navigate among the network of country roads, and I was weary and famished.

'A barn,' Marie Antoinette said, 'lead me to a barn with a little straw and perhaps some cheese and wine in the farmhouse first.'

But we found nothing of the kind and spent a wretched night in the car. Next day we did our five hundred kilometres to Lisbon, telling each other our troubles were over. Was not Portugal a neutral country? Was there not that most reassuring of institutions, a British Embassy, in Lisbon? And would they not welcome us with our ton of precious metal in a manner altogether befitting the occasion and the deed? Would they hell!

As we rolled down the main road from Coimbra southwards to the capital, I regaled Marie Antoinette with tales of what we would do together in London.

'And all this, you have sufficient money for us to do it?'

I had talked about Sundays on the river at Maidenhead, colourful evenings at the Embassy Club and shopping expeditions of wild extravagance to Bond Street. Also tea at the Ritz.

'No,' I said.

'But surely they'll reward you handsomely for bringing them the treasure.'

'Heavens, no.'

'Then you will sell the car?'

'Don't be silly. How can I get the car to London? We'll have to leave it in Lisbon.'

'Sell it there.'

'After what it's done for us? I couldn't. I'll have to find someone to keep it for me until the war's over. Then we'll come back, reclaim it, and go touring. We'll see all the castles of Spain and I'll take pictures of you in the harem of the Alhambra.'

She seemed pensive and not much taken with my sketch of the future. She looked as if she were doing sums in her head and coming up with dusty answers.

'What will we live on?'

'I expect they'll take me in the service somewhere. Probably take you too.'

'I don't think I want to be a soldier.'

'Anyway,' I said, 'promise you won't leave me for a fat Portuguese with money.'

'It's a tempting idea but I think I prefer my Englishman. Also, I've never been to London. You know Schlesser has always hated the English.'

Actually, I hadn't known it.

Chapter 18

In the public gardens there were actually peacocks squatting in the feathery branches of the jacaranda trees, and the bougain-villaea, the red and yellow cannas and the geraniums were in flower. There were cedars, eucalyptus and cypress and there was the deafening screech of trams as they took the curves in the busy streets. In the Rossio the eighteenth-century palaces were decorated with black and white mosaics, and in Alfama where the eaves of the ancient houses actually met high above the alleyways, you could hear the raucous cries of the *varinhas* with their creels of fish balanced elegantly on their heads like out-rageous hats. They wore dark green shawls, vivid kerchiefs at their throats and they went barefoot. They were not beautiful unless you count vitality and peasant strength as beauty.

Lisbon was packed with refugees but we had bribed our way into a decent hotel in the Avenida da Liberdade. Six people were sleeping in the corridor outside our room and the head of reception, who was making his fortune while he could, had tried to book a small Frenchman into our bath. The price of our room had been multiplied by four.

'How did you get it?' Marie Antoinette had asked when I called her in from the car.

'There was this shifty character behind the counter looking at me with a good deal of contempt on his face as if to say I was the tenth stupid bastard to bother him in the last thirty minutes. "Are you a betting man?" I asked. "*Senhor?*" he replied. "A bet-ing man – a man who will accept an interesting wager?" He asked what wager and I told him: "I will bet you a thousand escudos in ready money that you haven't got a double room for me." He had small greedy eyes – pale and definitely greedy. He never looked at his register. He just looked at me and said, "Show me." I showed him and like the true sportsman he was, he accepted the bet. He won.'

We had slept like innocent babes, side by side in a great bed with brass knobs, and next morning we wandered among the varied and extravagant beauties of Lisbon. The hotel conveniently boasted a garage and I had run the Bentley in, removed the distributor head and hidden it under the tool kit deep inside the boot. Admittedly not what Lloyd's would have regarded as an A1 risk, but the best I could think of at the time.

'Today is ours,' I told Marie Antoinette. 'We will get back to affairs of state tomorrow morning.'

'What will you do?'

'I will go to see the ambassador and he will do what has to be done.'

'An English *milord?*'

'Possibly.'

'I knew a milord once. That was in Cap Ferrat in the winter. He had beautiful manners but no money at all. A pity. Also, he wore spats and gloves in a most delicate shade of grey. That was all right, of course, save that he wore them to take tea on the terrace of the hotel. A little excessive.'

'A charming vignette from your past. I'll watch for the ambassador's spats.'

We went down to the Praca do Comércio and stood looking at the great stretch of the Tagus as it broadened into the Sea of Straw and then narrowed again before spilling its waters into the Atlantic. In Alfama we found a tiny eating place just below the medieval battlements where they served us *bacalhau* and then peaches with sour cream. Later we walked, together with everyone else, in the Chiado and took tea and cakes in an English tearoom where the lady in charge complained that as a result of a serious dereliction of duty by the shippers she was completely out of Lipton's, save for China. In the bird shops the vivid green parakeets with their scarlet heads hung upside down in their cages, watchful and irritable by turns. The crowds were polyglot, the Lisboans outnumbered. That night we made love in a kind of frenzy of relief.

'God meant us to do that,' Marie Antoinette said.

'You think so?'

'Why else would He have designed our bodies as they are?'

'And those ingenious ideas of yours just now, are they His, too?'

'Of course. I think He is particularly pleased when it's as wonderful as that. It shows him He designed well, doesn't it?'

'Do you hold God, poor soul, responsible for everything you do?'

'Naturally. I am a good Catholic girl.' A wild burst of laughter, which she smothered at last on my shoulder.

I ignored her faulty theology.

Suddenly serious, she said: 'You will take me to England with you?'

'I promised and I will.'

A moment later she was asleep.

Next morning at the embassy over in the Lapa district matters proved not to be all that simple. In the first place, the building was besieged by my fellow-countrymen trying to get home and a lot of foreigners in search of UK visas. The queue stretched out of the building into the garden and thence into the street and along the pavement. I couldn't see myself queueing for half a day in order to tell a clerk at a counter that I'd come on a little matter of smuggled bullion and could he call up an aeroplane or similar to pick it up. There was a retired petty officer type keeping a semblance of order at the front door. I put my problem to him.

'I'm not after transport. I need to see the ambassador.'

'I advise you to write in, sir.'

'The matter is highly confidential.'

'I'm afraid they all say that, sir.'

'I can't help what they say. This can't be put into a letter.'

'I'm sorry sir, but I have my orders.'

'Could I call the ambassador's secretary on an internal phone?'

'I'm sorry sir, but visitors are not permitted to use the telephone.'

'What about a first secretary?'

He shook his head. 'Same regulations sir.'

'Second secretary?'

Now he was only shaking.

'Suppose I were to write a note. Would you get it upstairs to someone?'

'I might do that sir, though you'll appreciate it's irregular.'

'Does anyone have a sheet of paper?'

More shaking. 'Afraid not sir.'

It was comforting to know His Britannic Majesty's missions abroad were defended with such zeal.

I found a receipt for some forgotten object in a pocket, tore off the bottom half and wrote my note:

I have arrived from Paris with an important communication for the ambassador, relating to the war effort, and wish to see him as soon as possible.

W. Quinton

I folded it and handed it to my friend at the door.

'I'll see what I can do, sir.' He barked an order back into the building and a young Portuguese appeared, took the note and retreated. Fifteen minutes later I was beckoned from where I was standing under a tree, shaded from the scorching late morning sun.

'Someone will see you now, sir.'

I was ushered into an office where sat a gangling, bespectacled young man behind a battered oak desk, Office of Works regulation issue, junior foreign service personnel, for the use of. He was holding my scrap of paper.

'Most frightfully sorry, Mr Quinton, but the ambassador's in London just now.'

'The first secretary, then?

'He's in Oporto on leave.'

'With all this going on?' I nodded my head in the general direction of the milling crowds outside.

'He doesn't deal with visa and repatriation matters, you know. One has those matters under control.'

'Ah.'

The young man was inclined to be helpful. 'Is there anything one can do?'

'One can pass me on to the chargé d'affaires, whoever that might be.'

He appeared flustered by the speed at which I was driving the matter to a conclusion.

'I'm very much afraid that would not be a fruitful course for us to adopt in the matter. You see, one needs some idea . . . some indication of the nature . . .' He contorted the upper part of his body in a paroxysm of deference and protocol both.

'But the nature is highly confidential.'

'And that is precisely our problem, Mr Quinton.'

'A vicious circle, wouldn't you say?'

'Indeed yes, admirably put.' And he emitted a braying laugh of quite extraordinary violence.

'So?'

'So one simply does not see how one can help.' He was still holding the paper, waving it slightly from side to side. 'Most frightfully sorry.'

'Supposing,' I said, 'that I were to tell you that I had information from Paris which was vital to the war effort? What then?'

'I would have to ask you to tell me what it was so that it could be referred to the proper quarter in due form.'

'Well, I *have* information vital to the war effort and I can't tell you what it is because it's top secret and with every respect I have no idea who you are.'

'Quite.' He paused and jerked his torso about. 'I quite see your point. On the other hand, I hope you see ours.'

'Actually, I don't. It seems to me the Foreign Office must be the most difficult body to smuggle for in the world.'

The young man appeared shocked. 'We do not involve ourselves at any point in illegal activities in the host country. At any
point.'

'I think,' I said, 'we are probably losing the war in an excess
of politeness and diplomatic niceties. What about the military
attaché – he must be a more adventurous type?'

'Major Hattersley does not deal with intelligence matters.'

'Can I see him anyway?'

'I'm afraid not. Not unless one knows the nature of your
business.'

It was a stand-off. I wouldn't tell this young man I had a ton
of treasure in a garage downtown, and he wouldn't tell me how
to find someone to whom I *was* prepared to tell it.

'Supposing,' I said, 'I were to write down on a sheet of paper
what all this is about and seal it in an envelope addressed to
your Major Hattersley and marked "strictly confidential".
Would you give me your word of honour that it would reach
him unopened?'

The proposal seemed to present him with an enormous con-
flict – ethical, moral or procedural, I had no way of telling.
Again he screwed his body into impossible shapes and his eyes
appeared to glaze over with the sheer effort of reaching a
decision which could be seen to fall within the traditions of HM
Foreign Service, not to mention international law and the 39
Articles. Then he said something like 'humph' and a moment
later 'urrgh'. After which, 'I see no reason why something of
the kind could not be arranged.'

I threaded my way through the double negative. 'I take it you
mean you'll do it?'

He couldn't bring himself to say anything as undiplomatic as
yes, but he nodded and waved his hands about. Upon which I
bade him good day and made my way back to the hotel.

To HM Military Attaché, Lisbon.
Strictly private & confidential.
*I have arrived from Paris with a substantial quantity of gold and
platinum, the property of the Bank of France and destined for the use of*

French representatives in the UK for the prosecution of the war. This treasure is naturally greatly at risk until it can be transferred to Britain and I am therefore seeking your co-operation in the matter. I would appreciate an early opportunity of talking to you about it and can be contacted by phone: 415–821, Room 14. I would appreciate a call by return.

W. Quinton.

By mid-afternoon I had delivered it to my ex-naval friend at the door of the embassy. Then I made my way along the tree-lined street outside the embassy building, searching somewhat idly for a taxi but heading towards a tram stop. It was when I reached the stop, having failed to encounter a taxi, that I realized I was being followed. A nondescript young man in a white shirt and black trousers, who had been making a show of queuing outside the embassy, joined me at the stop and got on the tram behind me.

It needed a change of trams and some rather clever footwork to get rid of him.

Chapter 19

Major Hattersley proved to be a very languid person in grey alpaca, a Dunhill pipe clamped permanently between his teeth and impeding his conversation. His moustache was a pleasure to behold, so perfectly trimmed was it. His eyes belied the rest of him. They were very pale and shrewd. His voice on the telephone had sounded world-weary, or it may have been simple boredom. My arrival was not, after all, a specially exciting event, and no doubt he was bothered almost daily by people who thought they had things they ought to tell him. But he had been civil enough and here we were, strolling in the Império garden, looking nonchalant. I had given him an account of what had been happening to me and it had sounded deeply unconvincing.

'I can show you the car,' I concluded weakly, as if hard evidence was going to be needed.

Major Hattersley was busy messing about with his pipe, which had gone out at just about the moment in my story when I was coming down into Catalonia. He got it alight again before answering me.

'Splendid show,' he said. 'Splendid cars, Bentleys. Had a '31 myself, back in England. Tell me, how did she steer with all that metal aboard?'

'A bit of understeer, which I suppose you'd expect, but otherwise perfect.'

'Jolly good.'

'If you want to see her — '

'Not necessary, old boy. I'm sure she has a ton of bullion

aboard if you say so. Point is, though, what on earth are we to do about it?'

'I thought you would be able to tell me that.'

'Me? Not in my line, old boy. I've a UK military mission on my hands just now. Over here to do a deal with the Portuguese. Meetings every day with the ministries, the general staff, some with Salazar himself. Up to here.' He indicated a point just below his chin. 'No time for undercover stuff like this. No time at all.'

'Perhaps you could cable someone in London for instructions, suggestions, I don't know . . .'

'But who, old boy, who, for God's sake? I don't think the War House would really want to know.'

'The Treasury?'

He shook his head. 'Book-keepers.'

'What about the Foreign Office?'

The idea seemed to intrigue him. 'Foreign Office, eh? An idea, that. Then, if they thought fit, they could get Transport or even the Admiralty to rustle up a conveyance of some kind. What would you say, a plane?'

'There's a ton of the stuff. Perhaps it had better go by ship, you know, car and all. Like that we wouldn't have to unload and manhandle all those bars and things.'

'Brilliant,' he said. Through his clenched teeth the word came out like an ill-suppressed burp. One had to listen carefully to catch the major's drift.

'So you'll cable the Foreign Office?'

'Good heavens, no. I couldn't do that without clearing it with the ambassador.'

'Is that a difficult thing to do?'

'Damn near impossible.' He sighed and I didn't ask why.

Something was bothering me. A few minutes before, as we reached the end of a path and turned to walk back the way we had come, I'd caught sight of a familiar figure. A young man in black trousers and a white shirt, with dank hair falling over a thin, sallow face. 'Tell me, Major, has anyone at the embassy had me followed since I called yesterday?'

'Good heavens no, old boy. Why ever would we do that?'

'And would you have a security type keeping an eye on you right now?'

The major laughed through his teeth. 'That sort of stuff comes from novels.'

'Well, when I left the embassy yesterday afternoon a young man was following me. I managed to shake him off. But now he's about fifty yards behind us and doing a second-rate shadowing job. I know he didn't follow me here so he must have followed you.'

'Very rum, that,' the major said. 'Let's see what all the fuss is about.'

He turned suddenly on his heel and marched off in the direction of the young man, who developed a hasty interest in a splendid azalea bush. The major strode up to him.

'Who the devil are you?'

'*Senhor?*'

There was an exchange in Portuguese, the major suddenly military in the extreme, the young man deferential but not at all intimidated.

'What does he say?'

'He says he wasn't following us.'

'But he was.'

'I told him that but he keeps saying, "The *senhor* is mistaken." That's all I can get out of the fellow.'

'What do you make of him?'

'I think you're right. He smells of the DGS. I've had to deal with these johnnies before. We won't get anywhere.' He turned back to the young man and appeared to be issuing orders. They had their effect. The man turned on his heel and walked quickly away along the river bank.

'He must have followed you,' the major said. 'We're very much *persona grata* right now. They wouldn't want to offend, don't y'know. So they'd never put a tail on me – not an incompetent youth like that.'

'What,' I asked, 'is the DGS?'

'Secret police. It's what keeps Salazar in the saddle. The

johnnies are everywhere. Half the staff at your hotel will be informers of one sort or another. Police state, old boy.' The colonel munched on the stem of his pipe and sent up a modest smoke signal.

'What I don't see is why they should suspect me of anything?'

'Probably got a message from France about you.' We walked in silence for a moment. 'Or Madrid.'

'Why Madrid?'

'Everyone here will remind you that Portugal is Britain's oldest ally, but look at the geography of the place. She's hemmed in by Spain and Franco is Hitler's ally. Of course, he's announced non-belligerent status, but that's because it's the convenient thing just now. The day an invasion of Britain looks like succeeding, Franco will declare war on us and try to take Gibraltar. It's what the Italians did to the French once it was clear they were beaten. Then, if that happens, Salazar will be at the mercy of the Spanish and their German friends. So what does he do meanwhile? Talks to our military mission on the days when he's not talking to the Germans. And above all he keeps his nose clean. The place is packed with agents and most of them are known to the DGS. They've only one interest: maintaining neutrality by granting a favour here, balanced by a favour there, and treading on no one's toes. Difficult, that.'

I agreed that it was difficult, but where did I figure in these power politics?

'Must have heard something about you and decided to keep an eye, don't y'know. Then, having established that you're in touch with us, they'll tread damn carefully. Otherwise you might have found yourself run in and given a going over, just to find out what you had to say for yourself.'

We were walking back towards the centre of the city. No one appeared to be following us. The major was displeased. He stowed the pipe in a jacket pocket.

'Very inconvenient, all this. Very inconvenient from my point of view. Last thing I need is to be linked to someone they have under surveillance. Afraid we'd best not meet again.'

'I'm sorry, but I'm only trying to deliver stuff which doesn't belong to me. Are you saying you'd sooner I disappeared with it?'

'Not at all. I simply wish you'd settle it with the political people at the embassy, since it's no concern of mine.'

'It's exactly what I've been unable to do.'

The major grunted and walked on in silence for some time. 'I'll get 'em to cable,' he said. 'God knows who will do it and where they'll send the cable. The ambassador will have to decide.'

'But they tell me he's away.'

'Back next week. Then we'll see. I suggest you keep in touch, old boy. Maybe in a couple of weeks or thereabouts there'll be some news from home and we'll be able to set something up.'

'Will you take the car at least? The embassy must have somewhere for the ambassador's Rolls. An extra Bentley wouldn't get in the way.'

The major appeared quite shocked at the idea. 'Quite out of the question, I'm afraid. Irregular and liable to lead to God knows what trouble.'

'Maybe God knows but I certainly can't see why there should be trouble.'

'HM embassy in possession of French national assets without an official request – good God, no!'

We had reached a crossroads. Keen to rid himself of me, Major Hattersley came smartly to a halt, extended a hand, shook mine vigorously, and turning on his heel set off at a brisk pace down a side street, leaving me standing.

As I entered the lobby of the hotel a plump man with a drooping Mexican moustache rose from a chair and joined me at the desk. The look on the concierge's face told me all I needed to know.

'Excuse me, *senhor*, I am from the police.' The fat man drew a heavily thumbed identity card from his pocket and showed it to me. On such occasions one should always look very carefully, if only to impress upon the policeman, if indeed one's interlocutor *is* a policeman, that one is not to be trifled with. I, however, did no such thing. The man had police stamped all over him anyway.

'What can I do for you?'

'We would deem it a favour if you were to come to our offices for a chat.'

'Can you tell me why?'

'A routine matter, merely. A question of papers. These are troubled times, you understand. We have to look after our foreign guests.'

'I appreciate your concern, but I'm fine and I don't need looking after.'

'Nevertheless, I must ask you to accompany me. I have a car outside. My fellow-officers are waiting in it.'

'I would like to go to my room first.'

'I am afraid I must ask you to come with me right away. You will see the *senhorita* at our offices.'

So they had already collected Marie Antoinette. There seemed no point in going upstairs.

'Do you have your passport with you?'

I nodded. Then we went out to the car. There was a driver with another man next to him. Both were in uniform. My fat friend and I climbed into the back.

'Where are we going?' I asked, by way of making conversation.

'To the headquarters of the security police.'

'Is that what you call the DGS?'

'It is.' Then he snapped an order to the driver. We were driving down towards the Tagus and then along its bank, back towards Belém where I had taken my walk with Major Hattersley. Behind the royal palace we stopped outside a heavy neoclassical building. There was a portico guarded by two policemen with automatics. The fat man and I got out of the car, marched inside and past the security desk with a nod. Then to the second floor, along a corridor and into an anteroom. There were hard chairs against the wall and at a small desk sat a man in uniform, writing in an exercise book. We sat down. Nothing was said for maybe ten minutes. Then a buzzer sounded on the policeman's desk. He nodded to my man.

'We are to go in.'

The policeman got up and opened a door for us, signalling me to go through. It led into an altogether more opulent room, carpeted, chandelier above, well-filled bookcases against the walls and large windows on to a courtyard. Seated at an ample desk, his back to a window, was a heavy man in a rather splendid uniform with a good deal of gold braid on the lapels. There was absolutely nothing on his desk save for a telephone. It somehow emphasized his importance, since he clearly didn't deal in trivia. By the side of the desk, on a straight-backed chair, sat Marie Antoinette looking composed and rather pleased with herself. Had she been practising her dubious techniques on this over-decorated policeman?

'My name is Ribeiro. I am a colonel in the security police and my responsibility is to look after our foreign visitors. Please sit down.' The tone was polite but not polite. Colonel Ribeiro waved towards a chair on the other side of his desk without looking at the chair or at me. What had Marie Antoinette with her skills in this department been able to achieve with the colonel?

'Hallo there,' I said to Marie Antoinette as I sat down.

She smiled and gave me a small wave with her fingers.

The colonel produced a box of cigars from somewhere, selected one and lit it carefully, taking his time. Then he looked at me for the first time through a puff of smoke. He must have seen a good few B movies in his day.

'Mr Quinton, welcome to our country.'

'Thank you, Colonel.'

'I have been speaking with your charming friend here. It has been a delightful but not especially illuminating experience.'

I said nothing, on the principle that the man must perforce come to the point sooner or later and was not entitled to any help from me.

'Tell me, Mr Quinton, at which frontier crossing did you arrive in Portugal?' The tone was friendly, always a bad sign with policemen.

187

'We came in by car at Fermoselle.'

'Your passport, please.'

I handed it over and he flicked through it like a man who knew he was wasting his time.

'I see no Portuguese visa – only the stamp. Now how did you achieve that?'

'Your frontier guards were very kind.'

The passport snapped shut and the colonel looked up. 'What did it cost?'

I'm not sure, but I think I achieved a suitable mix of surprise and indignation. 'I would never dream,' I said, 'of attempting to bribe a Portuguese official.'

The colonel's laugh was brief and quite genuine. 'The going rate at the frontier is three thousand escudos. Mademoiselle here tells me it cost you four thousand. I'm afraid you were taken advantage of. Some of our petty officials are greedy, I am sorry to say.'

I looked across at Marie Antoinette. They must have been having quite a conversation before I arrived. I wondered how many more little lies she had told him. She smiled at me encouragingly. I shrugged in the direction of the colonel.

'Tell me, Mr Quinton, why exactly are you in Portugal?' The tone was harder now, altogether more like the sound policemen like to make.

'We got out of France just ahead of the Germans, like a lot of other people. We're trying to get to England.'

'No other reason?'

'What other reason could there be?'

'Why have you been talking to my friend Major Hattersley?'

'I'm trying to get transport back to England and someone gave me his name. You know, a little inside influence . . . It can't do any harm, can it?' I nearly winked.

'Inside influence can be very useful indeed.' The colonel injected heavy emphasis into the words. I glanced at Marie Antoinette. The fact that she blinked might or might not have significance. Was the colonel running up a discreet signal at the yardarm? Could influence be acquired here? What might it

188

cost? Would it be useful? And if so, how was one to go about acquiring it?

The psychology and anatomy of bribery is, to me, an endlessly fascinating topic. Sometimes there is a mythical third person who has to be looked after, or a favourite and equally mythical charity which would welcome a donation. Or again, there is a whole category of officials who would be horrified by a straight bribe but perfectly happy to accept absurdly inflated Christmas presents. The bundle of crisp notes handed over in a plain white envelope comes later, when mutual confidence has been established and greed has somehow lost its nasty smell. Your effective purchaser of favours knows how to judge such stages of the process to a nicety, so that no face is lost and no one either has to ask for money or, God forfend, refuse it. A kind of *pas de deux* is danced to the sound of an infinitely delicate minuet played *con amore* by the strings. It can be a beautiful exercise in empathy and human communication.

But how did Colonel Ribeiro of the DGS like to dance? And was he worth dancing with? It seemed to me that he had a very clearly defined negative value. That is to say, bribed he might be useful, but unbribed he could be deadly. *Ergo* . . . let us dance. I had a sudden wish that we were nearer to Christmas.

'You must understand,' the colonel was saying, 'what a difficult situation we find ourselves in as neutrals amid the turbulence of this unfortunate war. After all, are we not allies of long standing, we and the British? Are our sympathies not with you and your compatriots? On the other hand, we must think of our neutrality – a neutrality for which your Mr Churchill has shown the greatest understanding. Did you know, Mr Quinton, that a British military mission is working closely with us on the re-equipment of our armed forces?'

'Yes, I did know that.'

'No doubt Major Hattersley told you. But *vis-à-vis* the Germans we must show correctness. And when they inform us that something is happening on Portuguese soil which is inimical to their interests, and thus an infringement of our neutral status, why, must we not do what we can to accommodate them?'

Was this it at last, and were we now approaching some kind of nitty gritty?

'Surely you haven't had a complaint about me?'

The colonel made a big play of taking a sheet of paper out of a drawer in his desk and spreading it before him. Then he took reading glasses from a breast pocket, adjusted them on his nose and started reading as if he'd not seen the document before.

'William Quinton, age thirty-four, British subject . . . yes, yes . . . escaped from detention in Reims, where he was serving a four-year sentence . . . car believed to be stolen . . . charged with acts against the security of the state . . . and so on.' He looked up at me. 'Dear, dear, Mr Quinton, they appear to attach great importance to retrieving you and your car.'

'Where does all this nonsense come from?'

'From the German AST in France via their embassy here.'

'And what is the AST?'

'The *Abwehrstelle*. It deals with matters of this kind where they are believed to affect the military situation in occupied countries.'

'I'm afraid it's all lies.'

'But why would they bother to transmit lies to us?'

'You have me there.'

'Pardon?'

'A colloquial expression. It means I have no idea. Mistaken identity perhaps?'

'It seems unlikely, Mr Quinton.'

'So what will you, as one of Britain's oldest allies, do about it, Colonel?'

'The legal position is frankly obscure. We have an extradition treaty with France but it is not the French authorities who have contacted us. The French government is no longer in Paris and it is not clear whether they will have jurisdiction in the occupied zone. As to the *de facto* position, it is not easy for me to ignore such a request from the German Embassy.'

'But what exactly are they asking you to do?'

The colonel picked up his piece of paper and read slowly from it: 'You are requested to prevent Quinton from leaving the

190

country until the arrival in Lisbon of a representative of our legal department in Paris. You are also requested to impound his car pending arrival of our evidence that it is a stolen vehicle.' The colonel looked up, removing his glasses. 'That is what I am asked to do.'

'And do you intend to do it?'

An expansive shrug. Then silence. Marie Antoinette rose to her feet. 'Colonel, do you have a ladies' room here?' It was beautifully timed.

The colonel called in the policeman from the anteroom and Marie Antoinette was shown out. The colonel and I settled down again. I decided on a full frontal assault on his integrity.

'If it were possible for you to ignore this absurd communication I would naturally like to make some contribution to a suitable cause. Perhaps there is a staff association here? A charity for security policemen's families in need?'

Colonel Ribeiro responded like a man who knew from experience how to accept a bribe with dignity. 'Do you have dollars?'

'I have francs, pesetas and escudos.'

It would be an exaggeration to say that his eyes lit up, but he certainly looked interested. We chatted for a while like a couple of dealers in the foreign exchange department of a respectable bank, and being dealers, we made a deal. It was not unduly expensive.

'I will inform you, of course, of any developments in this unfortunate matter,' the colonel said as Marie Antoinette, with further exquisite timing, rejoined us. 'My man who brought you from the hotel will be the contact between us. His name is Soriano. From time to time he may appreciate a modest gift. You may rely on him.'

We shook hands warmly and the colonel gave us a car to take us back to the hotel.

In the lobby of the hotel I asked Marie Antoinette: 'What did you say to the colonel before I arrived?'

'I said you were very rich.'

191

'Why did you say that?'

'I thought it would make him want to be on our side. He looked like a man who would go to the highest bidder.'

'I hope you didn't do your little whoring act.'

'He likes boys.'

'How on earth do you know that?'

'Well, I let it be understood that you and I . . . you know, finished. I said I was lonely. I have never met a normal man who wouldn't offer to eliminate my loneliness. But the colonel said he was sorry to hear it and how rich were you? So you see, he must like boys.' She smiled sweetly and squeezed my arm. 'I have not been obliged to be unfaithful to you.'

Chapter 20

For me two institutions, and two only, epitomize sanity, decency and security in a mad world. The first is the nursery with nanny starched by the fireside, and the second is your English teashop with its brasses and polished oak and the smell of scones hot from the oven. Nor are these images, or more particularly the second of them, as incongruous as it might seem in the midst of this account of greed and mayhem in the deadly summer of 1940. Of nurseries there were none that I knew of in Lisbon. But having sent Marie Antoinette off to the Rua Augusta to buy clothes, I went back on the day after our encounter with the colonel to the English teashop in the Chiado. Everything there inspired confidence – the faded chintz at the window, the horse brasses from some corner of rural England, the doileys, the silver and the very English lady in charge who had been so captious about the lack of Lipton's tea.

It was early for tea and there were no other customers. There was a pale green card on the table which announced in gothic script that the English Teashop (sole proprietor Miss E. Gilpin) was pleased to serve English Teas and Light Snacks, Mondays to Saturdays, English Spoken. Miss Gilpin was a rather etiolated lady of uncertain age with severe hair and the hygienic appearance favoured so often by your English spinster. Nonsense, it was clear, was something she would not stand for, be it from the shippers of Lipton's tea or anyone else. I judged that though she may well have lived among foreigners for many years, she did not like them. Nor was she someone with whom to crack a jest. Not at all.

I ordered scones with raspberry jam and a nice pot of tea, and when it arrived I commented on the weather (too hot) and the city (too crowded). These modest prejudices were met with cautious approval. Miss Gilpin showed no immediate inclination to leave me to my tea.

'I have only just arrived in Lisbon,' I said.

'I fear it is not a friendly city,' Miss Gilpin said.

'I know absolutely no one here.'

'Are you on your way to Blighty?'

I didn't think anyone used the word any more. I nodded. 'To London.'

'London, too, is an unfriendly city.'

'Where are you from, Miss Gilpin?'

'I,' she said with a touch of asperity in her voice, 'am from Eastbourne.'

'A charming place. Very nice weather.'

'I have been in Lisbon for seventeen years. There was an event in my life and I shook the dust of Sussex from my feet.'

The moment wasn't suitable to inquire about an event appalling enough to cause Miss Gilpin to take such extreme measures and land among foreigners.

'Miss Gilpin,' I said, 'it is a great pleasure for me to meet an English lady in a foreign land. I have just come from France. It is terrible there just now.'

'I was in Paris once. I did not find the people friendly.'

'I do so agree with you,' I said. 'Your scones, by the way, are quite delicious.'

This being no more than her due, Miss Gilpin simply nodded. Others had come into the tearoom and she allowed an emaciated Portuguese waitress to attend to them.

'I wonder,' I said, 'if I might presume on your kindness. I have a problem.'

'There is not much kindness about nowadays,' Miss Gilpin said. 'I'm afraid I speak as I find.'

'Indeed there isn't.' I was anxious to pull the conversation down from the general to the particular. 'Would you by any chance know of somewhere secure and not too expensive where

I could garage my car for a while? Maybe somewhere away from the centre of the city. Perhaps you have friends who would like to let their garage. It would only be for a week or two. I'd pay by the week, or the month if necessary.' Was Miss Gilpin an Eastbourne snob, I wondered? I decided that she was. 'I'm afraid it's rather a large car,' I added. 'A Bentley.'

'Very nice cars,' Miss Gilpin said.

'Very.'

'I could ask Mr Gomes.'

'Who is Mr Gomes?'

'He is my landlord. I rent a flat in his house. I know he has others, and always a very good class of property. I would say a garage is a possibility where Mr Gomes is concerned.'

'I would deem it a favour, Miss Gilpin, if you would ask him on my behalf.'

'I will ask this evening. You have had the last of the Tiptree.'

'Pardon?'

'The raspberry jam. I fear there will be no more Tiptree until this wretched war is over.' And she left me to my tea.

Next morning, while I drank a coffee and sank my teeth into an excellent bun, Miss Gilpin told me that she had indeed spoken to Mr Gomes, who had a garage vacant which he was prepared to rent by the month. The price she quoted on Mr Gomes' behalf was extortionate. I told her I would take the car over this very day and she instructed me on how to find the place. 'A distinguished gentleman,' she said, 'with a very good class of property.'

After lunch I drove the car northwards, following Miss Gilpin's directions. Mr Gomes' property was a rather large white stucco house in a quiet residential street close to the Edward VII park. There was a garage by the side of the house. Mr Gomes himself turned out to be distinguished in an Anglo-Portuguese manner. His English was beautiful and his suit was of an English cut. His greying beard and waxed moustache, in particular, conferred the distinction to which Miss Gilpin had referred. I could see that if she had to deal with foreigners then

195

Mr Gomes, the embodiment of the ancient Anglo-Portuguese alliance, would probably suit as well as anyone. I showed him the Bentley and he showed me his garage. The one fitted neatly into the other. Money changed hands and we cemented our new-found relationship with a handshake. 'It is always a pleasure,' Mr Gomes said, 'to do business with an English gentleman. Mr Churchill is a great man.'

'And your Salazar,' I said glibly. Upon which we parted, I with the key to the garage in my pocket.

I picked up a taxi and returned to the hotel. As far as I could tell no one save Miss Gilpin, Mr Gomes and myself now knew where the car was to be found.

'Where is it?' Marie Antoinette asked.

'I don't think you really need to know. Like that no one can extort the information from you.'

'So you don't mind if I am tortured to death because I cannot give the information they want?'

It was a point. 'Look,' I said, spreading my street map on the bed. 'Here – the Rua Redondo, number thirty-four.' It was the first spot on the map that hit my eye and I felt bad about it.

'Are you sure our friend Soriano didn't follow you?'

'Positive.'

'Nor anyone else?'

'Nor anyone else.'

'Good; then I have a plan.'

'What plan?'

'First, you haven't asked to see my new dress.'

'If you want that sort of attention you should find yourself a *couturier*.'

'I did once. It was no good.'

'So show me your new dress.'

She slipped out of what she was wearing and extracted a vivid red affair from a mass of tissue paper and pulled it up over her hips. Then she came to me and with her slender arms around my neck rubbed her body against mine like a cat.

'I can't see your dress from here,' I said, 'but the colour suits you beautifully. You should have worn the red that night in Paris.'

'Tonight, you may take me to a place where they sing the *fado*.'

'Let's go to the *Poisson d'Or* instead. I've been trying to get you there ever since we met.'

'When the war's over and we're in Paris together we'll go there and stay for breakfast. They do a great breakfast.'

'I know, I used to go there with Francine.'

'That bitch,' biting savagely on the lobe of my ear.

'I'll ask the concierge where we should go.'

When we got to the lobby I announced that I'd left my wallet in the bedroom and went back for it. I took the garage and ignition keys from my pocket, unscrewed one of the knobs of the brass bedstead and dropped the keys into the hollow brass tube. They fell to the point where the bed frame was joined to the bedhead by means of a screw through the tube. How to retrieve the keys was something I would worry about later. I screwed the knob back on, took up my wallet and went down to join Maire Antoinette.

The concierge recommended a *fado*-house up on the Bairro Alto. 'Take the funicular,' he said. 'Then ask. It's in the Rua da Rosa, number sixteen. The food isn't bad. The singing is very special. You will eat at nine and the singer will appear after ten.' He picked up the phone. 'I will book you a table, *senhor*.' He seemed determined that I should go there.

And so we took the funicular, Marie Antoinette attracting attention in her red dress, and then we asked our way to the Rua da Rosa, found it, found the restaurant at number sixteen, which proved to be small and nondescript, and were led to the table. The food was as forecast by the concierge and soon after ten the lights dimmed and two guitarists appeared on the tiny stage and gave fifteen minutes of Portuguese-sounding tunes which tended towards the mawkish.

'And what exactly is the *fado*?' I asked Marie Antoinette.

'I read about it in a guide book. They say it is a form of singing which may have come from Brazil or Africa – no one knows. It's full of *saudade*, and they say *saudade* is a mood of gentle melancholy, nostalgia and despair. Also tragedy and longing. These are all things that I love.'

'No laughs?'

'No laughs. The English are impossible.'

A middle-aged woman appeared in the spotlight. She was dressed in severe black and her face had no expression at all. Immediately, the audience was hushed. The guitars sidled into a plaintive sequence of chords and then she sang. It was the most haunting, the saddest and at the same time the most erotic thing I had ever heard. The audience was mute as the chant developed, the harsh voice rose and fell, now lamenting a lost love, now angry and now resigned. I glanced at Marie Antoinette. In the reflected light of the spot, tears were glistening on her cheeks. She sat absolutely still, her wonderful head strained slightly forward, her hands immobile for once in her lap. She had never been more desirable and yet more elusive. It was as if the singer and her song could speak to her and no one else could do so. *Saudade!* Endless sorrow and longing. She and I had made love with infinite tenderness. We had 'known each other' as the phrase has it. And it was perfectly clear to me as the singer sang and Marie Antoinette wept quietly that I had never known her and never would.

When the songs ended at last and the audience had clapped and shouted their bravos, she turned to me, dabbing at her eyes. 'Let's go quickly. The *fado* has made me frightened – I don't know why. So let's go.'

We walked out into the street alone, ahead of the rest of the crowd from the restaurant. In the heavy warmth of the night there was no moon and the Rua da Rosa was virtually unlit. As we reached the corner of the Calçada do Tijolo I noticed a car parked ahead of us, its lights out. It was impossible to see whether there was anyone inside. My instinct was to cross the road and give the car a wide berth, but such moves, in the absence of any direct evidence of danger, smack of paranoia and cowardice – and how one hates to be thought crazy or yellow. And so we walked on and came abreast of the car. It was at that point that I saw the three men sitting impassively inside and by then it was too late. Both front doors and the rear door of the car were flung open at once and we were trapped on the narrow pavement between a wall and the car, with two men in front of us and one behind. I saw the flash of a knife and one of the men snapped '*Jetzt! Schnell!*' The operation was expertly conducted and it was soon over. We were thrust violently into the car – Marie Antoinette in front, I in the back – and as she screamed a hand closed over her mouth and the scream was strangled. I lashed out, but the knife blade glinting close to my eyes soon shut me up. In seconds the driver had taken the car down the Rua da Rosa and into the network of streets dropping down from the Bairro Alto.

The heavies on either side of me each had one of my arms in a half nelson behind my back, pressing me backwards against my own arms and causing quite astonishing pain. Then I felt the stab of a hypodermic in my shoulder and the rest was oblivion.

At first I couldn't recall what had happened. Then I felt euphoric and didn't care. Then I wondered why I was in an unfamiliar room with no window, with my limbs as heavy as lead and my eyes unwilling to focus. It took me about ten minutes to get my mind functioning in some sort of order, though my legs still felt too heavy and my hand trembled when I raised it to look at my watch. It was just after nine – a.m. or p.m., I'd no idea. The room had no furniture save for the camp bed on which I was lying and a stool. It was lit by a naked bulb hanging from a flex in the ceiling. The painted brick walls seemed to indicate a cellar. Marie Antoinette was not with me.

It was nearly ten when a key turned in the lock, the door opened and a man came into the room. By then I was sitting up on the bed, my back against the wall. I was still having trouble with my eyes but my brain seemed to be working and my memory had returned. At a guess the man was in his early thirties. His blond hair was cropped short and he had very pale blue eyes. The dark grey suit fitted perfectly over his broad shoulders and narrow hips. A soldier? Possibly. Indeed, he struck me at once as everyone's idea of an officer in Hitler's Waffen SS.

He locked the door behind him and dropped the key in his pocket. Then he sat down on the stool and treated himself to a long examination of my person. When he spoke the English was pedantically exact but the accent was not German at all. Austrian? It had the ingratiating softness of Viennese.

'Mr Quinton, I must first apologize for bringing you here in this unorthodox fashion, but I am acting under orders and had no choice in the matter.'

I decided to say nothing, being too busy toying with the absurd notion that I might leap from my recumbent position, overpower this athletic-looking person in some undefined manner, seize the key and escape. The notion, as I say, was absurd and I abandoned it at once.

'We would like to know where your car is,' the blond man said. I noticed that he had beautifully manicured hands. He sat on the stool with his legs drawn back, the knees together, as a woman would sit.

'I would like to know where my friend is.'

'She is with us and she is safe.'

'And who are you anyway?'

'I will ask the questions, Mr Quinton, and you will answer them.'

'This is not Berlin,' I said. 'This is Lisbon. The German disease hasn't reached here yet.'

'Mr Quinton, I must tell you I cannot be provoked. Please, you will tell me where is your car?'

'That injection has made me very thirsty. Bring me something to drink.'

'I earnestly advise you to deal with me, Mr Quinton. I do not use violence. But if you will not answer then I must tell you that you will be handed over to someone who does.' He had a girl's long, golden lashes and they curtained his eyes when he talked and only lifted when he fell silent. He had thin lips and perfect white teeth. I found him disgusting. 'The violence,' he went on, 'is extreme. I will tell you about it.'

If this sinister hermaphrodite was the good news, then his violent colleague, the bad news, must be dreadful indeed. I was in no mood to find out.

'The car,' I said on a sudden hunch, 'is in the hands of the British diplomatic mission.'

'We think not, Mr Quinton.'

'You can think what you please, but I handed it over yesterday morning.'

'Where do you claim to have handed it over?'

'Right in the middle of town. In the Chiado. An embassy driver took it over.'

'And where is it supposed to be now?'

'I've no idea but I daresay it's with the embassy cars in a garage somewhere. I hope so: it's a valuable car.'

'If you are lying,' the blond man said, 'we will beat both of you until you lose consciousness.' For the first time there was an expression on his face. He was smiling and his lips were wet. 'Whom do you know at the embassy?'

'The ambassador.'

'He is not in Lisbon.'

'I know that.'

'Who else?'

'The military attaché.'

'We are aware of your connection with Major Hattersley.'

'Then why ask?'

'Mr Quinton, I fear I will lose patience with you.'

'You said just now you couldn't be provoked.'

The long lashes came down again. 'What your lady friend tells us does not coincide with your story.'

'I would have to hear her tell it before I'd be prepared to comment on that. Anyway, she wasn't there when I handed the car over.'

'She tells us the car is at an address in the Rua Redondo. She says she cannot recall the number despite what was done to improve her memory. So you will tell us the number.'

At that point a wave of fury swept over me and I lurched forward from the bed and promptly fell back again. I had

201

overestimated the recovery in my legs.

'I will think about it,' I said.

'You will not think about it. You will tell me the number now or I will call my colleague.' The lashes came up. He was not going to say anything more.

'I gave her the Rua Redondo address for just such an occasion as this, so that she couldn't reveal where the car is. I don't even remember the number I invented.'

The pale eyes examined me for a time. 'I repeat, I do not believe your embassy has the car. On the other hand, I accept your statement that the girl does not know where it is. Our problem therefore becomes extremely simple. You will tell me or we will have to start all over with the girl.' Up came the lashes. 'We will also try some persuasion on you.'

During all this I had had a chance to do some thinking. It produced a lousy plan: the up-side of the thing was that it might gain some time: the down-side that it didn't seem to lead to a way out of the mess. I tried it.

'When I said the embassy had it just now, it wasn't quite accurate. My contact was not with embassy staff: Major Hattersley put me in touch with a member of the Intelligence Service. He said the embassy couldn't get involved in a thing like this. My contact doesn't work there.'

'Who is your contact?'

'I've no idea. He called himself John.'

'Where did you meet him?'

'Outside the hotel. Then we went for a walk. In the Edward VII garden as a matter of fact.'

'And he took the car?'

'Yes.'

'So where is it now?'

'You wouldn't expect him to tell me, would you?'

'How do you make contact with this John?'

'I am to phone and leave a message and we meet at an agreed time and place.'

'A prearranged time and place?'

I made a weak effort to look reluctant. Then I nodded.

'You will tell me the time and place.'

'You'll have to find out.'

'You have forgotten the girl, Mr Quinton.'

Another effort at acting the effete Englishman outwitted by the scum of the German lower middle classes in their brief moment on the stage of history. 'We meet at the eastern end of the Rossio at seven in the evening of the following day.'

A pause for thought. 'You will give me the telephone number.'

'You can have it if you like but I warn you that if they smell a rat at the other end, all contact will be broken off. Take me to a phone and I'll do what's necessary.'

'And what if you warn them off?'

'Why would I do that when my main concern is the girl? And myself, come to that. I rate us both above the Bentley.'

Further thought. It was complicated, but then it was meant to be. I was relying on my hunch that the man wasn't a fool, since a fool would go about it bald-headed and my fragile scheme would collapse.

'Come.'

He took the key out of his pocket and unlocked the door. I rose carefully to my feet and found I could get along by taking small tentative steps and holding on to walls and things. We made slow progress down a short corridor towards stairs leading upwards.

'I am only phoning my intelligence contact because you are forcing me to do so.' I said it good and loud in the hope that Marie Antoinette might be somewhere in earshot and would know I was alive. 'It's strictly on the understanding that the girl isn't harmed,' I yelled. 'Do I have your guarantee of that?'

'You have the word of a German officer.' He didn't seem to realize what nonsense that was.

'Good!' I shouted. 'Very good!'

We were labouring up the stairs and soon we'd reached an office of some kind on what I took to be the ground floor. He opened the door, went straight to the window and drew the blinds. I had had a glimpse of what appeared to be a waterfront,

203

with the masts and derricks of ships maybe a hundred yards away. Then I was led to a chair next to a heavy desk and handed the phone.

'You will telephone and I will listen on the extension.'

'I must have a glass of water first if you want all this to be relaxed and convincing.'

He went to the door and shouted something in German. While he was doing it I managed to glance at the little card the hotel had given me with my room number. It also gave the hotel's telephone number: 415–821. The water arrived and I drank the lot: the stuff they had pumped into me had dehydrated me. Then I picked up the phone and when the exchange answered I struggled with the Portuguese: '*Trees um cinco oito dois nove.*' I reckoned a number as close to that of the hotel was very likely to exist. That was the first gamble. The second was that someone would answer. The third, that whoever answered didn't speak English and try to start a conversation. On the far side of the desk the German had the extension against his ear.

I got a ringing tone and it continued for a long time. I felt my hand trembling and I tried to steady it by pushing the earpiece hard against my ear. Finally, the earpiece was lifted from the hook at the other end.

'*Esta?*' The voice was female, anonymous, giving no clue as to how the thing would go.

'This is William. Please tell John I will see him tomorrow. Goodbye.'

As I rang off I heard squeaks of surprise coming from the instrument. The German must have heard them too.

'I will check.'

'If you do, the mission will abort. It's arranged like that. Any unexpected call will warn him off.'

'We shall see tomorrow. I will now return you to your room and some food will be served in two hours.'

'Lunchtime?'

He nodded.

'May I see my friend?'

'You may not. Now, follow me please.' And I was returned to

204

the basement, conscious that I had set something up which I had no idea how to control. But I happen to know what Napoleon said when they asked him how he went about winning battles. 'You engage,' he replied, 'and then you see.'

Chapter 21

One thing had stuck stubbornly in my mind: the alacrity with which the concierge at the hotel had booked me a table once he had headed me towards the restaurant of his choice. It was as if he had to be sure that I would go there and nowhere else. *Ergo,* he would be telling someone where we would be that evening. That was one thought which wouldn't go away in the long hours of the night and the following day. The other thought was this: if by some lucky chance I was able to make a run for it, what would happen to Marie Antoinette? I came to the conclusion that they wouldn't touch her, since their main hope of getting me to tell them the whereabouts of the car was the threat of violence to her. There would be no point in their harming her until they had me again. Sound reasoning? Was I putting her at risk? Did I care?

Yes, I found myself caring quite passionately. For this wayward, devious and totally unreliable creature had manoeuvred her way into my mind and wherever one's emotions are stationed in the body. If someone wanted to call it love they were welcome to the use of the substantive. Perhaps it was.

When the blond German came to my room the following day I laid down my conditions. I wanted a wash and shave and I wanted proof that Marie Antoinette was unharmed. The shave was provided, with a squat and totally silent German in attendance. Then they took me to a door on the ground floor.

'She is in there. You may call to her.'

I did so. There was a sound from the other side of the door.

'Are you all right?'

'Not bad.' Her voice sounded strained. She was making an effort to sound cheerful.

'I'm doing what I can.'

'You must get me out of here or I'll go crazy.'

'Sure, sure. Try not to worry.'

Then I was pulled away and back to my cell downstairs.

Soon after six they blindfolded me, tied my hands behind my back and marched me up the stairs again and out of the house. On the outside we walked a yard or two and I was pushed unceremoniously into a car. There was someone next to me. I could hear the wail of a ship's siren and the occasional noise of heavy vehicles passing on the road. Then we were off, and after twenty minutes or so, in the course of which we turned a lot of corners, the bandage was removed from my eyes. The blond German was next to me and the squat one was up front next to the driver. We were driving through a residential district towards the centre of town, and as we slowed down in the rush-hour traffic, my hands were untied. Then we were in the busy Rua da Prata and turning into the Rossia. The great square was awash with pedestrians and vehicles of all kinds and the cafés along three of its sides were already filling up with the usual early evening crowd who would sit over a coffee or aperitif, watching everyone else do the same.

'The south-east corner,' I said, 'outside the big café.'

The driver drove round the square and managed to park almost opposite the café. There were plenty of people at the tables on the broad pavement and waiters were scurrying about among them. The pavement itself was filled with the crowds on their way home from shops and offices. It was four minutes to seven.

'This,' I said, 'is the most stupid thing you've done so far. If John sees me get out of a car full of people who so clearly belong to the master race, he'll simply take to his heels. If you want anything to come out of this you'd better drive on.'

There was a hurried consultation in German. Then the driver restarted the engine and drove the car on fifteen yards or so along the eastern side of the square. The café was now behind us, with the car facing away from it.

'You will make the contact and you will be under the closest surveillance,' the blond said. 'You will say you wish to recover the car. You will give whatever explanation is most likely to satisfy him.'

Surely they didn't believe that a half-baked story like that would work with 'John'. And suddenly I understood what was afoot. A group of three policemen had been standing a short distance away. As we came to a halt they moved casually towards us and while one of them lingered near the car, the other two moved in the direction of the café. I looked round Nearby were two more policemen and a police type in plain clothes. The plan was not to fool my contact but to arrest him. Either Colonel Ribeiro, whom I had bought, was a man who did not stay bought, or the Germans had bought someone else and their man had nosed ahead of my man.

I climbed out of the car and walked slowly towards the café. There was an empty table nicely placed near the entrance, I made for it, sat down and ordered a coffee. Then I tried to look like a man who was waiting for a friend. The police were hovering on the pavement a few yards away and two of the Germans were walking back and forth, inadequate imitations of casual tourists. One thing was clear: I would never get away from the place by making a run for it. My legs still felt inadequate and I didn't even know if I could run.

I looked at my watch. It was five past seven. A man asked if he could have the empty chair at my table and I shook my head. I had the odd feeling that I was indeed waiting for 'John' and that he had let me down. Then I decided what to do. I got to my feet in the most offhand manner I could summon up, turned and walked into the café. It was full of people. Waiters were hurrying to and from the swing doors into the kitchens. At the bar others were calling up coffees and drinks. There was plenty of noise and just about enough movement for my purpose. I made for the service door, went through and found myself in the metal and enamel surroundings of the busy kitchen. Chefs and kitchen hands were going about their business amid a good deal of shouting. A couple of them looked up at me, puzzled, and then got on with their work: they must have thought I was something to do with management. Resisting the enormous temptation to run, I walked on past the kitchen battery and work stations and on into a corridor with doors opening into the cold store and other storerooms. If this was not the way out of the place I was probably done for.

But it was the way out. A heavy metal door led out into a narrow lane and the moment I was through it I started to run.

Five yards on and I realized I couldn't run. My legs simply gave way under me and I had to grab at a ledge to stop myself hitting the pavement. I paused for breath, feeling like the man in the dream who has to run from an unseen menace but finds his legs impossibly heavy, as if he were wading through treacle. Holding on to the wall, I walked up the lane rather like a drunkard. My progress was slow and felt slower. I had to work my way round the Rossio, using the streets lying behind the buildings on the square. As I skirted the great bulk of the National Theatre along the north side I felt sure the police must have been alerted and were already fanning out into these mean back streets. In the distance I heard the wail of a police car and decided it must be wailing for me. I tried once again to run, or trot, or shuffle midway between walking and running. A shuffle was the best I could achieve. I looked like a drunk or a cripple, and progress was dreadfully slow.

Twice I hid in doorways – once as a police car raced by, and once because a man loitering on a corner looked like DGS. It took me fifteen minutes to reach the Chiado, where the evening crowds were thick on the pavements. A few minutes later I was in the English Teashop and installed at a table well away from the window. The Portuguese waitress was in attendance. I ordered another coffee and asked for Miss Gilpin. That lady was summoned from the kitchen and in a restrained way seemed quite pleased to see me.

'I wanted to thank you for putting me in touch with Mr Gomes,' I said. 'We came to a very convenient arrangement.'

'Yes, so he told me. I always like to help where I can.'

'Indeed, you have been most helpful, Miss Gilpin. So much

so that I'm venturing to ask you to help me again.'

'In these troubled times,' said Miss Gilpin simply, 'we must help one another.'

'I'm afraid I'm in quite a spot of trouble,' I said. 'It's connected with the war and I can't really tell you the details. But I need to phone our embassy and I can't do it from my hotel. I wonder if I might use your phone here.'

'I know Mr Fosset-Bankes at the embassy,' Miss Gilpin said. 'A very nice gentleman. He is in the commercial department and I am on his list for Empire Day.'

'What happens on Empire Day?'

'They have a charming garden party and the ambassador and his wife are our hosts. Some of us in the British community are privileged to attend. I am on Mr Fosset-Bankes' list.'

'And may I phone?'

'We must all pull together for England, mustn't we? The phone is at the back.'

She took me out to the back, looked up the embassy's number for me and asked the operator for it. Then she handed me the instrument and retreated to the kitchen. I asked for Major Hattersley.

The clipped voice could have been more amiable. Perhaps he didn't like working so late.

'Yes?'

'Quinton here. I'm sorry to bother you but I'm in a spot of trouble. Both my friend and I were seized in the street two nights ago and taken off to some German hideout. I've got away but my friend is still with them and in considerable danger, I'd say. I need help.'

Humphing sounds came from the earpiece. Was the major chewing on his pipe?

'I don't actually see that I can do anything for you. Isn't it a job for the police?'

'I don't like to babble too much on an open line, but I fear the law has lined up with the other side.'

'And your car?'

'Safe – so far.'

More humphing. Then, 'Trouble is, old boy, I don't see that I can get mixed up. You know – guests in the country, tricky negotiations, all that sort of thing. I think you'd best go to the police.' And the bastard rang off!

I thanked the admirable Miss Gilpin and moved out cautiously to join the crowds sauntering in the Chiado, my second coffee untouched.

In the narrow street behind the hotel I took up a position in a doorway almost exactly opposite the hotel's service entrance. It was close to eight, and from time to time hotel staff came out and made off to their homes. I was feeling a little stronger: maybe all the shuffling around had brought some life back to my legs.

It was half past eight when I recognized the figure of the concierge. He came through the door, hesitated for a moment, then set off to his left, keeping to the far pavement. I gave him a few yards' start, then slipped out of my doorway and kept pace with him on my side of the road. Some hundred yards ahead the back street gave on to a busier thoroughfare. I had to carry out my little plan before he reached the intersection.

I hastened my pace until I was level with him and crossed the road just as he came abreast of a carriage entrance which presumably led to one of the internal courtyards which can be found in many Lisbon streets. As I stepped on to the pavement he turned and saw me for the first time. He had no time to react. I threw myself at him and hustled him into the carriageway, one hand over his mouth and the other gripping the back of his collar. I was a good deal heavier than he was and the thing wasn't really fair. His shifty eyes were opened wide in alarm and he waved his arms to no useful purpose. Then I had him hard up against a wall.

I shifted my grip to his tie, with the other hand still over his mouth. Then I brought my knee up into his groin and he doubled over with a grunt.

'If you make a sound I'll do it again.'

I removed my hand from his mouth and pulled him upright.

211

The poor fellow was in agony, gasping and holding his crotch with both hands.

'That was just to show I am in earnest. Now you will tell me who you are reporting to.'

There was just enough light for me to see that whatever else he was, he was no hero. I had never seen such terror in a man's eyes.

'*Senhor*, I will tell whatever you need to know. But please, not again . . .'

'So tell me.'

'What am I to tell you?'

'Don't waste my time. I want to know who it was that you told of our visit to the *fado*-house two nights ago.'

'The DGS, *Senhor*. You understand, one has no choice.'

'Who in the DGS?'

'Captain Soriano. You saw him at the hotel.'

'I did. And why do you think Soriano wanted to know about me?'

'Truly, I have no idea, *Senhor*.'

'How do you contact him?'

'He often comes to the hotel. The other night I phoned a number he gave me and he did not come. He just said "good". That is all I know.'

'Are you paid for these services?'

'Almost nothing, *Senhor*.'

'And if I pay you more, will you do something for me?'

A shrug and an attempt at a smile. 'One tries to satisfy, *Senhor*.'

'You will go back to the hotel now and you will bring me the key to my room. Can you walk?'

The man tried to take a couple of steps and managed it. He nodded.

'Good, now off you go, and if you are inside for more than sixty seconds I will assume you have contacted Soriano again. If less than sixty seconds I will give you five hundred escudos.'

'It is not much, *Senhor*, excuse me. I am very hurt down there, and only five hundred escudos . . .'

'There will be other tasks, each for five hundred. It's damn good money – certainly more than you get from Soriano.'

He shrugged again, hesitated, decided that I was a hard case, and hobbled away towards the back entrance of the hotel. It took him less than a minute to fetch my key. I took it from him and handed him the money.

'Now tell me how I can reach my room through the service entrance.'

'Just inside the door is a corridor. There is a pair of swing doors to the left and through there a service staircase. It will take you to your floor. But *Senhor* . . .'

'Yes?'

'They have been to your room. They came yesterday. I fear all your things – smashed up.'

'Who came?'

'Some men, with Captain Soriano. I do not know who they were.'

'Portuguese men?'

'They did not look Portuguese. I do not know for sure.'

'A tall blond man with pale eyes?'

'One of them, yes, I think so.'

'That is worth another five hundred.' I gave the poor wretch the money and he hobbled off to nurse his balls.

'If you say you've seen me,' I called after him, 'they'll be the next ones to hit you there because you gave me the key. So keep your mouth shut.'

His nodding head told me message received and understood.

I had no trouble reaching my room, which looked as if cavalry had passed that way. Our stuff was strewn over the bed and the floor and the bed itself had been stripped, with slashes along the edges of the mattress. They'd pulled every drawer out and searched under the carpet, which had been pulled into a heap in the middle of the room. Face cream and powder had been scooped out of Marie Antoinette's collection of pots and the lining of my suitcase had been ripped out. But when I gave the brass rod at the head of the bed a clout there was a reassuring tinkle within. On the other hand, I had nothing with which to extract the keys, which lay at the bottom of about thirty inches of hollow tubing.

I removed the brass knob and had the idiotic notion that I might have to buy fishing tackle to do the job. Then the very mess in the room gave me a better idea. Have you ever tried turning a double brass bedstead upside down without dismantling it? It is very hard work. But the keys fell out and I left the bed that way as my contribution to law and order in the Portuguese capital. A couple of minutes later I was out in the street again and heading north.

It was dark when I reached Mr Gomes' street. I walked the length of it, past the Gomes house and back again. There was no one about. Why was I there? Simple: I wanted the gun which I had left in the glove compartment of the car. I'd left it there because I never imagined I'd need a gun in neutral Lisbon.

Mr Gomes' garage gave straight on to the pavement. It had white-painted double doors secured by a mortice lock. I toyed with the idea of making a social call at the house first to announce my presence, but I'd no idea whether Mr Gomes lived there or merely acted as landlord. Miss Gilpin had referred to his properties in the plural. I decided to unlock the garage, retrieve the gun, lock up and depart.

The nearest street lamp was some forty feet away: I had to feel my way to the keyhole. The door yielded and I stepped inside the garage. I would have to feel my way round the car, doing the whole thing by touch. I advanced carefully, to make contact with the rear of the car. I reckoned on three steps. I took three. Then a fourth; a fifth. My hands were pushed out in front of me like a blind man's. Nothing! Nothing at all. The car wasn't there.

It was as the enormity of it dawned on me that I heard the faint squeak of the door hinge behind me, and then the beam of a torch hit my back, throwing a weak light into the recesses of the garage. There was certainly no car there.

'*Maos as alto!*' The voice behind me was full of the kind of authority that goes with a torch and a gun. It sounded like an instruction to raise my hands, so rather grudgingly I raised them a little way.

'*Vire se!*'

I turned round, carefully, scowling into the bright light of the torch. For a moment there was silence.

'Sorry, old man, I didn't know it was you.'

'Who the hell are you?'

'Never mind who I am. Let's say I'm a friend of the major.'

'But my car's gone.'

'It's all right. We've got it.'

'I think this needs explaining.'

'We can go to the house and I'll fill you in.'

I followed the major's friend out into the street, locked the garage door, followed him again to the front door of the house, which was open. We went inside. The dapper Mr Gomes was in the hall, smiling and full of old-world hospitality.

'Please come in. I am so very happy to see you again so soon. Please . . .' He ushered us into a drawing room crammed with mahogany and velvet, sat us down and proposed brandy. The major's friend proved to be pretty much like the major himself. I imagined him to be straight out of the Shires, just off his horse, recently with one of the better regiments, most probably between pipes. He had pocketed his torch and his gun. And there we three sat in the uncomfortable armchairs, each with a balloon of very good brandy, looking at each other.

'Please tell me all,' I said.

'I can tell you this much. We came to the conclusion that the setup here wasn't secure enough. We'd planned to talk to you about it but when the other side lifted you we felt we ought to act. So we towed her out to a safer place, and here we are. I must say, I'm glad to see you're at large again.'

'I am, but my friend isn't and I'm worried sick.'

'You'd better fill us in.' There was a pause. 'Mr Gomes here is a very good friend. Please speak freely.' Mr Gomes gave me one of his charming smiles. A nice little man.

I filled them in. The major's friend occasionally brought the brandy glass to his nose and on one occasion took a sip. Mr

Gomes had shed his deference and kept a steady and penetrating gaze on me. When I had finished he asked: 'This house, what chance have we of finding it again?'

'It has to be in the port area; I glimpsed ships. But that's all I know.'

'The car is down at the docks,' the major's friend said. 'Absolutely secure. Handy for shipping.'

'So London has responded already?'

'Not at all. The FO can't work that fast, you know. So I'm taking the initiative. We'll ship the car on the SS *Galatea*, which docked this evening. She'll be bunkered and loaded immediately. She has to join a convoy which is assembling now. So we've told the dock labour to get a move on, and we'll be putting our people aboard in the next forty-eight hours. She'll be crammed with repatriates. Her derricks will be able to cope with that car of yours and they'll stow it on deck. I've fixed all that.'

'And there's a couple of tickets for me?'

He nodded. 'Booked a double cabin. Best I could do. Thought you wouldn't mind.' His face was expressionless.

'I don't mind,' I said, 'but I do have a question.'

'Shoot, old man.'

'How did you get involved in my little venture and how on earth did you trace the car?'

'Well, you see, Major Hattersley took the view that if you had all that bullion here in Lisbon we might as well get it back to England. Could come in handy. But obviously, he couldn't involve himself in an operation like that. He'd be *non grata* in no time if the Portuguese authorities found out. Very touchy, old Salazar. Probably illegal to take gold out of the country anyway.' He turned to Mr Gomes, who nodded.

'So Hattersley handed the thing to me. We have no official links with embassy people. We sweep up after them, deal with the tricky ones, stuff like this.' He paused. 'Another department altogether.'

'So why didn't he tell me, instead of pretending he'd washed his hands of the whole thing?'

216

'Cautious bird, Hattersley. He wasn't going to risk you letting it be known he was giving you a hand. Particularly as Portuguese security tap his phone. No flies on Portuguese security. He's a bit upset about your phone call.'

'Sorry.'

'As for how we found the car, the answer's pretty boring. No clever detective work on my part, save that we kept an eye on you and by a stroke of luck, really, saw you pay your visit to Miss Gilpin the day before yesterday.'

'Miss Gilpin is a good friend,' Mr Gomes said. 'A patriotic lady. She sometimes helps in these little affairs, you know.'

'She told us she'd put you on to Gomes and the rest was easy. She said she thought you were a very civil person.'

'I would hate not to be in Miss Gilpin's good books.'

'So would we all.'

A curious thing, really. Major Hattersley of the clenched teeth, his military-type friend whose name I didn't even know, the dapper Mr Gomes of the trim beard and Savile Row suit, and Miss Gilpin of Eastbourne with her worries about Lipton's and Tiptree – all four of them could easily be laughed at, and yet they had turned out to be people of consequence, perhaps of greater consequence than my German hermaphrodite with the long, long lashes. I felt a bit sheepish.

'I don't know your name,' I said to the military type.

'Let's say it's Matthews.'

'Well, Mr Matthews, what do we do now?'

'First, the Huns' safe house. What did you see?'

'Inside, it was just a house – nothing special as far as I could tell. Through the window I saw ships' masts, maybe a hundred yards away, not more.'

'Cranes?'

'Not sure. You'd better not count on cranes. And I never saw any funnels that we could identify.'

'Smells?'

'A faint tang of the sea, I suppose, and that was about all.'

'Hot tar, the smell of cargoes, anything like that?'

I shook my head.

217

'Noises, then: when you came out to the car, what were the noises?'

'Just traffic, some of it heavy goods vehicles. But it wouldn't be a stream of traffic, just quite a few cars and lorries passing.'

'How long were you in the car?'

'About a half hour, I'd say, and we turned a lot of corners, so maybe they were following a tricksy route. It would be the sensible thing to do.'

'None of this is useful.' Gomes said. 'Our waterfront is many kilometres long, with about fifteen kilometres of docks. Probably somewhere up towards Sacavem there is this German house, but we will never find it by driving around.'

'This tame concierge of yours,' Matthews said, 'do you think we can get to him again?'

'I don't see why not.'

'What we have to do is somehow get him to say something to this Captain Soriano which will provoke Soriano into telephoning his Huns, but in such a way that we can trace the call.'

There was a longish and gloomy silence during which Gomes went round refilling our glasses like a man trying to make a dead party come alive.

'How's this?' I said, and proceeded to outline a scheme which sounded more and more improbable as I dug my way deeper into it. I expected Matthews to respond with a military snort, instead of which he announced that it was a capital idea and should lead us unerringly to the Hun.

I slept that night in one of Gomes' spare rooms – slept, to my surprise, like a baby.

Chapter 22

I was in the street behind the hotel next morning at eight, tucked into a doorway opposite the spot where the unfortunate concierge had suffered my attack on his manhood. I was gambling on his taking the same route back from his home. Just before eight-thirty I saw him coming up the street from my right. He was still inclined to waddle as a result of what had happened to him. I crossed the road as he drew level with me, and he started like a terrified rabbit.

'No, no,' I said, 'I don't plan to attack you, but I do want to have another little chat.'

He allowed me to guide him firmly into the carriageway we had used the last time.

'*Senhor*, please, I must go to my work.'

'Indeed you will. What we have to discuss will only take a minute – unless, that is, you prove to be difficult, in which case I doubt whether you'll feel like working today.'

'*Senhor*, I beg of you . . .'

'Begging will not be helpful. Only obedience will serve, my friend. And in any case, there is good money to be made.'

Maybe his eyes glistened: I couldn't see in the gloom. He just said '*Si, senhor.*'

'Now listen carefully. I want you to phone Captain Soriano as soon as you reach the hotel. Tell him you have very important news for him but can't give it over the phone. Tell him he should come round right away. Make it sound as if you're frightened, afraid of being overheard, stuff like that. Can you do it?'

He nodded miserably. It wasn't going to be a role he'd enjoy.

'Then, when he arrives, this is what you say. You saw me

come into the lobby with two other men. They looked English. All three went upstairs and you haven't seen them come down yet. Got that?'

'*Si, Senhor.*'

'Then I reckon Soriano will want to use the phone. Does he usually use the instrument on your desk?'

'*Si, Senhor.*'

'Will you be able to hear the number he asks for?'

The man shrugged. 'It depends. If there are many guests seeking my services I may not hear.'

'The hotel telephonist – is she a good friend of yours?'

'She is a decent woman.'

'Would she tell you what number he asked for if you warn her in advance?'

'*Si, Senhor.*'

'Then you will do that, but you will also listen yourself. And when you have the number you will come out to this street, where I will be waiting, and you will give me the number, right?'

'Right, *Senhor.*'

'For this service I pay five hundred escudos now and a thousand when you deliver the number. Out of that you may wish to give your telephonist a little present with my compliments.'

'That is very kind, *Senhor.*'

'It isn't kind, it's payment for a service rendered. Now let me tell you what will happen if you do not render this service, or if the telephone number proves to be a false one, or if Soriano and his mob appear to have been told by you where I am. In any of such cases, my friends will pay you a visit and I'm afraid they will treat you very badly indeed. Is that clear?'

'I would never double-cross, *Senhor.*'

'Good. Now here's five hundred.' I gave him the notes. 'I will see you again when you come out to give me the number. That's when you get another thousand. And take good care that Soriano doesn't follow you. I shall be with friends, by the way, just in case anyone is tempted.'

I was astonished at how smoothly the whole thing went. My concierge must have played it by the book. At any rate, soon after nine-thirty he appeared at the hotel's service entrance looking furtive. I was sitting with Matthews in his car, which he had parked a few yards away. The sudden appearance of the concierge interrupted our discussion of the merits of the respective batting styles of Hobbs and Hendren.

The concierge handed me a slip of paper with a phone number scribbled on it. 'I think he is waiting for the foreign gentlemen,' he said. I handed him the thousand escudos and he darted back inside the hotel.

'I know how to trace the number,' Matthews said. He drove quickly to a café in the Avenida da Liberdade and disappeared into a phone booth. In a few minutes he was out again, climbed into the car and pulled away from the kerb without a word. After a while he said: 'Gomes was right. It's on the waterfront up towards Sacavem.'

We drove for a while in silence, down to the Comércio, then along the boulevards which front the great river. It took us about twenty minutes to reach a stretch of road which was a mixture of solid but deteriorating mansions, and warehouses and offices connected with the activity of the port. The road ran parallel to the docks along this stretch of the Tagus and it carried a good deal of heavy goods traffic.

Matthews nodded suddenly. 'Over there – the big house set back from the road. That's where your friend is.' He drove on and stopped the car some fifty yards beyond the house. We got out.

The place was like a fortress. There were bars on the windows at ground-floor level and the windows themselves were about six feet above the gravel path which appeared to run right round the house. If the house had ever had a garden it had long since been swallowed up by the port: a warehouse wall was separated from the back of the house by only a few feet of space. The flat roof of the warehouse was about level with the first floor of the house.

221

'We should have known they had this place,' Matthews said. 'We usually keep tabs on them but the *Abwehr* has put a lot of agents into Portugal since the offensive started and we're hard put to keep things under control.'

We were back in the car, discouraged by our reconnaissance, and Matthews was making notes on a bit of card which he then stuffed back in his pocket.

'Do you think Colonel Ribeiro at the DGS would give us a hand?' I asked. 'He already has quite a lot of my money.'

'Given the choice, Ribeiro chooses us. We look after him on a modest scale. But he can't afford a scandal, with the German ambassador stamping into the Foreign Minister's office and shouting threats and abuse. A squalid little Nazi from some Bavarian slum; I don't know where the Wilhelmstrasse finds them nowadays.'

'Should I try him?'

'Probably not. If I know Ribeiro he'll tell you to get out while you can, since there are plenty more women in the world.'

'Not like that one.'

Matthews looked hard at me. 'Bad show,' he said, 'when the ladies get mixed up in this kind of caper. Always ends badly.'

'She saved my life – a couple of times actually.'

It shut Matthews up. But after a while he said: 'We'll have to do the job tonight. You'd better come with me now and meet the lads who'll be doing it.'

We drove a mile down-river and on to a quayside where a couple of ships were tied up. One of them – a fifteen-thousand-tonner badly in need of a coat of paint – was loading stores. SS Galatea, Liverpool, it said in faded lettering on her stern. We got out of the car and Matthews had words with a ship's officer who seemed to be in command of the gangplank. The officer nodded and we both climbed up the steep incline on to the ship's main deck. Instead of heading for the bridge as I'd expected, Matthews led the way down through a couple of decks as if he knew exactly where he was going.

'We have a tricky job to do here in a day or two,' he said. 'I've

222

managed to squeeze a squad of a dozen men out of London. They'll be wasting their time on booze and gambling so we might as well use them on this little problem of yours tonight.'

'What's the job?'

'You may have seen in the local papers that the Duke of Windsor and that woman are in Portugal.'

'Oh?'

'What you won't have seen is that there's a German plan to get them to Germany. You know the duke has a soft spot for Adolf Hitler.'

'Oh?'

'So we have to see no luring takes place. Now let's get on with this other business.'

We walked along a passageway and when we came to a door at the far end, Matthews knocked a couple of times. There was a shout from beyond the heavy iron door, he heaved it open and we climbed through.

There were two men inside, sitting on either side of a small table. They both wore trunks and nothing else, and in the foetid heat of the cabin they were sweating freely. A card game was in progress, but when they saw Matthews they jumped to their feet and stood rigid until Matthews told them to be easy. Stools were pulled up and the four of us sat round the table. The cards were cleared away.

'This is Sergeant Willis and Corporal Powers,' Matthews told me. 'It isn't necessary to identify their unit. I reckon we'll need a six-man group tonight.' The two men said nothing. Matthews had not introduced me. It is not a comfortable feeling to be an anonymous amateur among professionals.

Matthews was explaining about the house and how we had to get in and rescue what he called 'this detained person'. The two listened silently and a couple of times Sergeant Willis asked questions.

'This gentleman is to come with us?' he asked, nodding in my direction.

'I think that will be necessary,' Matthews said. 'He will guide you to the room where the person is detained.'

223

I was asked to sketch the interior and I did my best. We decided the room where Marie Antoinette was held was on the ground floor at the side. There was some discussion about what to do if they'd moved her to another room.

'Do we shoot Jerry, sir?' Sergeant Willis asked. He was stocky and very pink and there was not a hair on his head. Whether it was a neat shaving job, some genetic trick or a case of alopecia, it made him look like a monstrous and very dangerous baby.

'If you have to, you shoot Jerry. And in my estimation you may have to.'

Then there was talk of weapons, such items as ropes, grappling irons and ladders, followed by personnel, transport and timing. It was impressive.

'You will go in at two a.m.,' Matthews said. 'I want a clean operation and I want speed and silence. Detail a man to cut the phone wires where they leave the house on the right-hand side. They're about ten feet up and he'll need a ladder.'

I hadn't even noticed the wires, let alone drawn any conclusions from them.

We were to get in via the flat roof of the neighbouring warehouse. A ladder was to bridge the gap to a first-floor window. They made it sound simple, even safe. For a moment I started to enjoy the prospect, but the feeling didn't last.

'Excuse me sir, do you shoot sir?'

'Hardly,' I told Sergeant Willis.

'I think you'd best carry a revolver, sir. We'll provide one.'

'I think you'd better get dressed, Sergeant, and go over to take a look,' Matthews said.

'Yes sir, very good sir.'

'Do that this afternoon. We'll meet you and your men at one-thirty a.m. down on the quayside. I'll see there's transport.'

'Very good sir.'

The sergeant and his corporal sprang to their feet as we got up and left them.

'I have to give you these,' Matthews said as we stepped back on to the quayside. He handed me an envelope. 'Your steamer tickets and a paper which will get you past immigration in

England. Made out in the names of Mr and Mrs Quinton. You'll have to do your best with the bureaucrats back home if they get awkward about the lady's name.'

'No problem, not after the frontiers we've been crossing lately.'

'You sail the day after tomorrow, on the afternoon tide. That should be about three p.m.'

There were six men and a pile of gear waiting for us at the quayside. The time was just after 1.20 in the morning and there was very little light from the brand-new moon which hung over the sleeping city. Matthews had rustled up a lorry and the ladders and stuff were loaded in silence. A torch was shone briefly in my face and I felt a gun being pressed into my hand. 'Safety catch is on, sir,' Sergeant Willis said. 'Six rounds. Only to be used in extremity.'

We drove north towards the German safe house, Matthews at the wheel of the lorry, the men piled in among the gear at the back. We rattled forward for fifteen minutes or so, then we turned off the main road and stopped in an unlit side street. There was no traffic about.

'The house is a hundred yards further on, on the far side of the road. You'll have to manhandle the equipment and hope there's no one to see you. I'm not bringing this thing any closer.'

Everyone got down and the ladders and stuff were distributed among the men, with Sergeant Willis issuing a whispered order now and then. There was a pleasing businesslike air about the whole thing which tended to reassure. Then we walked the short distance to the house, which was in darkness. A moment later we were at the back between the house and the dark mass of the warehouse. One of the men made off with the ladder and returned very soon to report the telephone wires had been cut. Then a grappling iron was thrown up and caught the low parapet on the warehouse roof. A rope dangled from it.

'Charley, up you go.' It was the sergeant, scarcely audible and completely invisible.

Charley, whoever he might be, shinned up the rope like a

225

man who had been made to do it countless times in training. Two more men followed him. 'Now you, sir,' Sergeant Willis said. 'Use your feet to keep well away from the wall. You walk up it, see, as you haul yourself up on the rope. Take it easy, now.'

The climb proved as difficult as I had expected. The last few feet drove knives through my biceps and I felt a fool as willing hands hauled me over the parapet from above. 'Jolly good, sir,' someone said. It had not been jolly good at all. The sergeant followed me up and then the ladder was handed up to us.

The ladder was extended to bridge the ten feet of space between the roof and the ledge of the nearest window in the house. The ledge was maybe a foot lower than the roof, giving a gentle slope on which to make our way over.

'You sit astride the ladder,' Sergeant Willis told me, 'and then you heave yourself forward bit by bit – easy like. It's easier than you might think.'

'It couldn't be harder,' I said.

'Know how you feel, sir,' said the admirable sergeant. 'I suggest you follow me, then if you get a bit worried in mid-stream you can grab my shoulder. First time's always tricky.'

The first man over must have been a cat burglar in Civvy Street. The dim outline of his figure disappeared almost at once. There was a pause of a minute or so and then he was back.

'Window open,' he reported. 'Latch yielded to the old knife. No problem at all.'

'Good lad. Back you go; then Pete, then me, and this gentleman will follow me and Charley will bring up the rear. John will stay this side.'

Charley bumped his way back on the ladder and we heard a scraping sound as the window was opened. A moment later a torch flashed twice.

'Room's empty and we can follow,' the sergeant said. 'Right, Pete next.'

When it came to the sergeant's turn he got astride the ladder and stopped a foot or so out from the ledge. 'Follow me sir, and stay close behind. Easy does it.'

Getting astride the ladder, feet dangling on either side, was

226

difficult. Propelling myself forward, a couple of inches at a time, was harder still. I have no head for heights and thanked God for the dark. But the thought of the drop beneath me and a conviction that someone would jerk the end of the ladder off the window ledge made my stomach churn. The sergeant slowed down to my pace and offered murmured words of encouragement. An excellent fellow. And then he was across and through the window and into the room. Soon I was hauled after him.

The plan was to go straight down to the ground floor to the room Marie Antoinette was in, break the door down and get her out, dealing with any hostile Germans who might appear on what Matthews had called an *ad hoc* basis. We left one man on the first-floor landing and the rest of us tiptoed down the stairs, following a thin pencil of torchlight from the sergeant in the lead. For powerfully-built men they were amazingly quiet. We got to the ground floor without a sound being made. Now it was my turn to justify my presence. After a bit of feeling around and peering by dim torchlight I located the door at which I'd spoken to Marie Antoinette. The cat burglar came forward with what looked like a jemmy in his hand. First he tried the handle very slowly. The door yielded. I followed him in. By the dim light of the torch I could see a camp bed in a corner and a few bits of furniture. Marie Antoinette was no longer there.

Although we'd thought of such a possibility and had decided what to do if it confronted us, I still felt a sense of deep foreboding. Why would they have moved her? Where to? And would we find the place? I still clung to my belief that it was in their interest to keep her alive.

Now our contingency plan went into operation. Charley was sent back to the first floor to join the man we had left there. Then the lights on the ground floor were switched on and every door was flung open and the rooms lit up. The men were carrying revolvers. The ground floor and basement cleared, they raced up the stairs, no longer bothering to keep quiet. The first floor was subjected to the same treatment by two of the men while the other two raced to the second floor and went through the same routine there.

227

Our bag of *Abwehr* men consisted of my former friends the blond and the silent one, plus a small middle-aged creature I hadn't met before. All were in varying types of night attire and all looked confused and frightened. They were assembled on the first-floor landing and addressed by Sergeant Willis, who stood pink and hairless, a gun held loosely in his right hand, a nasty expression on his face.

'Right, where is she?'

No reply. The blond was fidgeting. He wore only a pyjama top and his spindly legs were detracting from his dignity.

'Stand still, you,' Sergeant Willis said, 'and answer my question. Where is she?' He took a step forward and poked the German in the stomach with the barrel of his gun.

There was still no reply. 'He speaks good English,' I said. 'I think he's in charge here.'

'No longer, he isn't. *I'm* in charge here, begging your pardon sir.'

'You'd better answer him,' I told the German. 'He can be very brutal. That profile of yours is a wasting asset right now. And I will be only too pleased to help him spoil it.'

'She has gone,' the German said. I thought I detected a kind of sneer on his face.

'Wipe that look off your face,' Sergeant Willis said. Apparently he'd noticed the same thing.

'I protest,' the German said. He was beginning to regain some composure despite his bare legs. 'This is an outrage and it will be reported to the Portuguese authorities.'

'Stop wasting my time. Where's the lady?'

'I do not know.'

'Hold him while I hit him,' the sergeant said to Charley.

'It is not necessary to hit me. I will tell you what I know, which is very little.'

'Then get on with it.'

At that point the front doorbell rang three times. 'Fetch it,' the sergeant said to one of the men. A few moments later Matthews was with us.

'I saw the lights go on so I thought I might join the party.' He took a look at our three Germans. 'Ah, Herr Dr Müller of the trade department at the embassy.' He was looking at the third German, who was wearing a long nightgown beneath which his rather gnarled toes could be seen. 'The Portuguese authorities will be interested to know you are an *Abwehr* VT,* eh?' The man shrugged and said nothing. 'So where are we?'

'Lady's not here, sir. This fellow says she's left and he's about to tell all.'

'I demand the right to dress myself,' the blond German said.

'Right refused,' Matthews said. 'Now get on with it, there's a good chap. We all want to get back to bed, don't we?'

The long eyelashes went down. 'First, I make my protest. I am an officer of the *Wehrmacht*, Captain Otto Wassner, on diplomatic mission in a neutral country. I protest against being detained in this manner and I shall make my report to my ambassador and to the Portuguese Ministry of Foreign Affairs.' The lashes came up. 'An outrage,' he added.

'Now please get on with it, Captain,' Matthews said, 'and I don't think you'll be complaining to anyone.'

The German sniffed and pulled his pyjama jacket round his shanks. 'The girl,' he said, 'has left of her own free will. She is with Monsieur Schlesser, a member of the French Senate. He arrived in Lisbon last night. He had an interview with the girl and she left with him. I was not empowered to intervene.'

Matthews looked at me. 'It must have been under duress,' I said.

'She appeared to be perfectly willing. They talked for half an hour. I do not know what was said. Then they left.'

'Where did they go?'

'That I do not know.' There was an awkward pause. 'Monsieur Schlesser said he would like to meet you today. If I saw you I was to say he can be contacted at the French Embassy.'

---

* *Vertrauensmann:* Military Intelligence Agent

229

Chapter 23

'I am disappointed in you, Quinton.'

Schlesser put me in mind of a malevolent toad as he sat, completely immobile, the rolls of fat about his jaw and neck pulsating slightly as he talked, his eyes scarcely open but always watchful and utterly without emotion. The strangely delicate hands were folded on his waistcoat. His black suit was crumpled loosely over his great bulk. A glass of champagne stood untouched before him on the low table.

'I am sadly disappointed. I would have given you credit for more . . .' – he searched for a word, seemed to find it – 'more sense of opportunity.'

'Max used that phrase.'

'I daresay he got it from me. His death is a sad and at the same time an interesting event.'

'It doesn't interest me.'

'It should. You knew he was dead, of course.'

I shook my head. 'It could well have improved him.'

'Never mind Max. What about you? What are your plans?'

'They are none of your business, Monsieur Schlesser.'

'I take a different view.' He leaned forward heavily, took his glass and sipped the champagne. 'I am here to offer you some new possibilities.'

'Where is Marie Antoinette?'

'Is that what she calls herself when she is with you?'

'Her name is of no consequence. Where is she?'

'On the contrary, this little matter of her name has its significance. You will have observed that she is a pathological liar. A psychiatric case, really.'

'Where is she?'

'We may come to that later. But it will depend, of course, on your response to my proposal.'

'If we were not in a public place, Monsieur Schlesser, I would ram my fist into your face, quite regardless of the fact that you are a far older man than I am.'

'Threats of this kind are not worthy of you, my dear Quinton. In any case, I arranged to meet you here precisely because I thought your emotions might triumph over your sense of decorum.'

We were in the bar of the Imperial. It was eleven in the morning. I had telephoned the French Embassy at nine-thirty and they had put me on to the ambassador's residence. Schlesser, it appeared, was staying there. We had talked, made an appointment, and here we were, each with a glass of champagne before him.

'So what are these new possibilities of yours?'

'First I must tell you that in these matters I am now collaborating closely with my German friends here and in Paris. It gives me – what shall I say – certain physical resources I would not otherwise have.'

'I've had a brush with the resources in the last twenty-four hours.'

'I must congratulate you on being here, still able to drink champagne. They underestimated you.'

'I also have certain physical resources.'

Schlesser opened his eyes wider for a brief moment and creased his face into a smile. Then he leaned ponderously towards me and tapped me gently on the arm. 'My dear fellow, don't you see that it is only a matter of time? England against the whole of Europe – absurd! Utterly hopeless, my poor friend. It is mere posturing to line oneself up with a loser who is to be crushed by a more vigorous civilization, just as we in France were crushed.' He leaned back in his chair. 'Deservedly so.' The words were murmured and there was no regret in them.

'Monsieur Schlesser, we have discussed politics before and we got nowhere. That was in Paris, with the Germans in the

231

suburbs. I'm afraid you'll do no better in neutral Portugal.'

'Nevertheless, I hope you will consider my words carefully. And now for my proposition. It is very simple. The car for me: the girl for you. Consider before you reply. The bullion is in any case utterly without significance in the balance of forces between England and Germany. Furthermore, from your personal point of view it is meaningless, since none of it is yours and you will receive no reward for delivering it. The girl on the other hand – now that is a different matter. She is a remarkable creature, as you must know by now. A sexual animal of great potency. A fascinating woman. Sick in the head, of course, but then many of the most seductive women are a little . . .' He made a gesture with his hand which could have signified almost anything. 'The impression I get is that you and she . . . shall we call it unfinished business? An affair which has not run its course? Something, let us say, that you would wish to pursue. I think so; definitely. And to show that I bear you no malice, I would add a useful sum of money to enable both of you to set yourselves up in a suitable manner once you get back to London. A fine city. I weep to think of what will be done to it before your Churchill is brought to his senses.'

'How do I know that she will come with me?'

Schlesser took an envelope from his breast pocket and handed it across the table. I tore it open. The letter inside was in Marie Antoinette's immature and disorganized handwriting, climbing crazily up the page.

Englishman!
No time or space to say all that I feel. Also, I cannot be sure this will reach you. But if so, Monsieur Schlesser has asked me to say that I will be able to come with you to England and this is the desire of my heart. And so I say it. I hope you will accept this offer that I make out of my love for you. If you refuse it my heart will break. I cannot explain more now, but there is much to tell you. Please take me with you – please, please, please. Otherwise I do not know what will happen to me.

I love you.
M–A

232

What was I to make of it? A cry from the heart? Or a move in a game? Whose side was she on? Just for once, was she telling the truth? And even if she was, what was I to do?

'Neat,' I said.

Schlesser allowed himself the trace of a smile and bowed his head very slightly in acknowledgement. 'I do not know what is in the letter,' he lied, 'but there you have a woman's heart laid bare, I've no doubt. And so you have a decision to make and you had best make it now. I understand your ship sails to-morrow afternoon. It leaves us little time to settle all this.'

'What if I cannot meet your terms? Others are involved now, you know.'

'I know that. I am tolerably well informed. However, I have to say that that problem is yours and not mine. I believe you are resourceful enough to resolve it.'

'And if I fail, what happens to the girl?'

'She will return to Paris and stay under my protection. Unless, that is, she is brought to trial as an accessory to murder. I am not all-powerful and I cannot always impose myself on a situation.' He paused, his eyes almost closed. 'Her mother, by the way, was Jewish. I believe even the Jews themselves would say that makes her Jewish too. You may know the National Socialists intend to cleanse Western Europe of the Jews. They are to be resettled in the east.' He paused again. '*That*, my dear Quinton, is what may well happen to the girl.'

'Unless she stays here.'

'She has no possibility of staying here, believe me.'

I got up. 'I will telephone you at your embassy at two this afternoon.'

'Very well, and do not make it any later.'

I left him drinking the rest of his champagne.

A half-hour later I was with Matthews in his car, pouring out my troubles. When I'd finished he sat in silence for so long that I thought he expected me to say something more. So I said, 'What the hell do I do?'

He looked round at me for the first time since I'd started

233

talking. 'Tell me something,' he said. 'Which matters most to you, the bullion or the girl?'

'The girl.'

'But she doesn't seem to be a very reliable lady.'

'She isn't.'

'And yet . . .'

'And yet.'

'So you're willing to allow a ton of gold and platinum to fall into the hands of the Nazis and their friends?'

'Would it make that much difference?' I asked lamely. I knew I was echoing Schlesser's argument.

'We think it would.'

'We?'

'You don't imagine I'm doing all this on my own, old boy, do you?'

'I suppose not.'

'My principals are very interested in the bullion. They consider you have done quite a job. They would be very, very disappointed if it all fell apart now.'

'I daresay.'

'As a matter of fact, old boy, I am under strict instructions not to let any such thing happen.' He sat in a kind of gloomy silence for a moment. 'Not under any circumstances whatever.'

'I see.'

'I wonder if you do.'

'Meaning . . .?'

'Meaning that decisions in respect of the contents of your car are henceforth being taken by HM government and by no one else. I'm afraid I have to tell you that officially.'

'So as far as you are concerned the girl can go to hell.'

'I would put it differently. We have to work for the greater good.'

I grunted. There was another long silence. 'It seems,' I said, 'that as a result of this lunatic odyssey of mind I am now out on my own. To the right, Captain Wassner and his thugs. To my left, Schlesser and the dregs of the Third Republic. And here right in front of me, Mr Matthews of who knows what department in Whitehall.' I brought my fist down hard on the fascia of his wretched little car and the sharp pain in my knuckles seemed somehow to do me good.

'I am sorry,' Matthews said, as if he didn't mean it. 'This is wartime.'

'You don't say. I thought it was Halloween.'

'This won't get us anywhere. I think we should calm down and see whether we can't have our cake and eat it. It's been known.'

After that I came to my senses and we started talking.

'Where would you reckon the girl is?' Matthews asked.

'I'd say at the French Embassy or maybe with one of their people.'

'I think so too. It gives us a lead.'

'I don't see how.'

'Let's put it this way: not everyone in their embassy is in love with Marshal Pétain. We make it our business to keep in touch with those who might place their bets on General de Gaulle. All this is very new, of course, but we do a fair job here and I know who to talk to among the French. As I say, it should give us a lead.'

Then we talked about the car.

'I think,' Matthews said carefully, 'that we may have to go through the motions of handing it over.'

I had a suggestion to make. Matthews screwed his face up, grunted, fell into one of his silences. 'Worth a try,' he said. 'Go and talk to Colonel Ribeiro at the DGS. You never know. Oh, and by the way, old boy, you don't have plans to fool me, do you?'

'You can check later with Ribeiro.'

At two I called the embassy and was put through to Schlesser.

'You win,' I said.

'I would not wish to express it in that way. Let us say you have come to see my point of view.'

'So what do we do?'

'We end this conversation and we meet again at the same place, say at four?'

'Very well.'

Then I found a taxi to take me back to the DGS building in Belém, where after much gesturing I was shown in to the colonel's office. We met as old friends, and as old friends we concluded our business in a satisfactory manner.

I reached the Imperial bar first and having tried and failed to get a cup of tea, settled for brandy. Schlesser, when he arrived, seemed much encouraged by my capitulation. I thought I would add a little motivation.

'I am indebted to the girl,' I said. 'I pay my debts. Also, I have come to agree that the French national treasure isn't really any concern of mine. Not after the Reims prison.'

'Very wise.' Schlesser had ordered brandy for himself. He put his nose in the glass, pulled a face and replaced the glass on the table. 'Now for the practical arrangements. Of course, in a transaction of this kind one needs an honest broker to hold the stakes – in this case the car and the girl. However, no such broker is available to us. So we must do the best we can. My first question is therefore this: would your people trust the word of honour of an officer of the *Wehrmacht?*'

'No.'

'I feared as much. And what of my word as a member of the French Senate and an officer of the Legion of Honour?'

'No.'

There was a silence. 'You must understand,' I said, 'that my people cannot agree to releasing the gold in return for a girl. I therefore have to pursue what you might call a personal policy.'

'I expected as much. Can you get access to the car and move it without being intercepted?'

'I can.'

'I take it they know nothing of my proposal.'

'Of course not.'

'Will *you* accept my word?'

'No, Monsieur Schlesser, I will not.'

The half-closed eyes beneath their puffy lids opened a shade and he spent a moment considering me as one would consider a laboratory specimen. 'No, well, perhaps I can see your point of

236

view. A pity.'

I pretended to have a sudden idea. 'Look, what about . . .' I shook my head and relapsed into silence.

'What?'

'Just a crazy idea, but I don't think it would work.'

'I am willing to hear it.'

'Since I arrived I have had some trouble with a certain Colonel Ribeiro of the DGS. He's responsible for keeping an eye on us foreigners and he clearly has considerable resources at his disposal. He had had a note about me from the German Embassy and it cost me a fair amount in cash to get him off my back. He strikes me as the kind of man who might be willing to play the honest broker. At a price.'

'Please elaborate.'

'Well, if both of us paid him he might see there was fair play. As you know, the Portuguese are terrified of offending either of the powers. I don't think the colonel would want to double-cross either the Germans or the British. I also think he would be pleased to be rid of me, the car, the girl, and for that matter, you. We all spell trouble for him, and we could make it clear that if he doesn't help us out of this fix, there could be shooting in the alleyways, as there very nearly was last night.'

For a full minute Schlesser sat in silence, his eyes fixed on me. Then, to break the silence, I added: 'I don't suppose it would work, anyway.'

'On the contrary,' Schlesser said, 'I think it might work very well. And the fact that I say so surely proves that I am after an honest deal. You may not give me credit for much heart, my dear Quinton, but I have no doubt that the girl would be safer with you in England than with me in occupied France.' He sighed. 'I will naturally be sorry to see such a charming creature go.'

'I'm sure.'

'Tell me,' he said, 'how much would this colonel want?'

'I would offer him ten thousand escudos.'

'Each?'

'Each.'

'I will come with you.'

Such was the warmth of my friendship with Colonel Ribeiro by now that we had reached the stage where money could be openly discussed and openly passed across his impressive desk with no camouflage more elaborate than the traditional sealed envelope. Next morning Schlesser and I were seated, one at each corner of the desk, each with an envelope in his breast pocket. It being part of the necessary ritual to talk about this and that, Colonel Ribeiro was expatiating on the impossibility of documenting the vast influx of foreigners into the capital. Then I went into my act.

'The Senator here and I have a problem, Colonel. We would like to impose on your kindness and . . .' – here I hesitated to what I fancied was good effect – 'your understanding as a man of the world.'

The colonel, who had gone into his act too, kept his eyes on me, frowning in a professional manner. From time to time he would glance across at Schlesser with the deference that a policeman owes to a politician.

I explained the background – an exchange on neutral territory which met the needs of both powers . . . the honest broker bit and the suitability of Colonel Ribeiro of the well-respected DGS for such a role . . . Then I came to the delicate part.

'We do not believe we should thrust such troublesome tasks upon the DGS without compensating you and your colleagues in some suitable fashion. Such compensation naturally comes both from the Franco-German side and from the British, in equal sums since we seek equal treatment.'

'Very proper,' the colonel said.

I took my envelope out of my pocket and Schlesser did the same. Together we slid them across the desk towards the colonel. They lay there, halfway towards him, for the rest of our little conversation.

'In what way can we help you?'

I let Schlesser do the explaining. I wanted him to feel a part of the thing. Logistics were discussed.

'I feel sure you will be glad to be rid of us and our potentially explosive problems,' I said.

The colonel made a charming deprecatory gesture. We all smiled. Then we got up to go, and as we did so the colonel scooped up the two envelopes in a discreet and practised gesture and slipped them into a drawer. Then he came round his desk and showed us out with an amount of charm which I judged to be proportional to what he already knew was inside his envelopes.

'That was satisfactory,' Schlesser said to me as he grunted his way down the stairs. 'Though I did not like the man. However, one must make allowance for the fact that he is a Portuguese.'

'Is this sort of thing done better in France?' I asked.

We had reached the door and he didn't bother to answer.

Chapter 24

Later I talked to Matthews.

'It's set up for eleven tonight,' I told him. 'Ribeiro doesn't fancy parading his little adventure in daylight. Even he has superiors at the DGS.'

'Money changed hands?'

'It did. What about your side of the thing?'

'I'll be seeing him at seven. What do we offer as a sweetener?'

'Gold coin. But it's impossible to value them. He'll have to trust us to do the decent thing. I can get some coin out of the car ahead of the exchange.'

'And what if the other side offer him the same thing once they have the car?'

'I daresay they will. That's the point on which we have to make a judgement about Ribeiro.'

'As I told you, Ribeiro's a friend. As long as he isn't made to look pro-British in public, he'll stay friendly.'

'All we need now,' I said, 'is reasonable luck.'

The weather turned against us. The heat had become unbearable through the day and things were working up for a storm. By nightfall the clouds lay heavy over the city and the humidity was oppressive. It started to rain in torrents soon after ten. I first heard it pattering and then beating wildly on the tin roof of the warehouse as I prepared the car. I replaced the distributor head and she started at the first pressure on the starter button. No problems. I prised open a corner of the interior trim and extracted one of the rolls of coins. Maybe the colonel would strike it rich with some priceless issue – say some nice twenty-rouble pieces of Catherine the Great. Then I settled down to wait for zero hour.

The plan called for me to drive the car out on to the quayside, where a DGS driver would take her over. Colonel Ribeiro would be in attendance. He would then drive in the car to the dock gates where Schlesser and his Germans would be waiting with Marie Antoinette. There the exchange would take place. Marie Antoinette would come to me and the Germans would drive the car away.

It was simple. Its philosophical basis lay in my estimate that whereas the fate of the treasure and the fate of Marie Antoinette were of equal importance to me, in the case of Schlesser and his friends the treasure counted for a great deal and Marie Antoinette for comparatively little. Her importance to them, really, was only a function of her importance to me: she was their hold over me, and once that hold was no longer needed they had little enough reason to renege on their deal. Which meant that they were more likely to honour the arrangements with Ribeiro than I was. And not being fools, they would know it. And so they would have to believe they had sewn me up in such a way that I couldn't double-cross them. And if Schlesser had accepted the Ribeiro plan it was because he did so believe. All he had to do was check the car when it reached him. He was to be given ten minutes to inspect the chassis and the interior hiding places. If the bullion was there he would agree that Ribeiro could accompany Marie Antoinette back to me on the quayside. All of which was very clever stuff; but anything – a sudden suspicion, a mistake about Ribeiro and the extent of his greed, even a mechanical fault in the car – any of these and no doubt other things could flush my reasoning down the drain.

'Nothing goes according to plan,' Matthews had said in a moment of doubt. 'After all, old boy, both sides have their victory logically planned before every battle, but something has to go wrong, otherwise every battle would be won by both sides. Which would be nonsense, eh?'

Shortly before eleven I heard the sound of a car's hooter. I heaved back the big doors of the warehouse and came out into the rainstorm. The storm lamps of a ship tied up nearby were reflected in the great puddles of rainwater ahead of me. Over towards the dock gates I could see the sidelights of a car. Soon two figures loomed out of the blackness.

'Quinton?'

It was Colonel Ribeiro's voice.

'Yes, Colonel.'

'The car is ready?'

'I can drive her straight out.'

'The Senator and two others who seem to be Germans are out on the road. Also the lady.'

'Have you checked that it is the right lady?'

'You don't want a change just yet, eh?' The colonel laughed at his little joke. 'Don't worry, it is the same lady. I have spoken with her.'

'Good, then let's get on with it.'

I started the Bentley and drove her out on to the quayside. The other man came forward and replaced me at the wheel. He spoke some English; it took a minute to show him the controls and explain how to drive her. The colonel climbed in beside the driver.

'Stay here. We will come back with the lady when they have checked the car.'

'Okay.'

'You will have something for me?'

'I will.'

The driver put her in gear and drove slowly towards the gates. As she went I suddenly realized that I had lost my nerve. Why should I be the one to win out in this complicated and unprincipled game? What was to stop this highly dubious colonel driving off with the Bentley and its millions, thumbing his nose at all the rest of us? After all, we were in Portugal, where the secret police were above the law, where atrocities were perpetrated in the DGS interrogation centres, where corruption went hand in hand with torture. And yet I expected this particular secret policeman to play by the rules. He was a friend, Matthews had said. But was that a word that Colonel Ribeiro of

242

the Portuguese DGS understood?

I spent the next ten minutes getting soaked in the downpour and working myself into a condition of extreme pessimism. Then I saw figures approaching. A moment later, laughing and crying, Marie Antoinette was in my arms. Stage one of the bargain had been honoured.

I detached myself gently and handed the colonel his roll of coins. He took them without a word.

'Your men at the gate understand what is to happen next?'

'Of course.'

'I will come with you.' I led Marie Antoinette into the warehouse. 'Stay here. I won't be long.' I kissed her wet face and again had to detach myself as she clung to me.

'Come back soon, Englishman.'

'Of course I will.'

I followed Ribeiro to the gates. Schlesser was sitting in the Bentley next to the driver. Captain Wassner sat behind.

'So we have done our little deal?'

'We have, Monsieur Schlesser.'

'It was the wise thing for you, Quinton.'

'Perhaps.'

'Will you shake hands?'

'No.'

'The girl has the sum which I said I would provide. I honour my obligations.'

'I hope you will be happy with your new friends, Monsieur Schlesser. I shall retain an image of you, a member of the French Senate, being driven away in a looted car by a couple of Nazis. I hope you never have to answer to your people.' Then I yelled '*Los!*' and the driver responded like an automaton and the car drew away and after a moment its tail lights were lost in the swirling sheets of black rain.

Stage two had been completed.

'I hope there will be no shooting,' the colonel said.

'We cannot guarantee that. It must depend on the response of the Germans.'

The colonel's hope was not to be fulfilled. A few moments

later a shot rang out and then two more. Then silence. Through the rain we could see nothing.

'Three shots,' the colonel said unhappily. 'They could mean three inconvenient corpses. It is what I feared.'

'Let us hope,' I said, 'that they were warning shots. Our men had strict instructions.'

'Let us hope.'

But only one had been a warning shot. As the car came to a stop before Sergeant Willis' barricade across the narrow road leading out of the docks, the sergeant had yelled 'Hands up!' and fired a single revolver shot over their heads.

'The silly bastards thought they could shoot their way out,' he told us later. 'Blondie in the back fired in our direction and I winged him. Then the fat Frenchman in the front shouted in German and it was all over in two ticks. We turned a light on them. Jerry was *kaput*: I'd reached him through the head. We told the other two to clear off and the Frenchman made a hell of a fuss as he went. We disposed of Jerry.'

But all I knew of this at the time was the three shots. Then the Bentley's lights loomed dimly through the rain and she was back with us, driven by Sergeant Willis. That was stage three. The operation was over.

'A satisfactory outcome,' Matthews said.

We were on the quayside next morning, watching them fix tackle to the Bentley's axles ready to lift her off the quay. Passengers were shuffling aboard in an orderly line and baggage was being hoisted by the ship's derricks in heavy nets. Marie Antoinette and I had spent the night at Mr Gomes' house, and that amiable personage was with us now.

'When do you sail?'

'On the tide just after lunch. Then we have to join the convoy.'

'You'll be happy to return to your country,' Gomes said.

'Yes.'

'And you, Mademoiselle, you are pleased to be going to England?'

244

Marie Antoinette nodded. She had said little since the night before. No doubt she must be in a state of shock. Apparently they had told her I was still in the hands of Wassner and his friends and would be liquidated unless she agreed to write her letter. 'I didn't want you to die,' she said. 'I wanted to come to England with you.' She said it listlessly, as if she were so tired that she no longer cared greatly where she was to be. She had not wanted to make love. 'I am sorry. It is the first time I haven't wanted you. It will pass and we will make up for lost time.' I kissed her and she slept peacefully.

'Well, goodbye, old man,' Matthews said. 'You'll be met by one of our people when she docks and no doubt they'll ask you for a report on all this. I suggest you don't dwell too heavily on the details where the colonel is concerned. They like to keep costs down, you know.'

'Goodbye and thank you.' I shook hands with Matthews and Gomes. 'Please give my regards to Miss Gilpin and tell her I hope to be back to see her with the Tiptree and Lipton's when all this is over.'

Gomes looked mystified. Maybe he thought it was a piece of intelligence jargon.

They said goodbye to Marie Antoinette and Mr Gomes kissed her hand. 'You will fall in love with London,' he said. 'In the buses you go upstairs. It is very nice.'

We watched them walk away along the quayside and then, arm in arm, we joined the queue, made our way up the gangway and so to our cabin. We had a couple of hours before the SS *Galatea* was to sail.

So the whole thing was over at last. Schlesser and Max, Captain Wassner and Colonel Ribeiro – all these grotesques were done with and life would be different now. I suddenly felt very tired.

'I'm going to lie here for an hour, then we'll have lunch.'

'I feel restless,' Marie Antoinette said. 'I shall go up on deck to watch the people.'

'See they fasten that car down properly, won't you?'

She bent over and gave me a lingering kiss, tender and

245

somehow sad. 'You are a very fine Englishman,' she said. Then she left the cabin and I heard the click of her heels on the metal companionway outside.

I must have slept for more than an hour. I was wakened by the insistent blare of the ship's siren, and the faintest of movements. We must have cast off and were already getting under way. I shook myself awake and made my way up on deck. The ship was packed and hundreds of people were leaning on the rails as the tugs pulled and shoved her gently from the quayside and out into the river. In the crowd it was impossible to see Marie Antoinette. I wandered aft to inspect the car: it had been fastened to the deck and seemed secure enough. Then I went to the lower deck. Marie Antoinette was nowhere to be found.

I returned to my cabin, since she would know she could find me there. Ten minutes later there was a knock on the door. It was the purser and he handed me a letter. On the envelope my name had been scrawled in Marie Antoinette's unmistakable hand.

I sat on the bunk to read it and I found I couldn't stop my hand trembling as I held the two sheets of paper.

Englishman!
When you read this I will be gone and perhaps you will hate me. But I want you to understand and I know it is hard for you. I am not a good person. I am not truthful. I make love too easily, often without affection. I must have comfort in my life and beautiful things. In short, I am a trivial person and not at all worthy. I asked you to take me with you to England and I truly meant it. But then you told me we would not have an easy life there, and I know I cannot bear that and so, one day, I would go to some other man. For me, a life like that in a foreign country is not possible. And so I have decided to go back to France.

You may ask: when you wrote the letter which Schlesser brought, did you mean it? I don't know, Englishman. I meant it and somewhere in my mind I didn't mean it. Perhaps I only wrote the letter because they told me they would kill you otherwise, and I couldn't bear that.

We had a wonderful adventure together, didn't we? Do you remember

246

meeting in Chateaudun, that terrible German corporal, being together in the mountains, the fado *in Lisbon . . .? I thank you for all that. I hope you have a safe voyage, that you have a lot of happiness in your life and that your country wins. Going back frightens me but I think Schlesser will look after me. There are worse fates, you know!*

When you have won the war come back to Paris and find me. We'll go to the Poisson d'Or *at last and stay for breakfast.*

I don't think you will believe it but I have to say now, at last, as you sail away from me, that I have truly loved you, Englishman. I have never loved any other man.

Tous mes baisers.

M–A

PS: I have kept the money Schlesser meant for us in London. I hope you will understand.

Two thoughts remained with me.

Matthews had said we could have our cake and eat it. One can't.

And I had intended to ask Schlesser for Marie Antoinette's real name. But no doubt he didn't know it either.

When I came up on deck at last we had joined the convoy.

On 28 June 1940 de Gaulle's Provisional French National Committee was officially recognized by the British government. It had been allocated a dingy two-roomed office and started life with £100 in the bank. Shortly afterwards a young man named Pierre Dennis found himself in charge of the finances of the Free French Movement and was introduced to an old gentleman sitting at a rickety table who told him that whereas they had had fourteen shillings in the till on the previous day, the General had decided to send some telegrams and the fourteen shillings had gone, plus a further ten shillings out of the old gentleman's pocket. But soon afterwards the Free French finances were put on a sounder basis out of what were described as 'secret funds'. Their origin has not been revealed.

On 5 July the Pétain government broke off diplomatic relations with Britain and on 3 August de Gaulle was condemned to death in his absence by a French military court.

On 2 August operational instructions were issued to the Luftwaffe *and on the tenth the Battle of Britain opened with massive German attacks on convoys approaching British ports. They were followed by daylight raids on the mainland. Of 2,830 German planes engaged, 1,733 had been lost by the time the Germans withdrew defeated a month later. On 12 October Hitler cancelled his plans for the invasion of Britain and the scene had been set for four more years of war, culminating for the French in de Gaulle's entry into Paris with the Free French forces in June 1944. By the time of his arrival Resistance forces in the capital had chased the Germans from their barracks, offices, interrogation centres and* Soldatenheim, *including the Hotel Crillon in the Place de la Concorde. The noble façade of the building still bears the marks of bullets from the rifles and automatic weapons of the people of Paris.*